The Psyman

Nick Bruechle

Contact the author:
www.nickbruechle.com
nick@nickbruechle.com
facebook.com/nickbruechlebooks
@nick_bruechle

Production and proofreading by Hourigan & Co.
http://hourigan.co

ISBN 978-0-6485699-8-5

Set in Adobe Garamond

Acknowledgements

I'd like to thank the many people who provided advice, guidance and encouragement in the writing and completion of *The Psyman*.

The story and my writing ability have benefited greatly from the patience, expertise and assistance of Lyn Tranter, who showed me how to improve the early drafts.

My editor Justin Evans made this a much more readable and enjoyable story, and in this he was significantly helped by Ben Hourigan.

And my darling wife Rachel as always provides the inspiration, the support and the love that drives everything I do.

About the Author

Nick Bruechle is an Australian surfer, writer and 'hausfrau'. He has spent over thirty-five years in the advertising industry, loves to travel, and is married to the most wonderful woman in the world, Rachel.

Prologue – Particle

Particle, it must be said, is a precocious child. To look at him you would say he is like any three year old – almost a metre tall, with depthless blue eyes and a shock of blonde hair that waves and rolls in curls that fall almost to his narrow shoulders. But there is something different about him. You never catch him looking distant or vacant; he is always present, and those blue eyes are always enquiring of their surroundings. In his citiburb, all the other kids are – like their parents – given to periods of utter absenteeism that come on in an instant and linger on. Times when their minds have gone wandering so far from the here and now that their brains have neglected to arrange their features into some sort of expression. Moments, minutes, time-less intervals when nothing is going in, nothing is going out, and nothing is going on inside.

But Particle is always focused. He loves learning, creating, exploring, discovering. This ceaseless activity annoys his parents. Truth be told, they only had a baby because one time a pregnant woman appeared on YouStar. She had been so spoiled, and people seemed so excited about the fact that she was having a baby, that Flaunch and Pound, Particle's eventual parents, decided to have one too. Who knew? If Pound should fall pregnant, maybe she would jump up the rolls and be on YouStar as well.

What the young couple had not realised was that having a baby would be so much work and worry. Especially a baby like Particle. His uncommon intensity and apparent intelligence distracts them from doing the things they want to do, which is usually lying in their comfortable black Cocoons, glued to the comings and goings of Famers on YouStar. So a lot of the time they leave him confined in the Babycoon where he can watch too.

But baby Particle has figured out to navigate the channels of his 'coon himself. He's found the frequencies for children much older than him, and he devours what he finds on them. Having taught himself to read, he is progressing through years of education each month, gorging on the thin, basic diet of intellectual tools, rules and factules, which is supposed to sustain children and young adults.

This most unusual child's viewing choices are unremarked by his parents, but they have not gone completely unnoticed. Those who know enough about independent learning to know that they must do something about it watch Particle's watching. They have already resolved to respond.

It is a cool summer's evening. Crickets chirrup with content in the yard, seeking mates that may be lurking in the sparse, spindly vegetation that struggles to breathe and grow in the unwelcoming air. There is much excitement in the household. Tonight is Changeover night on YouStar, the most popular, most important, and for most people the only channel of the InterFace. Tumor – Flaunch's sister, Particle's aunt – will be one of the ten Famers for the next thirty days. The lucky ten's fellow citiburbians will follow the Famers' every activity, their comings and goings, their doings and beings. The clamouring videorazzi will scrupulously document it all, and feed it down the line to the populace, which will endlessly evaluate, adjudicate and comment on the action, enviously imagining what they would do if they were in the Famers' places. Almost every Famer is worth the scrutiny and dissection of the Gobblers out in the citiburbs, but to know or be related to one, well, that gives the experience an exciting new dimension.

For the next month, Flaunch and Pound will identify and empathise with Tumor's tics and flaws, laugh and commiserate with her foibles and failings, cheer on her conquests and claim her victories as their own. After all, she is family, even if they rarely see her, or the rest of the family for that matter. How thrilling it will be to watch her and tell each other 'that is so Tumor,' or to comment online, with great authority, 'Tumor is always doing that,' or simply, 'that's my sister,' so that all the other viewers know that they know a Famer!

There is a risk that Tumor will not be rated on the A-list, that she will not get a lot of prime coverage. She is near-middle age. She tends to be cranky but she is not mean and so she might be seen as not entertaining. The younger demo might not be interested in her. Perhaps she might make the B-list. But Flaunch likes to think that his sister's goofy sense of humour will emerge, and that perhaps her clumsiness might lead to some good physical comedy, which could, fingers crossed, draw an unexpected audience. She was on YouStar eighteen years ago, when she was a lithe, athletic lass of just nineteen. Then, she rated very well. She was pretty, active and keen. In the meantime, her slender figure has filled out, and her sunny outlook has clouded somewhat. But looking back at pretty, active and keen nineteen-year-old Tumor, it's no wonder that she rated well in those past days.

Flaunch was on when he was a healthy, good-looking twenty-two-year-old, engaged to Pound but still single enough to cut a swathe through the female co-Famers. That's part of the fun of watching YouStar, knowing that in the past you've been that celebrity, and will be again when the random ballot to select Famers comes up with your name on it again. One day, you'll live the exhilaration of Fame for a whole month. Unless you're beautiful or interesting, you'll know the tension of having to do outrageous things so you'll be noticed and rate, but also having to make sure you don't go too far to gain attention and end up as a B-lister. Ratings are ratings, whether you are beautiful and kind or ugly and unpleasant, but the viewers can be very sensitive about people who try too hard.

So, Flaunch and his wife Pound lie back in their joining Cocoons, ensconced in their plush chairs, surrounded by their screens – one large and eight smaller – to keep track of what's going on over on the YouStar sub-channels. They are preparing for the Changeover, when the old Famers are seen off and the new ones are welcomed. Their keyboards project in front of them; they can fire off fan mail, contribute amusing or abusive comments, deride or endorse the new Famers, or chip in to debates and arguments started by the observations of others. Yes, Flaunch and Pound are looking forward to an absorbing night's viewing.

On this important night, a knock at the door is most un-welcome. It means that someone is outside, which is unusual and off-putting. Not that Pound and Flaunch are afraid; like all Gobblers they feel perfectly secure. Breathing the 37% component of oxygen in the atmosphere may make them a little light-headed and confused, but it doesn't make them worry or fret, or even think about things too much. But it is strange, someone being at the door now. Flaunch glances at Pound; Pound looks at Flaunch. Neither of them wants to move, but the knocking becomes quite insistent.

Pound gives in and drags herself from her Cocoon, opening the door to see two men wearing the semi-casual uniform of the Liberty Guard: light blue button-down hemp shirts with open necks, and dark blue trousers over heavy black carbo -leather boots. They smile pleasantly.

'Good evening. I am Officer Pinion and this is Officer Prompt. Sorry for interrupting you on Changeover night.'

Pound grunts and bids them come in. Without looking

back to see if they followed her, she bounds back into the living room and shoves herself back into her Cocoon, gluing her eyes to the screen to see what she missed. Flaunch looks up and smiles at the two officers, who stand mildly in the centre of the room, conscious that they have come at an awkward time, and obviously frustrated that they are missing out on Changeover night.

Flaunch is irritated that Pound only brought the men in, instead of dealing with whatever they want. She has immersed herself in YouStar again and pointedly ignores all three of the men in their living room. Flaunch asks curtly, 'What can we do for you?'

'We've come about Particle,' says Prompt.

'Oh?' says Flaunch absently. Tumor is at the back of the crowd of new Famers; Flaunch has to concentrate hard to keep track of her.

'Yes. The Babycoon surveillance team has been watching his InterFace viewing for some time. For a little boy, he spends a lot of time on education channels. Channels meant for kids much older than him. Kids who are already at school.'

'Really? I always thought he was just watching YouStar, didn't you dear?'

'Um, ah, yes, sure.' Pound does not take her eyes off her screens.

'Well the fact is, he's been doing much more than that. He's been learning.' The way Officer Prompt leans on the word *learning* startles them, and they look up. Is this a good or a bad thing? It's never happened to them or anyone they know before, a child voluntarily taking on his own education. They look at each other with concern.

Officer Pinion nods. 'Our surveillance people have passed Particle's viewing habits and accomplishments on to the folks at the Bastion, and they have identified the boy as a Prod.' This bombshell elicits two blank looks and a few seconds of silence.

'A what?' Flaunch leans out of his Cocoon, one elbow out over the black chrome gunwale. The officer now has his full attention.

Prompt repeats, 'A Prod.'

'Yes. What does that mean?'

'A prodigy. Or a productive. Or both, it depends who you talk to. In any case, a person of extraordinary intelligence, destined to live a privileged life in the Bastion, serving the community… Does any of this ring a bell?'

'I know what the Bastion is.' It is where the government leader Joe and the bureaucratic Sharps live. It is a mythical place, its operations virtually unknown. There are rumours that the occupants enjoy lives of unlimited privilege and un-trammelled luxury. Flaunch grins. His boy is special, for some reason. How or why it happened he does not know, and what precisely it means he has no idea, but it must be good. The boy is special. That may mean special treatment for his parents.

Of course, they've always thought that Particle was clever, but it isn't as if they've taken a lot of notice. He won't be eligible for YouStar for many years yet, and he's even a long way from the precursor, TeenStar, so he won't really need much more than their passing attention until then. So to find that all this time he's had this special talent and that he's important already and the Bastion needs him, well, what an unexpected belt of pride and pleasure! And one that's happened in real life, no less! If only this had happened while one of them was a Famer – wait, Flaunch wonders, is there a way to communicate this to Tumor?

'So, wow! What happens next? What do we do?'

'Nothing for now. We will take you all to the Bastion, where you will be looked after, and Particle will enter the Bastillion, where the Prods live and work together, inventing and creating. Even most the Sharps dont get to go into the Bastillion.' Pinion has made this announcement before. He enjoys it; the parents are always shocked and joyful, even if their Changeover night has been interrupted. The announcement of a Prod is better than Changeover night, after all. It's even better than getting a call-up to YouStar, which is saying something.

Flaunch and Pound are out of their Cocoons. They do not entirely understand what has happened, but they do know that Bastion life is a huge step up for them. No more of the required fifteen-hour workweeks; no more worrying that their credit will be revoked if they miss a week; no more worries at all. What could life in the Bastion mean other than free time and luxury Cocoons?

'Fren, that is incredible!' Flaunch's eyes bug out and his voice climbs a full octave higher than usual. He pumps Pinion's hand. Behind him, Tumor is on screen, but he doesn't notice at all. 'Just give us a few minutes to get a few things together. But we don't really need anything, do we? It's all at the Bastion, isn't it?'

'It's all there fren, don't you worry.' Pinion smiles; he doesn't even mind that Flaunch is still holding his hand. 'I've seen plenty of people like you go to the Bastion empty-handed, and I've never seen anyone come back for anything.'

Pound's face clouds over. 'But if we live in the Bastion, doesn't that mean we can't be on YouStar? We can't be famous?'

'That is true,' Pinion admits. 'You cannot be a Famer. But you'll be in the Bastion, the home of Freedom. You'll want for nothing, be denied nothing, and you can do anything you want, other than be on YouStar.'

'Or leave,' Prompt adds.

'Yes, quite right, Officer Prompt. Or leave.' Pinion gives his colleague a vaguely reproving look.

Flaunch and Pound are ready to go. Flaunch briefly wonders if they can get these officers to stop off at a message station so Tumor can announce it on YouStar, but the thought pops out of his mind immediately. In a few moments they have gathered everything they want to take – a few snacks thrown together by the automat in the kitchen, and a bottle of THC+ Flurient.

'For the journey,' Pound smiles.

'Okay let's go!' Flaunch is exultant.

But the Liberty Guards do not move.

'Um,' ventures Officer Prompt, 'the baby?'

The parents laugh at their silliness, and Pound goes into his room to collect their precious little bundle.

Outside, the summer night has cooled further, and there is a chill breeze. The atmosphere is so thin these days that it never really gets too warm any more. Pinion opens the levtrans bus doors for the family. Particle is cranky and irritable now that he has been roused from sleep. He cries and struggles as Prompt tries to secure him in the travel seat.

But Flaunch and Pound can't wait to get in. The levtrans is spacious, fitted out with luxurious travelling Cocoons, and the large windows are thoughtfully smoked all the way to blackness so the lights outside won't distract them from Changeover night. They hope they haven't missed much of Tumor's screen time. In no time at all, Particle has gone back to sleep, and his parents are absorbed in YouStar.

Eventually, the levtrans stops and Pinion invites them to leave the bus. They are in a huge, shiny garage, empty but for their transport. The ceiling is so high that they can't see it. It might as well be the sky, but its blackness is dense and solid, and they can dimly discern walls to either side of them.

The Guards show them through a door, and hand them over to three nameless people dressed neck to toe in black: Sharps. They seem nowhere near as friendly as Prompt and Pinion, who have already rushed back to their bus. This is no place for people like them.

Without words, almost without any signs of life at all, two of the Sharps lead Flaunch and Pound into a bright, well-lit room almost the size of their whole house. The third takes Particle, but the parents are too amazed by the room – lavishly endowed with gleaming Cocoons, fridges, snack counters and automats groaning with colourful foods, and a bar stocked generously with every flavour of Flurient – to even notice that their son is gone.

'Oh my god, it's beautiful,' whispers Pound. 'I've never seen anything like this. I'm gobbled.' She giggles.

'This is the staging area,' says the Sharp to the left. 'You are free to stay here and catch up on YouStar.' The Sharp waits for a second. 'Turret has taken Particle to the assessment area.'

It's debatable as to whether Flaunch and Pound haven't heard this last remark, or whether they simply don't care. They're already sharing a brand new double Cocoon, gorging on the fizzy madness of YouStar and sipping on a rare peppermint Flurient. The Sharps leave. The door's bolt slides into place behind them.

After a few minutes of looking for Tumor on his many screens, Flaunch starts to feel odd. It's like a fog is lifting, but he never knew the fog was there, and the clarity invading his senses is awful. He looks at Pound, who looks at him. They both feel the same thing. Neither can name it. In any case, the feeling soon passes, and in its place is a terrible headache. Again, they look at each other in confusion. The headache, thankfully, fades – and is replaced by an irresistible drowsiness. They fall asleep and dream of ratings and Fame and a lengthy retirement in their new, opulent Bastion home. Moments later, the carbon monoxide that has flooded the room claims their lives as they sleep on.

1.

The children repeated the words flashing up on the screens of their Educoons in full voice and with complete conviction. The small, egg-shaped Educoons were neatly arranged so that the teacher could see all of his students at all times, could see the whole gallery of Gobblers in their teaching machines, slowly absorbing their lessons.

The teacher, Gneiss, looked up from his screen while the children recited their creed. Joe was indeed their Father of Freedom, the sole leader of their society: unelected, unchallenged and apparently eternal. As the manifestation and personification of the practically invisible ruling elite of Sharps, he had led the Gobblers for more generations than anyone could remember. That he would be there for the rest of their lives and beyond was a given.

'Our Father of Freedom is Joe. Joe tells us all we need to know,' said the children. Gneiss turned his attention back to his controller. It was time for him to play his part in the lesson.

On the screens before the attentive students, Joe's homely, avuncular figure appeared, seated at a plain desk in a plain room. His eyes were bright and his gaze was sharp, but his features were soft and civil, framed by snow-white hair. He was wise but approachable. He was concerned about them, as a father might be.

'Hello, frens,' he said with a smile. The children listened eagerly. Everyone listened when Joe spoke, and he spoke to his people regularly through InterFace Joe-casts. His casts were pre-recorded, and they were played in every Educoon in every school at the same time, so every child believed he was speaking directly to them, and only them, and right then.

'It's an exciting time for you, now,' Joe continued. 'Over the last few days you've been given the keys to the rest of your life. You have your Manacle tattoos on your wrists, with micro-bots, transmitters, receivers, and GPS locators. You'll need them for almost everything you do from now on. They're the symbols of your Freedom, and you need to get used to how they work. Look at the light blue ring around your left wrist. Go on, lift up your left hand and look at it.'

The students all did as Joe asked, although most were so pleased to have finally been given their Manacles that they'd been playing with them and staring at them practically non-stop. The tattooing had been painful, as the various components and colours were injected under the skin, but it marked their transition from children to young adults and made them feel proud and Free.

'Whenever the blue Manacle on your left wrist tingles, like this –' Gneiss pushed a button on his console and they all felt an electrical pulse circling their wrists like a ticklish, intrusive wave, impossible to ignore but not uncomfortable '– there is a message for you in the Message Centre in your local Hub. You have twenty-four hours to retrieve your message. Who knows, it may even be your invitation to the most wonderful time of your life, an appearance on TeenStar, or later, when you're older, on YouStar itself.'

Gneiss heard, somewhere in the distance, beyond the classroom but within the school's carbcrete walls, a low rumble. It was unusual, and vaguely threatening.

'When you've finished school and been recommended a career,' Joe continued in his genial tenor, 'every now and then your left Manacle will throb a little, like this.'

Gneiss pushed another button and the students' wrists began to palpitate with subtle urgency. 'That,' said Joe, 'is the signal that you are required at your place of work in three hours. It will throb again each hour after that, a little faster each time, to remind you. You can miss the odd work shift here and there if you must, but if you miss too many, it will affect how the green Manacle on your right wrist works.'

The noise outside grew louder and more ominous. The echoes in the hall were unmistakable: the crash of heavy boots running at full pace, eight or ten pairs of them. It must be the Liberty Guard.

'Your right Manacle holds your credit information and a record of everything you buy, and it uses a GPS transmitter that talks to the cameras around you, so if anything bad should happen, we'll know where you are.'

Gneiss could feel the blood draining from his face. The thrumming of boots and the clank of chains and weapons came closer, growing louder and more sinister. He swallowed and stood up. This had never happened before, but he had long feared and even half-expected it.

The students watched Gneiss lapse into consternation – they all knew how their right Manacles controlled their access to credit, and seeing this unique reaction on their teacher's face was far more engrossing. The thundering boots were exciting but a little frightening, too. The running troops stopped right outside the door, and someone out there shouted breathlessly.

Gneiss looked at the two children occupying the two fron Educoon; Strabismus, who everyone called Biz, and the girl next to him, Bock. They looked back in confusion. There was a weird mixture of sorrow and pleading in his eyes.

'I… I'm… I just wanted…'

Bock and Biz, like the other children, were more concerned about the noise coming from the hallway than what he might be saying. The sudden silence outside their door was even more alarming than the running. Were the Liberty Guards about to burst in and give them all the Freedom Ride?

And then it was past them. The thunder of boots resumed and the troops ran off down the hall, where they stopped again. There was a terrifying cacophony of wood splintering and glass crashing, mingled with the screams of children and a bellow from Glia, who taught students a couple of years older. The boots retreated down the hallway, slower and more quietly now than on their arrival. Glia howled, but in a muted way, from a distance. A few seconds after that, the hallway was silent again.

Gneiss collapsed into his chair, dropped his head into his hands and tried to gather himself. His students stared at him, many with their mouths wide open, unable to fathom what had just happened and why Gneiss was in such a state of panic.

'So remember: left hand communication, right hand credit. Together, your two Manacles bring you everything you could want or need, and keep you Free.' Joe clasped his hands together in front of him and smiled handsomely. 'I thank you for your attention, and return you to your normal school programming.'

Joe faded from the screen as a frightening, familiar image appeared: a giant building, many times taller than any the students had ever seen in real life, crumbling to the ground in a billowing cloud of dust and smoke, while an equally tall tower next to it burned. A title appeared over this horrific image:

HISTORYCAST #379
The End of the War Centuries 1900–2122

This was followed by a montage of brutal scenes: men shooting at each other; planes dropping bombs that detonated in colossal, expanding balloons of mottled black and orange flames; running children, their arms outstretched so you could see the dangling shreds of burnt skin and the horror, fear and sickening pain distorting their faces into cruel masks; then fields of crosses, weeping women, children and men; and more and more scenes of death and destruction, culminating in an immense cloud with a ring of pure, malevolent energy pulsating around its grotesque grey stalk, rising up over a devastated landscape like a gigantic mushroom.

'By the beginning of the twenty-first century,' said the voice-over, 'the world had been more or less constantly at war for almost a century. The economy appears to have been dependent on the continuation of conflict, which was fuelled by disagreements over the ownership of the energy producing substance called oil. The so-called 'Clash of Civilisations' between three religions that were in fact variations of each other heightened the hatred and pushed aggression to new levels. The ongoing Religoil wars could only end in global disaster. But first, nature herself had a surprise in store for humanity…'

Like so many of the Eduvids that filled their school days, this was a repeat. Since learning to read and write, the children learned the same lessons for the next fifteen years. Without this repetition, nothing would sink in to their soft, Gobbler brains.

Gneiss remained silent, his head bowed and his hands, almost invisible in the oily curls of his hair, still shaking. There was a gentle knock at the door, and Gneiss at last recovered his composure. He sat bolt upright and said, 'come,' in the time-honoured tradition of teachers everywhere. The deputy Principal, Noll, entered the room, unassuming as ever. The kids peered out at him from their Educoons, perhaps hoping he would explain the recent ruckus, but he dismissed them with a wave of his hand.

'Eyes on screen, children.' Gneiss stood, and tried not to look alarmed.

'Glia,' Noll confirmed. 'It seems she has been telling her class that Flurient damages the brain, and warning them not to drink it. One of her students, Bint, mentioned this to her parents, and the parent passed it on in conversation in a levtrans. Of course the surveillance microphones picked it up, and the Liberty Guard investigated. Glia will not be returning.' He excused himself from the room, apologising to the students for interrupting their studies.

Gneiss turned back to his console, then looked up again. 'Turn to the front.' His students obediently spun their seats to face him. Gneiss turned down the sound levels in their Educoons a bit so they could hear him, but not enough to alert anyone who may be monitoring their output. The class was used to this situation. Gneiss often delivered lectures that were not on the curriculum. They enjoyed his quirky diversions.

'Children, we've had a security issue in the building, as we all heard. Sadly, one of our teachers has been taken away and will most probably be given the Freedom Ride.' The children snickered and passed knowing glances. The Freedom Ride had never been properly explained to them, but they all knew that the people who took it never came back.

'Now you know,' said Gneiss in utmost seriousness, 'that I have on occasion departed from the standard curriculum to share with you my own thoughts about a range of matters.' The pupils responded with a series of nods and smiles. 'Although I have never shared anything that would jeopardise the well-being of our community,' he said, 'the very fact that I have trusted you enough to take you into my confidence on these matters is frowned upon. So I must ask, hands up anyone who has ever repeated to their parents, other family members or friends outside this class, anything that I have said.'

Biz and Bock looked bemused and thoughtful, as though they were trying to decode what Gneiss was saying. The rest didn't seem to care about anything except the fact that they had been momentarily released from watching yet another tedious Historycast.

'Very good,' said Gneiss, as every hand remained unraised. He heard the relief in his voice, but the children would not have picked it up. No doubt to them he was always boringly the same. 'There's really no point in talking about what goes on at school when you're at home,' he continued. 'Your parents and friends already know all this stuff, and they don't need to have it repeated to them, do they? Besides, if you interrupt their free time, especially while they're watching YouStar, they'll probably get annoyed, won't they?' He'd get no disagreement on that point – every one of his pupils had been scolded or punished for uttering a word at the wrong time at home. His relief grew. At least for now, he was safe.

He looked at his screen and returned to the main lesson. 'So there you have it, your future. You're expected to work fifteen hours per week, the same number of hours you currently put into your schooling. But I'm here to tell you,' he continued with a confidential air, 'that if you're one of the lucky ones to go into the productive industries, you don't have to stick to those hours.' Even the distracted students looked up at him. Who wouldn't love to hear a way to work fewer than fifteen hours?

'If you're in a job you enjoy in an industry that encourages it, you can work as long as you like – thirty hours, or even more.'

Phage guffawed in disbelief, spitting out a few specks of partly chewed biscuit as he did so, and Necker groaned. That was no surprise; they were the two laziest students in the class. Although Necker might have just been having a nightmare.

'When I was a child, my father ran our local greenhouse garden, and he loved it.' He was getting wistful, but he couldn't help it. 'He used to spend as much time as he could in the greenhouse, sometimes up to forty hours per week.' A wave of incredulity swept the classroom. As if anyone could actually work that much!

'I spent as much time with him as I could. And even though it was strictly against the rules, we slept in the greenhouse most nights. And you know what? It changed my life. I wanted to be a gardener, like my dad. But one day, just after I finished school, I watched a Joe-cast. Joe was talking about the need for people to volunteer for jobs in what we call the caring careers, and I found that all I really wanted to do was become a teacher. All of a sudden it all made perfect sense, and I had a plan for the rest of my life.' He looked around. Biz and Bock were hanging on his every word, but everyone else looked bored or fidgety, or asleep. 'I still don't know how it happened. And looking at most of you now, I wonder why.' His gaze fell on his two star pupils, Bock and Biz. 'Then again,' he said softly, 'perhaps everything happens for a reason.'

2.

There were lots of things about school that Biz liked. There was Bock, for a start. Her green eyes had a spark of intelligence that he couldn't recall seeing in anyone else, and she even liked talking to him. He had been seated next to Bock ever since they'd started school, and he liked her more every year.

He also liked the teacher, Gneiss. This unusual and empathetic man had already taught him so much more than he thought he'd ever know, and he was getting smarter every day. Gneiss was squat, and his wavy, messy hair didn't just stop at his head, it grew all over and around his face in a lavish beard, covering his sometimes-flaky skin. He was the only person over the age of fourteen that Biz had ever seen wearing shorts, and that, added to his long white socks and scuffed up, scruffy faux leather sandals, accentuated his stumpiness. The whole outfit must have been specially made at the local Synthetron. The only normal things about it were that it was made of hemp, it was dark and dull coloured, and the shirt had the standard squared collar and V-neck.

Gneiss had been their teacher since the first day of school, when the students were just three years old. He had sat Bock and Biz together – another reason to like him – and it was just as well they both liked him, because he would guide them through their entire school lives. Gneiss seemed to like them more than anyone else in the class, and sometimes it seemed like the three of them were the only ones in the room, or at least the only ones that mattered. And they both seemed to advance more quickly than their classmates.

The only other person in his class that Biz liked was Necker. This powerful round boy with fierce eyes offset by cute, nearly girly curls and dangling ringlets, often stepped in to save the too-smart class pets Biz and Bock from the threats and actual violence of their classmates. He was at least as dim as even the dimmest of his classmates, but Necker had an ingrained sense of right and wrong, and he couldn't stand to see anyone bullied. So Necker, Bock and Biz were famous friends, sitting together at break times and sharing the walk home via the local Hub. Now they were teenagers with their own Manacles, they would of course share a Communalcoon at the local Cocoonery, watching TeenStar, which you could only see there. Although it was a long way off, they often talked about getting jobs in the same career, in the same place, so they could stay together forever.

The one thing that Biz didn't like about school was the testing. Every year strange, mean people turned up and took over the classroom to perform a battery of tests while Gneiss stood by, staring at the blank walls like a Gobbler. The strange men and women measured the children's growth and weight, tested eyesight and hearing, probed their skin and mouths and minds, asked questions, and ran tests in reading, writing, maths, science, electronics. They checked reflex times and got the children to run up and down, and throw things and catch things, and made them do all sorts things they were never allowed to do except during the tests. And always, there were more and more questions, not knowledge questions but about how the kids felt, what they liked and didn't like, what they wanted to do, what they didn't want to do, and what they could do but didn't really want to, but would if they had to. It was odd, intrusive and taxing, and Biz didn't like it at all, although like everyone else he just let it happen.

That is, until he was thirteen and in his eleventh year of school. After that year's tests, the school reported that Biz needed a doctor. This was a little odd, given that Biz had, as did everyone else, nanobots that meandered about the outside of his body in a nanomat, as well as a nanostream in his bloodstream. Between them, these autoatomic medics roamed every pore, organ, orifice, gland and bloodway of his body, seeking out and destroying any molecule that might cause trouble. Why would anyone ever have to see a doctor, unless it was to replace, reprogram or augment one's nanofriends?

His parents, Viand and Arbeit, worried for a moment. But they told themselves that the school, as an official instrument of the state, must know things they themselves did not and to be honest could not even imagine, so they agreed: Biz must see the doctor. And, even better, they would not have to deviate from their routine much at all – the doctor would come to them. They could watch YouStar while the doctor did whatever he had to do.

This was particularly agreeable, because they had both fallen in love with Strum. Like most of the top rating Famers, she was young and pretty, and just watching her go through her morning routine of stretching exercises, coffee and cereal in the Fame House kitchen, then choosing an outfit for that afternoon's event, gave people a thrill. Thousands of viewers stayed glued to the channel devoted to Strum, posting witty and wry observations or remarks. Arbeit and Viand could not wait to get home from their work monitoring surveillance cameras and logging data on people's movement to watch the fascinating, dreamy life of Strum and her fellow Famers. They loved her far too much to let a little thing like a doctor coming to see Biz interfere with their viewing, particularly since, they were sure, their fan mail about Strum would soon appear over the InterFace. Like everyone else, Arbeit and Viand sent messages of encouragement, love, anger, hate, distaste, bile, pathos or vitriol about the Famers parading around their screens on YouStar. They were each keeping one screen in their Cocoons dedicated to those messages, and occasionally ticked a post that they really liked. Sometimes their posts got ticks, and if one of them had enough ticks they would start trending up. Oh, to be trending up.

So Arbeit didn't take much notice when Viand let the severe, haughty man with drawn, furrowed cheeks and dark, aware eyes into the room. He seemed foreign, somehow, but Arbeit and Viand knew all they needed to know about him – he was a doctor from the government, he was safe and respectable, and he had arrived at a crucial viewing time, for Strum was wearing only a towel, which she was about to drop in order to take a shower.

Biz was InterFacing when the doctor entered his room, and, like his father, was deeply frustrated at being distracted from the screen. The doctor watched as the boy reluctantly extracted himself from his Cocoon.

'Doctor Psyllium,' the man said in a humourless voice that crackled like dry paper. He didn't like the boy, but he didn't have to. The boy was an object to be studied and understood, not liked, respected or otherwise accommodated. He was, however, an oddity, a Gobbler who, without any treatment at all, possessed some of the perceptive and analytical abilities of a Sharp: focus, attention, curiosity and memory. The question now was whether they should start the treatment that would prepare him for later induction into the Bastion.

Biz didn't think he needed a doctor at all, let alone a real live one who would in all likelihood want to look into his thoughts and hopes and jab and poke around his awkward adolescent frame. He felt well and strong and knew he would keep growing and getting stronger. His nanomat and nanostream were obviously working perfectly, because he had never suffered an illness or so much as a blemish on his perfect skin. His only problem was that he thought differently than his peers. He was interested in school and he wanted to learn, and the only people he knew who wanted to learn for the sake of it were himself, Bock and Gneiss. They liked to discover how and why things worked and work out how to make new things. One day perhaps they would be able to formulate new thoughts. But the doctor could not help him with that. So, when Psyllium began asking questions, Biz grunted instead of answering. There was no reason for this dour, intimidating man to interrupt Strum's shower.

Unperturbed by this feeble cantankerousness, Psyllium questioned the boy for ninety minutes, grilling him about his life, his thoughts, his actions, his reactions to school and what was being taught to him there, his thoughts on what he was learning and his opinions of how others in his class were progressing, his friendships and relationships, his enmities and apathies. He asked curly, probing questions that invaded Biz's mental space and excited him; here was someone whose mind worked like his own but who could control it much better. He became more animated in his answers.

The doctor was intense and clear in a way that Biz had never seen, and he envied. Psyllium knew Biz better than he knew himself, and while he was patronising and supercilious, as if he was sceptical that Biz could possess any thought processes at all, by the end of the interrogation Biz felt that the doctor had started to see him as an equal, or at least a junior equal. In some ways he even felt superior; he was smart enough to be guarded or evasive in answering questions about Gneiss or Bock, in whom Psyllium showed great interest. In fact, setting aside the doctor's gruff, relentless demeanour, he enjoyed the interview, and towards the end Psyllium's attitude started to soften. Then the doctor produced a large syringe and took blood from Biz's arm. The doctor said he would test the blood for anomalies, then let himself out of the house without disturbing Arbeit and Viand at all.

Psyllium was running behind time; he ran from the house to his preon drive. His left Manacle had buzzed twice during the interview with the boy, presumably something he needed to take care of back at the Bastion, but he still had one interview to go, with Biz's classmate Bock. Her test scores were on a par with those attained by Biz, but while Gneiss had strongly recommended the boy, he thought the girl was not really Sharp material. Psyllium looked at the clock on his dashboard. If Biz was the best the class had to offer, he wouldn't bother interviewing Bock. The young man had only just scraped in as a candidate, and if the girl was less gifted than him she definitely wouldn't make it. He headed to the Message Centre.

Two days later, Psyllium returned without warning just as Strum was preparing for the final dinner with the rest of the current YouStar Famers, and seemed quite likely to hook up with the handsome young baker. She had to choose the best outfit she could, and the audience was giving her suggestions. Arbeit and Viand were desperate to see if she would wear the one they'd voted for.

Viand dragged herself away to admit the doctor. As soon as he was inside, she stood edgily next to her Cocoon to see what was happening on the screens inside, half-listening to what the doctor was saying, but not really hearing him. She nodded and said yes to whatever he said until he insisted that both parents disengage from the InterFace, which they did with theatrical reluctance. They fetched Biz from his room; he, too, was dismayed at missing the resolution of Strum's fashion fix, but when he saw Psyllium, he smiled eagerly.

'Biz,' Psyllium announced, 'is afflicted with the Leadership Gene.' Viand looked anxiously from the doctor to her husband, but Arbeit stared back, uncomprehendingly, before trying to sneak a look inside his Cocoon. 'Leadership Gene?' he repeated.

'Yes. He has a degenerative condition that, if left untreated, could claim his life. The Gene is both a blessing and a curse: it endows the carrier with extraordinary intellect, but it also leads to the breakdown of vital soft tissue. The boy needs immediate treatment, and he will be required to continue taking it for the remainder of his life. But there is good news. Joe has decreed that anyone with the Leadership Gene is suited to government work. Not only will Biz be inducted into the Bastion when he finishes school, he will receive treatment for his condition starting immediately.'

This was a lot for Arbeit to take in. 'So you're saying he's sick, but you'll look after him until he finishes school, and then take him into the Bastion?'

'That's correct. The condition isn't serious as long as it is properly treated, and we intend to provide just what Biz needs to get better and better. And when he comes into the Bastion, he will be very well looked after indeed. He'll get the best care available anywhere. In the meantime, a crew will arrive tomorrow to fit a special air conditioner in Biz's room, which will distribute what we call free air for him to breathe – air that's free of any impurities that can cause the gene to mutate and kill the carrier. A smaller free air unit will be placed in his Cocoon, and one in his school Educoon. He should be alright when he is in transit or out of the home, as long as he is not away from one of his purifiers for more than a few days, and even then it takes quite a while for the effects to become noticeable. Any questions?'

Viand looked at Biz, then at Arbeit, then back at the boy, then at Psyllium. The whole medical thing had gone a fair way above her. 'So if Biz goes to the Bastion at age eighteen, he'll be removed from the YouStar rolls, yes?'

'That's correct,' said Psyllium, without rolling his eyes.

'Oh, I do hope he gets to be a TeenStar Famer before then.' Viand clasped her hands, prayer-like, in front of her.

3.

'Can you believe we've been together for fifteen years? I've known you all since you were innocent, delightful children – and look at you now.' Gneiss looked around the classroom and could see that the great majority of students had, as usual, no idea what he was talking about. In fact, most weren't paying the least bit of attention to what he was saying. Some were sleeping, more were daydreaming, staring at nothing, their minds as blank as their expressions. In the cool, still air he could hear Necker's susurrant snore. Even Gneiss thought the clock was turning the seconds slowly.

'Look, it's the last day of your school life, so I'm not even going to try and teach you anything.' He could see Necker drooling, now, too. 'But I would appreciate it if you would do me the courtesy of pretending to care about what I am saying, even if it is just a random rant.' No response. 'Things have changed so much since I first met you all.' He scanned the room. 'Back then you were short, scrawny, uneducated Gobblers who didn't care about anything but your Cocoons at home. Now, you're all much taller and most of you have learned enough to at least muddle your way through life. So, I guess even you would have to concede that I have succeeded in educating you, despite your efforts to avoid being contaminated by even the most modest facts, let alone infected by a modicum of critical thinking.

'The funny thing is, I am going to miss you all. Even you, Phage.' Flat-headed Phage looked up from his sandwich and smiled. 'And do you know why?' Phage shook his head and chewed his meat. 'Because although you never paid any attention to a word I said, and you ate your way through just about every class you ever attended, you always did it with a smile. At least when your mouth was not as full.' Phage grinned, showing detritus-covered dentition. A few of the students laughed, and Phage laughed, too.

'Seriously though, I hope in all sincerity that you have gained enough from me in our time together to get through what remains of your lives without too much trouble. I hope that you will take away more than just the knowledge of how to spell "slut" and to type it onto an air keyboard so you can insult or inspire some less than discriminating Famer. You may not know or care about it, but I have actually taken a great deal of time and care trying to instil in you some principles, some appreciation of the moral aspects of everything you do.' He looked directly at Bock and Biz. 'And for this, our final lesson together, I would like to reiterate the importance of integrity and inquiry, and most of all to remind you: you do not have to be Gobblers. Of course, you always will be Gobblers, with the notable exception of our fren Biz, here, who, as we all know, will be entering the Bastion.' Biz blushed, and Bock leaned out of her 'Coon, beaming at him with pride.

'So, you will be Gobblers,' continued Gneiss. 'But you don't always have to act like Gobblers. You don't have to be like everyone else you ever met. You can question what is going on around you. You can object to the way things are being done. You can disagree.'

'You can get yourself on the Freedom Ride,' interjected Allergen. He was rewarded with scattered laughter.

'Ha ha, very clever Allergen. If only you'd shown some spark of that wit in the last fifteen years, we might have made something of you. Nonetheless,' Gneiss announced to the whole class, 'Allergen is, perhaps for the first time ever, right.

You can, if you are not careful, find yourself taking the Freedom Ride, if you're not just a little bit sensible about how you disagree and with whom. But that does not mean you should just roll over and do whatever you're told without question. It doesn't mean you can't imagine and propose improvements in our way of living. It doesn't mean you can't think!'

He slammed his hand hard on his desk, making a loud bang that startled the class and shook Necker out of his slumber. The dribble on his chin spilled over onto his Educoon console.

'Necker! Must you slobber all over the school equipment? Kindly drool on yourself, fren, and let your nanomat deal with it,' Gneiss commanded. Necker looked vaguely sheepish, and grinned foolishly. Gneiss returned to his normal placid, modulated delivery. 'I want you all to know that there are things out there that are bigger than you, and that it's okay – it's more than okay, it's admirable – for you to dedicate your life to them.'

'You mean like the InterFace,' goofed Necker, wiping spittle from his cheek. He looked around, expecting laughter, but saw only blank, disinterested faces.

'I mean precisely the opposite, Necker,' said Gneiss. 'If you give your life to the InterFace, working in surveillance during the day and spending the rest of your time ogling YouStar, you will always be giving yourself to the status quo, to the way things are, and at its end your life will not have made a whit of difference to your planet or your people.

'The things that I am talking about are bigger than you, and the InterFace, and YouStar. But they're not things at all, they are ideas. Concepts. Principles. If you commit yourself to these important things – and I hope that I've taught you at least some of them – you stand a chance, however slim, of making a difference. If you act according to an objective ethical standard, even if it's one that you and you alone in the world uphold, you will be practically unique among your peers.

Gneiss stated pacing between the Educoons. 'Ours has long been an amoral society, where actions are judged not on their moral foundation, their principle, but on their expediency for the person carrying them out. In our time and nation, there is no longer any requirement for integrity, a word I doubt you have ever heard uttered beyond these walls. Most Gobblers wouldn't know what it means, and Sharps have long considered it a tiresome impediment to getting things done. But in our years together I've gone "off script," to try and give each of you a sense of what integrity is, and how you can use it to improve the lives of your fellow humans. No doubt I have failed miserably.'

He stopped in front of Biz and stared into the young man's eyes. 'But if I have succeeded with just one of you, I will consider myself to have done a fine job.' He nodded. 'Because I believe that the time is coming when integrity will make a comeback.' He turned back to the rest of the class. 'And if I can have helped in that, then I too will have made a difference.'

The students were getting restless. There were only a few minutes left, and Gneiss still had one important thing to do. 'Anyway, it's time for me to perform my last official act as your teacher, and then you can go.' He returned to his control desk and sat down to consult the screen in front of him.

'Each of you has been recommended a career, based on the results of the testing carried out throughout your schooling. But you don't have to go into the career recommended to you. You can choose a different occupation, and simply ask for a job at the appropriate workplace – unless it's in a forbidden place like the YouStar compound or the Bastion. And of course there are many jobs in what we call the caring professions – teaching, child care, the military, computer medico assistant, emergency response and Liberty Guard officer – that only recruit volunteers. In order to do those jobs, you really have to want to.

'So after today you all have one month to consider whether

the career recommended to you is the one you want, or whether you'd prefer to volunteer for a different job or a career in the caring professions. If, at the end of the month – your first and last holiday, I'm afraid – you haven't volunteered or applied for another job, you need to report to the nearest place of business for your recommended career.

'So,' he drew a deep breath, 'without further ado ... Allergen, Bock, Knop, Necker, Trope and Whorl, you're all headed for surveillance in your local Hub. Grabe and Smirk, you're in InterFace services in the CentreHub. Cosm, pack your bags, you're going to be a YouStar camera operator.' Cosm squealed with delight.

'Phage, you're going to be a sales assistant at your local fresh food provisioner, which I am sure will suit you very well.' Phage grinned and took another bite of his sandwich. 'Furn and Perk, you'll be in transport, working at the levtrans depot nearest to your houses. And Flens and Shun, report to work at your local greenhouse garden any time in the next month. That leaves just one, and as I am sure you all agree, our most outstanding student. Biz will be entering the Bastion and taking on the responsibilities of leadership. The school and this class take great pride in his selection, and we all wish him well. Who would have thought that you lot would produce a Sharp?'

The class dutifully clapped, and Gneiss smiled on Biz with fatherly pride. He had guided the boy's development, and he had shown interest and attachment rare in a Gobbler. The lad had been metamorphosing into a Sharp even more quickly since he had entered treatment. His attitude had hardened. The dreaminess in his eyes had been replaced by a more penetrating, less tolerant stare. His focus, his attention span and his memory were astonishingly far above those of his schoolmates, except for Bock. But so far he did not have the mean, selfish edge that so many Sharps take on. He was still pleasant to be with, and still a champion of honesty and responsibility, much to

Gneiss's delight. He had even stayed friends with that true Gobbler, Necker.

The bell rang, and without permission the students cleared the classroom as quickly as if there was a YouStar crew outside. Bock and Biz didn't join them. They wanted to thank Gneiss for his years of service. He had been more involved in their growth and development than their parents; he was easily the strongest adult model of their youth. He had witnessed their milestones, rejoiced and empathised through their highest and lowest points, had helped and advised them through so many crises that they were almost as close to him as they were to each other. For an ordinary Gobbler like Gneiss – even a teacher – to have such an active intellect, and to show interest in any-thing beyond YouStar, was unusual; he was almost like a Sharp, and although they didn't realise that, they were thankful for all he had done. For his part, Gneiss knew that he'd played an important role in their lives, and he was proud of what they had accomplished. He could see everything laid out before them, and felt their excitement.

They chatted for thirty minutes, staying long after the school had emptied. They laughed at him when he complained that he'd have to go back to a brand new class of year ones and start the whole cycle again – but he joined in the laughter. Then they talked about the rest of the class, their work assignments, and their overwhelming collective hope of a YouStar call-up.

'Surveillance drones are very often picked for YouStar, Bock,' said Gneiss. 'I guess it's because they can be spared for a month without anyone noticing, ha ha.'

Bock, who was philosophical about being assigned to surveillance, had been on TeenStar when she was sixteen. She was beautiful and smart, and clever enough to mask her real intelligence, so she had been a ratings star. Her friendly simpleton act and her emerging sexuality put her in the top two across a range of categories. She had received a huge amount of fan mail, and most of it had been positive.

'Oh, I hope I don't get called up to YouStar ever,' she said with a shake of her head. 'I can't imagine being surrounded by all those Gobblers, scrambling for the attention of the Gobblers at home in their Cocoons.' She hung her head a little. 'I'd much rather be sitting with you two, talking about things.'

Gneiss nodded. 'Maybe you should volunteer for teaching. We never get picked for YouStar.' He pretended to frown.

But Bock perked up a little. 'If I did that, I could help Gobblers, and I'd be close to you, at least. Even if Biz has gone into the Bastion.' She smiled at her intelligent friend.

'Absolutely. Think about it, seriously,' said Gneiss, putting a hand on her shoulder. He left it there a little too long for it to be merely paternal. Then he looked at Biz as well. He was so proud, and truly believed that they could be happy and successful. 'I'm serious when I say that working with you two made my time with the class bearable,' he said. 'I hope I have done enough to help you onto the right path, and I trust that you will remember what I've taught you, especially when it comes to the most important things.'

4.

The month of free time was an idyll for Biz, Bock and Necker. They could do nothing, or everything, without commitment. Then, they knew, it would be over. When Biz was transferred to the Bastion, as far as they knew they would not see each other again. People who went into the Bastion did not come out except for reasons of state, family or death, and Gobblers could not visit them there. This was easily policed because nobody knew where it was or how big or small it was. And when Sharps did come out, they did not talk about what went on inside.

The only thing any Gobbler knew for sure was that, like everything else the Bastion was ruled by Joe, but even he never spoke about it when he appeared on the InterFace to deliver messages of good cheer, or to report on developments in the War in the East, or to explain how a certain "frivolous liberty" made it easier for terrorists to plot dastardly deeds, and would have to be given up.

Joe did sometimes appear just to remind everyone who was in charge, which seemed unnecessary since everyone understood that he was the sole authority – even though he didn't have a title, hadn't been elected, and nobody seemed to know when or how he had become so powerful. If some other official from the Bastion appeared on the InterFace, it was to address a local situation that Joe didn't have time to deal with. In such cases, the official was usually not named, and they cited Joe's authority for whatever was said.

The three friends understood that when Biz went into the Bastion there would be nothing holding Bock and Necker together. They had little in common. Although they would both be working in the Surveillance Centre, they probably wouldn't see each other very often. They would drift apart, and if they did get together they would just share a few words about Biz and the old days. Their short Gobbler memories would soon cloud over, and after a little while they would have only dim recollections of each other. There would be no acrimony, but also no attachment. Their friendship would fall victim to apathy.

Only Biz was really worried about the future, and found it hard to embrace this final fling freely. He was about to leave his friends, his family and his Cocoon. The school life he'd loved was already finished, and he was about to take on the responsibilities of leadership in a place he knew nothing about. Ever since he'd met Psyllium he'd been able to see everything more clearly and focus his energies on the future, but he was determined to make the last weeks with his friends count, so he hid his stress and doubts. He did such a good job that his friends didn't notice anything different about him.

One afternoon the three of them descended on the local Cocoonery to drink teen-strength Flurient and watch some TeenStar together. They settled in to jeer and boo a Teen Famer whose shtick was to act like a dick in an attempt to attract views, votes and ratings. After they'd had more than enough Flurient and were well into the heckling, the screens went blank for an instant, and the words they knew so well appeared on the screen – *Our Father of Freedom is Joe. Joe tells us all we need to know* – before slowly dissolving into a close-up image of the man himself.

Everyone loved Joe. He was a friend to them all. Everything he said made sense, and put his listeners at ease. His messages were often repetitive, but it was obvious that he was giving them the information out of the goodness of his heart. He was a Sharp – indeed the greatest Sharp of all – but he was just like the people in his audience, too, so it was impossible not to adore him. Whenever he appeared, a sigh of devoted affection escaped every Cocoon. Every viewer watched with bated breath, waiting for him to begin. It didn't matter what he came on to say, his message had already been bought, taken home, and put in a safe place by everyone watching.

The camera tracked slowly around him, showing his snowy mane of white wavy hair tamed and tamped, his avuncular smile creasing his weathered face, his cool grey eyes staring at them with untainted sincerity. He took a deep breath, then began.

'Hello my fellow citiburbians. I come before you today to talk about Freedom. Don't you just love it? The Freedom to be. The Freedom to laugh. The Freedom to be entertained. The Freedom not to worry. We've got it all!' Joe smiled brightly, and every Gobbler watching smiled back. He was so right!

'And we're all equal!' he proclaimed. 'Everyone has an equal share of our Freedom. Under our wonderful YouStar system, you're all famous too. Not all the time of course, that would be far too much like hard work. People would press you for your views on things, and you'd have to take the time and trouble to formulate those views, and be responsible for the disturbances they caused.' He shuddered, and so did his audience.

'So you take turns in being famous, and being loved and watched and yes, envied. But just before it becomes a hassle, an almighty drag, you give it up and let someone else be famous for a while. And then you're free to enjoy your anonymity. Your insignificance. How free is that? To be so free you don't even matter! I tell you, it just doesn't get any freer.

'But frens, I'll be honest with you. There's a blot on our Freedoms, and that blot is that pesky War in the East. We have to fight that war, and you know why? Because those crazy folks over there, they hate our Freedoms. If it were up to them, they'd take your Freedom and trash it. Just take it away from you and never give it back. They'd like to burden you with responsibility for your own lives, and force you to make your own decisions. They'd even saddle you with the efforts and irritation of choosing your own leaders! How much of a chore would that be? How boring? How much drama would it cause between you and your friends and your loved ones, especially if you disagreed with one another over such a stupid, trivial issue? How much of your free time – yes, even your time has Freedom now – would you have to give over to learning and thinking and deciding?

'And then you'd have to spend the rest of your time keeping and eye on them to ensure that the leaders you put in place did what they said they were going to do, and didn't do things that upset you, which they would inevitably do, and which would cause you grief and sometimes anger, and rob you of even more of your Freedom. And you don't want to be robbed do you? No! You want to be entertained. You want to be famous, even if only for a little while. You want to be chilled and happy and just a little bit high on Flurient. And that's what our Freedom does for you. It lets you get on with just being, without the aggravation of thinking. As far as you're concerned, we live in a perfect world, and we want to keep it that way.

'So we have to keep fighting this war to keep our Freedoms safe. We really don't want to do it. Those crazy Sandrags, they all live in hell. They've got nothing better to do than sit around envying our Freedoms and trying to find ways of taking them away from us, and if they came over here, well I guess they would want to kill us all, or at least enslave us.

'Your government, my colleagues and I, and of course our wonderful boys and girls over there in the battlezone, we work hard at defending your Freedoms by invading Sandrag territories and killing them before they can work their evil designs on us. It's only fair – it's just plain self-defence.'

He was so warm, so sincere. So emotional about the wonder of their Freedoms and so offended by the dark plans of the enemy. It was just not in any way possible to disagree. Every heart swelled when he spoke of Freedom, and every heart hardened when he spoke of the necessity of invading their country and killing those horrible Sandrags.

'But we've got a small problem, frens.' Joe looked troubled. 'Recruitment rates have fallen off. I know, I know,' here he put his hands up in front of him defensively, 'you've got it so good here that there's just no reason for you to want to go join up. But I'm going to give you a reason. Me. Do it for me.' He paused and looked at the cameras, staring straight into every Gobbler's soul.

'Say yes to the War in the East. Say yes to defending our Freedoms. Say yes to aggressively promoting peace.' He smiled benignly and clasped his hands in front of him, creating a small flesh steeple. 'I just know that tomorrow many of you will take yourselves to your local Recruitment Centre and sign up, and to those of you who do, I say thank you. You are true patriots. For those of you who cannot or will not join up, if anyone ever asks, or even if they don't, just say you support our troops. Who knows, one day you may even meet one of them. Until then, stay happy, stay Free, and when your turn comes around, be famous. I know I'll be watching you. Good night'

The lights dimmed and Joe's shadow was visible for a moment, and then the screens all jumped back to the Fame House. Bock, Necker and Biz heaved a contented sigh in unison, then clambered out of their Cocoon, went to the bar, and ordered a fresh round of Flurient, which Biz paid for. After Necker had drained his, he turned to his friends.

'Right!' he said. 'That's it. Joe needs me to fight in that pesky war. I'm going to join up.'

Until that moment, Necker had never expressed a passing interest in the war, let alone wanting to be part of it. True, he had never expressed any interest in anything at all except for sex, Teen Star and YouStar, and talking about having sex with various Famers. His destiny was to disappear into the bowels of the InterFace in data surveillance. He was an average person, and that was the perfect path to a standard Gobbler's life. To hear him declare that he would deviate from that path startled his friends.

'Um, why would you want to do that, fren?' Bock asked.

'Didn't you hear Joe?' Necker's face was as animated as they'd ever seen it. 'Those ass-fuckers in the East hate our Freedoms! We can't have that. Somebody has to go and fight for us, and I guess it might as well be me.'

'But you don't know anything about fighting,' Biz said.

'I know I'll be fighting for Freedom. What more do I need to know? Besides, if Joe says it's important, I'll learn how to fight. The army will teach me, I don't know, maybe hundreds of ways to kill Sandrags.'

'Mmmm, true,' Biz nodded, doubtfully, 'but all the same I just can't picture you over there fighting.'

'Well, of course not. None of us has ever seen a real soldier.' Necker's brow furrowed. 'Nobody I've ever known has signed up, and sure as hell nobody I ever knew came home from the war. Shit, I've never seen any war or proper fighting on the InterFace, just desert and explosions and stuff. I don't even know what it looks like. But Joe tells us it happens, right?' At the mention of the leader, his expression softened again, and he smiled brightly. 'And if Joe says it's so, that's good enough for me. Besides, what else am I going to do?'

'Go and work for the InterFace, like Gneiss said. Your future is written, my fren,' said Biz.

'Watch the InterFace and prepare yourself for when you're a Famer so you can be the best famous person you can,' said Bock. She was shocked and scared. She had never been as close to Necker as she was with Biz, but that did not mean she would be happy to see him go off to war, and possibly never come home.

'Why? He's not going to,' Necker jerked his thumb at Biz. 'He's off to live in the Bastion and make decisions and be important. Why can't I do something like that?'

'Hey, I didn't choose to be a Sharp, it just happened. I don't even know if I want to be one. I don't want to be important and I sure as shit don't want to make decisions, but I can't get out of it. I just happen to have been born sharp.' He wasn't even smirking.

'Well I just happen to have been born to be a soldier fighting for *your* Freedoms, fren,' Necker said. There was heat in his voice now. 'And it just happened to me, just now, and there's nothing I can do about it.' He finished with a defiant stare.

Bock had an idea that she thought would stop Necker and make him think. 'But what about YouStar?' she asked. 'What if you're not here when your name comes up? What will you do then? Who knows when it will come up again?'

'Yeah, we've never seen a soldier on YouStar,' said Biz. 'What if they won't let you be on it?'

This struck him. The possibility hadn't crossed his mind, and for a solid ten seconds he stood there with his mouth open. But when he spoke again, he was resolved. He was firm. His mind was made up.

'Hell, who needs to be a Famer?' he said with all the fake contempt he could muster. Bock and Biz were aghast.

All their lives Necker had spoken of little else but when he would be a Famer. Day in and day out he raved about it, planned it, and played it backwards and forwards in his mind. It was easy to see that it practically killed him that it hadn't happened yet, and he'd been devastated when Bock had gotten the TeenStar call-up. The only thing that kept him going was the hope, verging on certainty, that it would happen any day now. Any day.

Bock and Biz exchanged glances. The unspoken understanding between them was that it was the Flurient talking, capped with a touch of the "Joes", which affected everyone when the leader came on the screen to talk to them. They were sure he'd come to his senses soon.

'Well, good luck, my fren,' Bock said. They finished their drinks in silence and split up to go home for dinner and an evening of YouStar dreaming.

Bock and Biz spent the next day together. Biz had expected a message from Necker, and when they hadn't heard anything by late in the day, they went to the Message Centre to send him an invitation to meet them at the Cocoonery. They got no response. Biz thought Necker was probably too lazy to write back – he would have had no choice but to go and pick up his message – so they just went to meet him anyway. The Cocoonery was crowded with noisy, flirting teenagers, but not Necker's familiar, bulky figure.

They started to feel edgy. Perhaps he had done it, after all. They took a levtrans to Necker's house and knocked on the door; his mother Goggle answered the door and invited them in to her untidy, strange smelling home.

Necker's father, Font, was ensconced in his Cocoon, watching a Famer in a limo on her way to a red carpet event, talking about how much she hated another Famer who was presumably in a different vehicle. Goggle, anxious to return to her Cocoon, told them that Necker had gone to a Recruitment Centre that morning, and that she had only found out when a pair of very amiable Recruitment Centre officers had knocked on the door. They said Necker had joined up and was being sent for training, and that they should be very proud of his commitment to the War in the East. The soldiers told them that he would not be back, and not to bother sending him messages because his Manacles had been effectively switched off. He wouldn't need them. Then they disappeared.

'They came during the mid-afternoon YouStar summary, so we really weren't paying much attention,' Goggle said. 'Really, to have two sets of visitors in one day, it's just so busy. If you don't mind, I'll let you go.' She slid back into her Cocoon, and they let themselves out.

Back at the Cocoonery, they toasted their absent friend, and hoped that he would return in one piece from the dreadful war. They admired his fighting spirit, which had saved them from bullying so often, but they were also shocked that he had followed through on his spur of the moment decision. But there wasn't anything they could do about it, so they downed another Flurient and climbed into a dual Cocoon.

A few days later, Biz was due to be collected, perhaps never to return from the Bastion. On their last night together, Bock cried and hung onto him dearly and said, 'I'll never forget you. I love you and I always will.'

Biz was shocked. For so many years he'd played the role of best friend reluctantly but patiently, hoping that one day, when they were older, Bock would realise how much he cared for her. Then, he'd thought, they would be together. And now, on their last night, on the eve of parting, she'd told him that she'd felt that way, too – and it was too late.

'I love you too.' He started to cry as well. 'But I'll probably never leave the Bastion. You'll forget me, it's okay.'

Bock looked into his reddened eyes. 'No,' she said. 'I won't.'

She came to see him off from his parents' house the next morning. His driver was a man named Knead, who had the angular, glowering look of a Sharp, but with some underlying friendliness, or at least an approachability that asked you to trust him and open up to him. It wasn't the goofy affability of your average Gobbler, it was more charisma than friendliness. In any case, it was at odds with his dark, close fitting clothing, the heavy, black, square preon drive that he piloted, and the mission he was on to separate Biz from his family and friend. But Arbeit, Viand and even Bock warmed to him, and after the vehicle had disappeared down the glittering black citiburbian street they all agreed that Biz was in good hands.

And he was ready to go. The way he saw things had been changing a lot since he'd met Psyllium. He was less interested in YouStar, more critical of it, and therefore less patient with it. He didn't become enveloped in the Famers' lives, and he wasn't fascinated by each new intake.

Instead, he found himself deconstructing the show's artifice and the way it manipulated viewers. Elements of the presentation that had escaped or enchanted him now seemed obvious and, on occasion, gratingly transparent: the way the focus softened whenever a Famer spoke sentimentally; the use of quick cuts between scenes to raise tension; the way an InterFace message or Joe-cast interrupted at crucial moments; the fact that even the most engrossing scenario would be shown for no more than six minutes at a stretch so as not to exceed the viewers' attention span; the way some Famers were relentlessly presented as "nice" or "good" while others had only their less attractive sides shown and their misdeeds were repeated, examined and analysed ad nauseam, while their redeeming features, if any, were ignored.

He found himself wondering what happened to outgoing Famers, too. How had their YouStar experience changed them? How had it affected their friends, family and lovers? How did they cope with the transition from Fame to anonymity? YouStar Fame was fleeting, but it was also intense and all-encompassing. Did recent Famers pine for a call-up even more than everyone else? Did not getting a call-up affect their well-being? Was a long gap between appearances bad for their health in some way? And when he had thought these questions through, he found himself wondering whether the supposedly random selections were really random, or whether they were influenced in some way.

That was not all. He'd started to find almost every aspect of citiburbian existence appalling. The expectation that almost everyone would disappear into the bowels of the InterFace to carry out some meaningless, unrewarding but facile task seemed to him more sinister than comforting. The Gobblers' lack of introspection, their unwillingness to investigate, evaluate or debate anything had become a source of deep frustration. Did they know where they were headed? The array of flickering screens that overwhelmed their senses; the yearning for Fame and the fleeting experience of it that dogged them; the pre-set, predetermined nature and direction of their very lives – did they not realise how it seemed contrived to divert and entomb them?

He was ready to leave all that behind. As he climbed into the vehicle, Knead handed him a drink.

'It's a long journey,' he said.

Biz felt that he was at last heading in the right direction. He was happy with the idea of a long journey with Knead. So, he was surprised to find that after just one sip he became light headed.

He was soon asleep. Knead took the cup from his hand. 'It's a long journey, and you're not yet allowed to know where you're going,' he said, and fixed his eyes on the black road ahead.

5.

Poor Bock. She'd lost her two best friends (three if you counted Gneiss) in the space of a few days, her holidays were coming to an end, and very soon the course of the rest of her life would be inescapably set. She would spend a few hours a day several days a week conducting surveillance activities, and the rest of her time anaesthetised by Flurient and YouStar, becoming less and less interested in socialising, conversation, and any new experiences that could not be delivered by a screen or automat. When she turned twenty she would be too old to watch Teen-Star in the local Cocoonery, and unless she found a permanent partner by then, she would live out her life alone. That left her only two years.

The evening after Biz left, Bock took a long walk. In her citiburb, like all the others, no resident was more than a fifteen-minute walk, or a five-minute levtrans ride, from the local Hub, the centre of their community. Each Hub looked like all the others: a local Surveillance Centre where many Gobblers worked, a defence Recruitment Centre, a TeenStar Cocoonery, a Message Centre, and a fresh food provisioner for those who preferred their vegetables greenhouse-grown rather than automat made. There was also a Medical Centre, where people who felt unwell could go to have their nanomat or nanostream reprogrammed or augmented, and a Synthetron, which custom-printed virtually any object in the world at the push of a button.

That night, the Hub's quietness and loneliness mirrored her own, except that the Hub was so well-ordered. Each store

45

carried a small but legible sign, the same size and colour and in the same typeface as all the others, telling people what was behind the black-smoked windows. There were no displays, only functional lighting, and very little colour. Only the camera trees, dotted about in careful geometric placement patterns so that each field of view was overlapped by at least three others, and the oxygen vents that towered over every corner, interrupted the monotony. The only people around were hurrying to or from the provisioner, or finishing or starting shifts at the Surveillance Centre. The wind crept down the wide black graphite road in discrete swirls. Only the muted din of the crowd at the TeenStar Cocoonery gave any indication of life.

Bock could only find a partner to replace Biz – until now she'd never thought of him as a partner, but they'd obviously been heading in that direction – if she spent more time at the Cocoonery. Communal TeenStar viewing was the main mechanism for facilitating permanent pairings and ensuring the survival of the society. Finding someone permanent was difficult, though. TeenStar actively promoted promiscuity, and the viewers indulged in hectic mating behaviour; they paired off and swapped partners, experimented, tested each other. Nonetheless, most Gobblers did eventually settle for a single partner with whom they could live in peace. And now Bock had to find one, or face permanent loneliness.

She slowly walked home, not seeing the homes made of coal bricks and carbcrete, graphene and lithicarb – tidy black boxes surrounded by sparse and poorly husbanded gardens desperately clawing their way into life. There was no sound coming from any home, just the dull glow of InterFace screens reflected off Cocoon casings onto ceilings and walls, casting eerie blue light that slow-danced into Bock's eyes. She was not sleepy. She had to think about her own future.

In one week, her unlimited credit would be cut off unless

she reported for work at the Surveillance Centre in her local Hub. To submit seemed her most likely fate. What would life be like inside the InterFace? She foresaw endless days, weeks, months and years monitoring the same set of fixed cameras, watching her neighbours' uneventful lives, searching for the slightest deviation from the norm.

The surveillance groups were not well-trained; any of them could misread an ordinary action and target someone for arrest. It didn't happen often, because a lifetime of surveillance taught people to live small, inconspicuous lives. But it did happen. And the Liberty Guard was no better. For the most part they were lazy and slipshod in their investigations, and usually found it easier to make up damning evidence than to recognise even the most obvious signs of innocence.

Bock didn't want any part of it, but she also had no choice. She knew it was inevitable, that she would become inured to the lifestyle and the process and at some stage, either through laziness or stupidity, make a mistake that sent an innocent on the Freedom Ride.

Again, her memories of Biz intruded. It was an annoying physical truth that Bock's memory was excellent, and it was particularly irritating that night because so many of those memories were of Biz, and they had all started rising unbidden from the unplumbed depths of her mind. She and Biz had spent so much of their lives together that they had almost become part of one another. He was odd and exasperating, and his recent tendency to analyse everything continuously exhausted her. But she would miss him. Miss the feeling of being with someone who questioned everything and who brought her own mind alive. She did miss him, already. If nothing else, the sedentary life of a Gobbler would deaden her thoughts and memories, and she would be free of Biz. As long as it didn't take too long, because it was starting to hurt.

*   *   *   *

It was a normal enough morning – Bock's parents, Trinket and Caper, watched a little InterFace over a cup of brew, talking without listening to the other's monosyllabic answers or questions, then went off to their shifts at the local Surveillance Centre. After they left, Bock settled into her own Cocoon for some YouStar therapy, making no further plans for the day. She was quite happy to fritter away her last days of Freedom. But almost as soon as she lay back, her left Manacle started to tingle. She thought, not for the first time, that there must be an easier way to communicate than sending everything through official channels. But there was nothing for it, she had to walk up to the Hub or risk a visit from the Liberty Guard.

She hoped the message was from Biz, but she wasn't sure if anyone was allowed to send messages from the Bastion, and was positive she wouldn't be able to respond. But it was most likely to be the message she knew was coming and that she didn't want to receive – details of her new career in the Surveillance Centre. She showered and dressed and walked up to the Hub.

The sluggard at the Message Centre looked at her with great respect when she told him her name, which was unusual. He handed her not the usual grubby, much-handled tablet, but a clean, gilt edged tablet with a green ribbon around it.

She was going to be on YouStar.

Her mind filled with possibilities. She knew from her time on TeenStar that she would get to step far, far out of her "normal" life, would discard her uniform of dark-green hemp slacks and dark or colourless hemp shirt. She knew that, being young and beautiful, she would be an A-lister, and as such she would be able to choose from the most exquisite couture, all gorgeous fabrics alive with colours and textures, sensually dripping with fringes, garlanded with delicate lace, bejewelled with glittering sequins and spangled highlights. She would revel in dresses – yes, actual dresses – exorbitantly indulgent, with design flourishes that ran the gauntlet from stiff, austere high collars to necklines plunging into daringly deep décolletage, or backlines that terminated millimetres above deliciously exposed derrieres. She would accessorise with the exciting and the opulent: strings of purest white, atomically perfect pearls; chains of gold studded with diamonds and rubies, emeralds and amethyst; elegant rings of silver, platinum, gold or all three intricately entwined; purses and handbags of softest leather; gleaming ebony carbon synthetics and sweetly sensual silk; and shoes that were so sleek and tall and dangerous and wonderfully dysfunctional that they surpassed even the wildest imagination.

She went home to watch YouStar, to "bone up" as it were. The current Famers would be leaving soon, and the coverage was in wrap-up mode. The new Famers, including Bock, would enter Fame House in just forty-eight hours. She watched the final group luncheons and dinners, retrospectives on what each Famer had "achieved", vote tallying and announcements. It was melancholy, but exciting for the viewers because soon they would have a new crop of people to love, hate, praise, and abuse.

Bock, obviously, wanted to be loved. The audience usually loved Famers who were young, attractive and female, although often they loved the paternally or maternally appealing, the ruggedly masculine, the outlandish dresser, the funny, the family-loving, the inoffensively eccentric, or someone who combined several of those features.

The viewers hated those who were ugly, inside or out, the mean of spirit and squinty of eye, those rude of face and uncivilised in behaviour, the relentlessly sour, ungrateful or ill at ease, or at least were made to seem so. Those who were hated knew that they had no chance to become one of the beloved, to make it to the A-list, and instead of trying to make it they made a conscious decision to be obstructive, angry, insolent or belligerent. Anything to gather ratings and to avoid being seen as a nothing – a Fame wraith. Far, far worse than being judged and hated by the YouStar audience was to not be judged but ignored, to not even be noticed enough to be disdained, to be invisible. Oblivion was the fate of those too stupid to formulate a plan to be hated, or too weak to carry it through. To be one of just ten people given the spotlight for a whole month and yet not have a single photon of interest fall upon you – this was as low as a person could get. The indignity and despair were so crushing that many of those who entered this lightless cave never came out, and preferred to commit suicide as soon as their YouStar hell was over. The only sign of their passing was the producers wiping their names from the YouStar rolls with a sigh of relief.

Bock had no fears on that front. She knew that all she had to do was play down her natural acuity. If she seemed too smart she would be perceived as threatening, perhaps even mistaken for a planted Sharp – every now and then a Famer turned up who was simply too smart to be true, and those few were usually hated or feared. But she would use her intelligence to spot ratings opportunities, and perhaps even score points off her less insightful fellow Famers. Her eyes were wide open, and her sights set high: she would be an A-lister!

Day one began as it did for every new intake – orientation. This two-day cycle would prepare the Famers for the whirlwind of Fame as much as possible, and allow the InterFace watchers to start forming judgements on them. There were fittings and trials, catwalk classes and dressing instructions, group gatherings and one-on-ones, dinners, breakfasts, high teas, meet and greets, and interviews with unseen, unknown interviewers asking typical Gobbler questions.

Once orientation was over, the serious business of being a celebrity would begin for all of them. They would not be required to do anything much beyond prepare for and attend celebrity events and be famous. All were excused from their work commitments for the whole month, as none could leave the Fame House until their time inside it was over.

The forty-seven-room Fame House was just the front end of a hundred-square-kilometre complex of studios, storage, staff and crew accommodation, and the Synthetrons that created the enchantment of YouStar. The walled facility had everything needed for complete self-sufficiency. There was a shed of vehicles, from the longest stretch limousines to the electro-carts the producers used to zip around or to ferry Famers from the House to the transport shed. There was a full-sized, functioning replica of a standard citiburb Hub, complete with a Surveillance Centre in which no one worked, a provisioner's stocked with fresh vegetables, and a Cocoonery with working Cocoons. The people who "worked" there were little more than props, but they were part of the magic of Fame.

There were dozens of dining rooms, all filled with opulent furniture, lavish accessories and plush fittings, none of which even appeared in a Synthetron catalogue, let alone were available to be synthesised for use in a Gobbler's house. And all the furniture and every surface and every crevice contained a camera to capture every moment from every angle. Several counterfeit streetscapes had been built, each a short road drawing up to the entry of a monstrous, lavish palace with red carpet laid on the long walk from the kerb to the door. They were magnificent, but only façades, built to suggest that somewhere out there, excess and luxury really existed. And even the Gobblers who had been on YouStar and seen the artificiality for themselves believed it.

Just about everything on YouStar was created on-site, except for the Famers' fashions, fabrics and magnificently useless accessories; these were delivered from the Bastion every few days. The source of these designs was known to very few, and they thought their secret extremely important. Deep in the Bastion lived a select group of Prods, isolated from their fellows. They combed through ancient texts known as Magazines, examined the images in those banned publications, copied them or even improved on them. Such provocative images and knowledge were clearly dangerous, and the existence of Magazines was one of the most closely guarded secrets in the Bastion.

But that aside, the YouStar facility was a city in itself, though only the Famers entered or left. The Gobblers who helped produce YouStar were forbidden to leave the facility or contact former friends and relatives, lest they share the secrets of YouStar production. They were willing captives, though, and most loved it so much that they willingly put in five or more hours of overtime each week.

The Famers took no notice of any of this, or of the army of production assistants, stylists, chauffeurs, chefs and valets struggling to keep up with them. They were too busy trying to garner ratings by fighting, flirting with or fucking their fellow Famers. Their job was to live and breathe their celebrity, to gorge on its excesses and choke on its restrictions, to revel in its riches and despair at its busy solitude. For some, like Bock, it would be a revelation and a joy. They would slip into the mantle of star; it would fit perfectly and they would wear it with pride. For others, Fame would be a bitter disappointment, a cloak of dashed hopes and unmet expectations, the world failing to love them as they loved themselves. The endless rush from event to event, the constant chaos of production people coming on- and off-shift, the need to make nice with Famers they hated or feared, the relentless intrusion of cameras into every moment – these were part of a dreadful trial. And yet almost every one of them, once outside Fame's glittering walls, would leap with near hysterical joy at another chance to get back to that torturous embrace.

Even those who had endured the crushing desolation of being a non-rater, those Fame wraiths of the lowest order, would beg and pray for an opportunity to do it all again, only better next time. Assuming they hadn't already taken the preferred non-rater's exit.

The only thing the Famers could not do was snuggle up in a Cocoon and watch InterFace themselves. They were the entertainment; they could not also be the entertained.

Bock entered the Fame House with trepidation, awe and excitement all swirling around her belly. As she passed them, the camera operators, sound recordists, lighting specialists, make-up artists and stylists, caterers, important looking types holding InterTabs, floor managers, everyone, all turned to give her a deferential smile, several looking her up and down lustfully. She took the stares with good grace. She was used to it.

The menacing looks from some of her fellow Famers were harder to take. It was obvious who would make the A-list and who would not. Plantar, a woman in her mid-twenties who oozed the kind of confidence that comes with complete ignorance of one's own shortcomings, would obviously be Bock's prime female competitor. Plantar was almost defiantly oblivious, but also naturally devious, and had clearly started plotting before she'd even made it to the facility. Arena, a big boned, powerful looking woman with delicious dimples and an irresistible motherly manner, had decided to rave on and on about her redoubtable child, Rune, in order to bring laughter and tears and empathetic sighs to many in the audience. Her gambit was successful and many of the viewers ended up feeling closer to Rune than their own children.

Among the men, only Swain, a handsome thirty-year-old charmer on his fourth YouStar appearance was a serious candidate for the A-list. He was familiar with the high-energy hustle of YouStar life. He was confident in his own good looks and apparently artless charisma. Viewers would be drawn to his ease with Fame, and imagine themselves as comfortable and cool as he seemed.

The others – Moot, Anvil, Dirge, Nib, Mandible and Pang – were either too old, too ugly, too shy or too awkward to present much opposition. True, Pang was capable of biting disdain and had mastered the pinched, venomous stare, but anyone could see that her outbursts were motivated by petty jealousy, which almost all viewers would find unattractive.

The only oddity among the ten was Nib. He seemed intent on becoming a Fame wraith. He kept his eyes downcast and his hair unkempt, shrugged off his handlers, ducked combs and shied away from make-up. He did not participate in any discussions or gossip sessions, and avoided the arguments that more forceful Famers used to snatch up screen time. He was a nonentity, and happy to embrace it.

But Bock soon saw that he was not nearly as backwards or dim as he made out. Most obviously, he was excellent at learning. Even multiple-time Famers like Plantar and Swain found it hard to learn how to slip gracefully out of a limo seat, how to walk with elegance, and how to make a stylish entrance. Bock picked all this up first time, every time – as did artless, ugly Nib. Beneath the lank curtain of straight dark hair that almost covered his eyes, he was observing everything intensely. When others grew bored, impatient or disinterested, Nib was alert, furtively registering the most inane details, even though he still appeared perfectly apathetic. He rarely spoke unless he was invited to offer an opinion or asked a question, but when he did, his diction was clear and his vocabulary was noticeably larger than anyone else's – except Bock's. Most troubling of all, he appeared to have an unhealthy interest in Bock, fixing his dark gaze on her while she tried not to get caught looking at him with the same inquisitiveness. Bock understood – in fact had always known – that she was smarter than most other Gobblers. Until their last year together, she had always felt

Biz's equal, and he was the only person who ever seemed to be different in the way that she was; along with Gneiss the only other high-functioning Gobbler she knew. Nib seemed to see that in her, as she saw it in him.

For the ratings, and to avoid his weird gaze, she would have to step up her Gobbler act – feign disinterest and boredom, use lazy language, forget words, ask for constant instruction for even the most basic of tasks. It was harder than she thought it would be. But, from almost the moment a camera first turned to her, the viewers warmed to Bock and watched her every move in droves. People of all ages favoured the Bock channel, and kept watching no matter how much or how little she did each day. They sat rapt in their Cocoons, as alert as Gobblers could be, to watch her eat, sit, stand, walk, laugh, relax and shower – everything except use the toilet. What Bock wore and how she wore it, who she talked to and what she said, how she got up out of a chair, brushed back a stray hair, shook a hand, straightened a skirt; every single move was documented, discussed and dissected.

But Bock also wanted to be more like her true self, and she sometimes forgot that she was supposed to be an average Gobbler. She was confident. Her wit was sharp. She could remember and process information. These things were hard to hide – although she noticed that Nib was hiding them much better than she was. But he found it easier, because he did not rate, whereas even when she let her real personality shine through, her audience loved her more. She was, as the production minions reminded her daily, a massive ratings success. So she, along with Plantar and Swain, received special treatment at every turn. Every day people thrust spectacular new outfits, jewellery and accessories at them – luxuries that further exaggerated the differences between the A-listers and everyone else. And Bock soaked up the adoration and the sense of entitlement that came with it.

Naturally, this aroused the jealousy and competitive instincts of her co-Famers, and none more so than Plantar and Pang. Plantar especially felt affronted by Bock's success, and this came to the fore only three days into the month, at a post–red carpet dinner. The Famers had all been dressed up in finery – some finer than others of course – and electro-carted to the transport depot to be scooped into five waiting limos. Swain and Bock took the first to drive a few hundred metres to the red carpet set.

A small, ragged crowd of tired but enthusiastic YouStar production crew, some of whom were into their second or third hour of overtime, cheered. Videorazzi crowded around the Famers as they arrived, shoving absurdly large cameras into the A-listers' faces – a pencil sized unit would have done the job but would not have looked the part – and asked irrelevant questions as the Famers swept by. A new limo arrived every two or three minutes, so within fifteen minutes everyone had walked the carpet. They waited by the fake doors of the gauche palace for the signal, then they all walked back down the red carpet in the order they had arrived, piled into the limos, and headed for the dinner location.

This was the Versailles Room, a huge open space surrounded by tall walls covered with creamy, thick-textured wallpaper striped with gold, and large gilt framed mirrors hung every few feet in gaudy repetition. The long, narrow, gold-washed dining table was piled high with delicacies – real roast chicken, quail and turkey, heaped bowls of fresh green salads, soft, creamy mashed potatoes, elegantly sweetened orange carrots, and carefully plaited loaves of freshly baked bread – all served on paper-thin bone china crockery and eaten with pure atomic gold cutlery. For the viewers at home, eating automat meals of carbon constituted into edibles of plainclothes flavour, it was almost pornographic, especially the liquid accompaniment to the meal. The red wine had been made from real grapes, and was famous for its soft, natural alcohol, which was only permitted in the Bastion and the Fame House. It was well-known that alcohol excited passions and inflamed sensitivities, unlocking aggression that could earn a visit from the Liberty Guard. But in the Fame House, it created the conditions for a storm of baiting, farce, philandering – and ratings.

The diners sat on chairs with tall, ornate, white-enamelled backs and plush red velvet cushions. They talked quietly at first, but by dessert they had grown raucous. Spot fires of anger and unhappiness flared up around the table, and a flood tide of spilled wine and flung food turned the glamorous setting into a shambles. Bock flirted sweetly with Swain; they giggled, clinked glasses, and patted each other on the arm or thigh. The viewers loved it, and their fan mail was even more sexually direct than Bock and Swain's conversation.

Plantar, on the other hand, was not enjoying herself. She sat on the other side of Swain; her ruby-red gown was cut so low you could see the dark hairs below her navel, and her breasts popped out of the shining sateen fabric. But Swain wasn't giving her so much as a second glance. To make matters worse, Nib sat on her right side, unobtrusively watching proceedings, ogling her breasts whenever possible, but resolutely failing to respond to her irritated remarks and vinegary observations. He was next to useless. Eventually she just had to shut up and sit, gloomily glaring across the table at Moot and Pang while they ate and drank everything in sight, chewed with their mouths open, smacked their lips, sloshed wine around and shamelessly overplayed their roles for the cameras. The waiters refilled everyone's glasses constantly, and since Plantar wasn't talking or flirting, she had little to do other than drink. Her drunken bitterness started to attract more attention than her dress. Viewers hated how she wasted that wonderful setting. She didn't know the specifics of the viewers' comments, but she felt that her ratings would be poor unless something changed. She might even fall into the B-list, and that would leave Swain and Bock alone at the top. She started to look for an opening.

'Fren, this room is incredible, isn't it?' said Swain merrily. 'It's so golden and silky, it makes me feel sexy. Does it make you feel sexy?' he asked Bock with a suggestive leer. He laid his hand casually across her bare shoulder.

'Oh, it's beautiful,' she agreed, with an innocent, wide-eyed and alcohol-glassy stare. 'But don't you think it's just a bit, um, ostentatious?'

This was Plantar's opportunity. 'Fuck my grandmother on a bicycle,' she exploded. 'You are such a fucking faker!' It was loud, it was rude, and it was explosive enough to stop every other conversation on the table.

'Osten-fucking-tatious?' Plantar knew that she had sent out a shock wave, and was dimly conscious that this might not enhance her likeability, but she was also drunk and angry enough not to care. 'Five days we've been in this House, and all you've done is parade around acting like you're some kind of fucking Sharp. Osten-fucking-tatious!' She almost spat her contempt. 'I don't even know what it means, but I can guess. But what I really don't know is where you get off with bullshitting everyone that you're so clever that you know. Why can't the room be fancy? Why can't it be, um, I don't fucking know, isn't fancy good enough?'

Nib was very interested in all of this, and the others were giggling. Two burly crew members stood up straighter, ready to restrain Plantar if she should attack Bock. Such things happened often enough.

Bock was taken aback. She looked to Swain for support, but he was staring at his plate, looking guilty. Perhaps he knew that ignoring Plantar and flirting with Bock would lead to some sort of row. Maybe he even planned it. Being the apex of a love triangle couldn't hurt his ratings.

Bock turned to Plantar directly. She managed to look

confused. 'Fren, why would you say that? Yesterday day the man who drops off the clothes and stuff said that something – I think it was the dress you're wearing – was ostentatious, and I liked the sound of it. I don't know what it means either.' Tears began to roll down her cheeks in large globules of sincerity. At home, thousands of hearts melted.

'I was just trying to be smart for Swain,' she said, daintily taking a napkin and dabbing at her tears, careful not to disturb her make-up. 'I know I'm not smart,' she said with heartbreaking honesty. 'But you're so smart and beautiful, I just wanted to be more like you.' She buried her face in her napkin – without letting it make any but the lightest contact with her skin – and suppressed a grin. In spite of the boozy haze, or perhaps because of it, she was turning in a winning performance and at the same time crushing her ablest female competition.

Plantar knew she was beaten. 'Fuck you,' she said. She finished her wine in a gulp.

'Get back in your box, you drunken slut,' Dirge said to Plantar. He laughed, as did all the people around him. He clinked glasses with his nearest neighbours and drank. The party resumed its former chaotic racket. Swain leaned close to Bock and whispered something while casting a sideways glance at Plantar. Bock giggled.

Unable to sink any further in her chair, Plantar stood and swayed for a moment, muttered something about the toilet, then weaved and crashed her way out of the room.

At home, the viewers clapped and laughed, and sighed for beautiful, fragile Bock. Messages of encouragement for her flew, while a new strain of support for Plantar emerged; plenty of viewers found angry, reckless Plantar alluring and amusing. The party raged on, the Famers grew still more lusty and salacious, and the wine was consumed in copious quantities. The producers patted each other on the back. These alcohol-fuelled parties really did make for terrific viewing.

In the middle of it all, Nib remained an island of aloofness. His eyes swept the room with an appearance of woozy, uncomprehending neutrality, often alighting on Bock. She saw him from the corner of her eye, and realised she would have to step up her Gobbler act.

This was getting easier and easier. With each day, the pleasant fuzziness in her mind grew. She had less to think about and almost nothing to worry about. The only thing that seemed to matter was the attention being heaped on her and the gifts it brought. Her brain seemed to be getting more and more blunt, as if some vital ingredient that had helped her maintain an edge was now missing. Her reactions slowed, almost measurably, day by day. Words that had once come easily to her now seemed out of reach or just forgotten. More and more she found her thoughts drifting aimlessly. She began to tune out of conversations, or lose the thread. Crew members had to repeat instructions to her, and she often stopped to ask herself where she was going and why. It was as though by acting like a Gobbler she was becoming more of one.

But then she would shake her head and tell herself that she had always been a Gobbler. Yes, she had felt more vitally connected to herself and to the world, and to knowledge itself, when she was at school. But that was due to the exciting and intelligent company she had been keeping – Gneiss and Biz. Now she was beyond their influence, her true Gobbler self was emerging.

The viewers didn't notice any change in Bock, and neither did any of her fellow Famers, or the production crew. It was, she told herself, just an internal thing. She didn't notice that Nib, after the second week in the House, stopped paying attention to her as he had previously – by then she'd forgotten how they had regarded each other in those first few days. Had she been watching him, she would have noticed that he was dealing with a nosedive in self-esteem brought on by poor ratings and the realisation that he would be just another Fame wraith. And he had lost interest in the habits and personalities of his fellow Famers.

For thirty days Bock and her fellow Famers lived in the glare of Fame. It followed them and burnished them and some-times seared and blackened them, and showed them in their best and worst and every other light. Then it was over. At the fare-well dinner, Bock and Swain were the featured guests, with the rest just making up the numbers. During the sumptuous feast, the InterFace channels cut away to recap and summarise the Famers' month, replaying funny, silly, horrible, embarrassing and enlightening clips.

Bock and Swain had loved being the superstars. Arena and Dirge had at least maintained their smiles in the face of their B-list status. Anvil had made a creep of himself – he'd spent the whole month becoming less and less agreeable, and he obviously planned to go out with a nasty bang. Which turned out to take place against a wall near the toilets and, in a final insult, with Plantar.

The outgoing Famers spent one last night at the Fame House, handed back the wonderful outfits and gorgeous accessories, and in the morning were shown the rear door as the new Famers came in the front. They left as they had arrived – in plain hemp, unknown and unloved by the masses, and yearning for the next call-up.

The anticlimax was shattering for all of them, including Bock. The loss was like an amputation. All the trappings of stardom fell away and left phantom feelings in their place – Bock felt she could reach out and touch her celebrity, but also knew that it was gone and might never come back. She was determined to get back onto YouStar, some way, anyway, and become an even bigger hit, show more cleavage, smile more dearly, forget her underwear more often, and fuck anyone who'd stand still for it, as long as fucking them added to more to her shine than it did theirs. Fame had banished all other ideas from her mind.

6.

Necker eased into a comfortable seat, picked up his drink, and sat back to watch the show. It was one of those local feast days that dotted the calendar with welcome regularity, giving him days off from all the training and drilling and filling those days with displays of joy and colour. These fireworks were a relatively new addition: the rockets flew high into the sky and burst into beautifully coloured cascades of spectacular shards, which floated slowly downwards, burning brighter and brighter until they winked out over the upturned faces of the locals and their guests, the Gobbler army.

Most of Necker's colleagues were watching with him, sipping Flurient. The festivals were about flying kites and cooking exotic dishes. To the astonished joy of the invading army, music and dancing were allowed. None of the soldiers had seen dancing or heard music like this. To them, music had always been the muted background noise that presaged a Joe-cast, or the ominous soundtrack to alarming news items. To hear it celebrated as a thing in itself – set free, as it were – was surprising. And it was uplifting. It stirred new emotions and exhilarated the senses; they felt the music as much as they heard it, and once it was gone they longed to hear it again. The fireworks added to the feeling that they were witnessing something special.

Necker could not believe that he was there. The journey had happened so quickly and inexorably it was as though his will had been suspended and a higher power had taken over his brain, or at least switched it off until it was too late. The day after Joe's stirring speech had awakened his patriotic spirit, he'd attended the Recruitment Centre to see what it might take to follow through on his intention to join up. He'd never seen anyone go into the Recruitment Office, or leave it, and it had always struck him as a lonely, neglected place even though it was kept clean and new. You couldn't even tell if there were people inside – the windows were tinted opaque and backlit. The door was always closed but unlocked, and the slogans painted on the windows in regulation signage type were compelling: 'Fight for Freedom,' 'Kill Fear,' 'Keep Our Country Safe for Freedom's sake'.

And yet in spite of all the light and gravity of the place, he'd always sensed a chill hanging over it. As he'd stood before it, the clarity he had felt after Joe's speech disappeared into a cloud of uncertainty. Yet, he was already there and he had committed himself without knowing how or why. There was nothing left to do but push the door open. He could always back out, right?

He walked into the spartan suite. The cleanliness and power of the lights assaulted his eyes. Two uniformed soldiers and one applicant sat at each of the Centre's three desks, engaged in a flurry of paper shuffling and loud, artificially good-natured banter, the two soldiers always smiling and bustling. The chairs around the walls for waiting applicants were all empty. He had an urge to leave, but also a deeper, more powerful need to follow through on his decision.

So he sat in a hard chair. An InterFace screen in the room's corner bled pictures, but without sound he couldn't track the action. He closed his eyes and straightened his legs out in front of him, putting his hands behind his head. He may have dozed, but it seemed like only a few minutes before a soldier was tapping him on the shoulder and directing him to a deskside seat.

The interview was swift and the induction immediate.

Before Necker could explain that he was just there for a look and a chat about the possibility of maybe considering talking about joining up, he'd been patted down, filled in, pushed through and signed up. The two soldiers who handled the red tape with such efficiency kept up an encouraging patter, smattered with probing questions. They barely waited for answers and studiously ignored any interjections or questions put by the applicant.

'You'll love the army lifestyle. You'll be protecting our Freedoms, isn't that awesome? What's your father's name?'

'Font.'

'Yessir, three square meals a day. Exotic locations. The satisfaction of taking Fear away from your community and implanting it in the enemy's. Mother's name?'

'Goggle.'

'Boy, I hope you enjoy travel. And being fit and sexy. And the taste of liberty mixed with the flavour of conquest. Sexuality?'

'Omni.'

'Men or women, or both at the same time, eh? Fabulous. You'll look great in a uniform. You'll score big time. 'Specially if you don't mind ruttin' with them Eastern trolls. They might be ugly but by golly they can fuck. Weight?'

Almost before he knew the interview had begun he was staring out the wide windows of a transport in the Recruitment Office's garage.

'Don't worry, we'll contact...' the soldier consulted his InterTab, 'Font and Goggle. They'll be fine. And so proud...'

The only occupants in the big transport were Necker and the other three recruits from the Centre. Necker took a large, comfortable seat in an empty row, and breathed out for what could have been the first time in an hour. It was difficult to gather his thoughts. He felt giddy, even nauseous. He had no idea where he was going or what was going to happen to him. He thought of Bock and Biz, and wondered if he would ever see them again. He hoped so. He wished he'd sent them a message, if nothing else, just to say goodbye.

The transport pulled up to another Recruitment Centre and three new recruits got on. One of them, a rangy red-headed man with stony blue eyes and spider hands, looked up and down the vehicle, and chose the empty seat beside Necker.

'May I?' he asked, with a deferential expression.

'Of course.' Necker was glad of the company. He didn't like to think too much, and hoped the other recruit would take him out of his circle of thoughts.

'Navel.' The new man turned awkwardly to extend his freckly, moist hand.

Necker took and shook it. 'Necker.'

They sat in silence for a few moments.

'So. What the fuck just happened?' Navel giggled ruefully. 'I mean, I thought I wanted to sign up – first time that's ever happened – so I went in to talk about it and BAM, next thing I know I'm on this bus.'

'Uh-huh, same thing happened to me. I don't even know if I said yes or no, or if it mattered.'

'The second you walk through that door, you're going to war, fren. I guess they have to make every one count.'

'Yeah, well, they sure made it count with me. But you know what, it feels right to me. I feel like going to war.'

Navel nodded. 'Snap! Me too.' He looked at the others. They all looked confused or shell-shocked. 'Freedom!' he shouted, and pumped his fist. 'We're in it, might as well make the most of it!'

'Freedom!' Necker agreed, less convincingly.

The bus stopped twice more to pick up four more recruits. As it drove out of the citiburbs, the big, crystal clean windows darkened and became inky black, blocking out the sunlight. They had no clue where they were going, and sat in dazed silence as the vehicle rolled on for hour after hour.

When the transport stopped, the windows suddenly cleared. They were in the middle of a vast, flat plain unmarked except by a tall, straight fence that stretched from horizon to horizon, and there was a gate with a guardhouse beside by the front of their vehicle. There wasn't an oxygen vent in sight. The driver was talking to an armed soldier by the little hut. They drove onto the base, a small community of buildings made of some material that reflected the dry, rocky plain around them, and the sky above so effectively that they were all but invisible.

The desert shone with hard clarity in the flashing early morning sunlight. As they got off the transport, the recruits gazed at their surroundings with varying degrees of excitement and curiosity

The pudgy driver ushered them into one of the small, mirror-like buildings. The high-ceilinged room was set up like an auditorium without stage or screen, just rows of seats all facing forward. They sat down. Navel whistled an endless, toneless tune. Necker told himself he was in a new place that he would get used to, as he'd gotten used to the old place. He was surprised to find that he missed the old place.

A man came into the room to look at the group of new recruits with proprietorial distaste. The recruits looked at him with curiosity; he had a head like a bullet shooting out of a chest like a gun barrel. He took their curiosity for insolence.

'You will stand to attention when a superior officer enters the room,' he barked. 'I am Sergeant Mandrill and I am your superior officer.'

They got to their feet and stood in approximations of attention. Navel giggled and elbowed Necker in the ribs. 'Ten shun!' he said. Necker tried not to laugh.

Mandrill gritted his teeth, but then seemed to calm a little. 'Alright, recruits. At ease.' Shoulders slumped. Navel giggled again. 'This is your training camp, Fort Manning. Here you'll learn how to play the game we call war. Then you'll get shipped off to the East and play it to the death. Do you understand?'

'Yes, sir!' they shouted, almost in unison. Navel almost kept a straight face, but winked at Necker, who grinned back.

'You will train in basic weapons, and more importantly, the fundamentals of strategy and teamwork, and above all how to win the hearts and minds of your enemy by kicking their heads and asses. Is that clear?'

'Yes sir!' The chorus was practically perfect and heartily enthusiastic. The recruits were getting better very quickly, and enjoying it immensely. This was what it meant to be a soldier – shouting as one their heartfelt agreement with whatever the drill sergeant said.

'Any questions?'

Necker raised his hand gingerly. 'Sir, how long will our training take?'

'Depending on how the recruiting drive goes – we need to ship off a certain number at a time – you should be in theatre in six to ten weeks, boy. Protecting the Freedoms of the good folks at home who are far too busy to ever know what you're doing for them. They'll be ignorant of your actions, and that's the way we like it.'

Navel, emboldened by the sergeant's attack of approach-ability, raised his hand with a jaunty fling. Mandrill, sensing a class clown, rolled his bulbous eyes under his single, bushy, overhanging brow.

'Sir, why are we fighting this war?' said Navel, a smirk besmirching his otherwise innocent face.

Mandrill rolled his eyes again. 'Son, because if we stop, we lose,' he said, shaking his head as though he had just explained that two plus two equals four. 'We're fighting for control, for mastery and most of all for Freedom. Not just over there but here at home too. Do I make myself clear?'

The recruits nodded in unison. 'Yes, sir!'

Mandrill coughed out an order and an orderly appeared

out of nowhere, a stumpy, swarthy woman with dark eyes and black hair in a short, shapeless bob.

'Follow.'

The recruits did so, but with much less discipline and unity than they had in the face of Mandrill's orders.

They trooped behind the slouchy, silent orderly to another practically invisible building. Entering through automatic doors, they walked down a long, spotless corridor with doors on either side. At each pair of doors the adjutant pointed to two of the recruits and said, 'Yours'. Navel and Necker were assigned apartments opposite each other about five doors from the entryway. Navel took the room on the right, Necker that on the left.

Instead of the ascetic accommodation he had expected, the room was spacious, comfortable and very well-appointed. It was fully self-contained, with its own kitchenette, comprehensive automat, a comfortable looking bed and a state-of-the-art Cocoon. It was almost too much; like home, only better. No parents, no talking, no sharing, just his own space filled with almost everything he could ask for. Even the bed was bigger than his old one. He paired his Manacles with the central control panel, which transmitted his identity and vital information to the base's mainframe computer and unlocked all his appliances. He toured his apartment, lingering over the light recesses and drawer handles, sitting on the stools and chairs, running his hands over the gleaming surfaces, getting a territorial glow as he did so.

The digital bulletin on the wall had instantly updated with his name, rank (recruit) and Unit number (4/25th Battle Group). The screen delivered digital orders and displayed the day's schedule as well as a range of other essential communications. At that point, it listed his own information and meal times:

Mess: *0645–0745*
            1200–1330
            1830–2030

He tapped the word 'Mess,' and the screen displayed a map of the base, showing his current location as a blue dot. The buildings were labelled Mess, Vehicles, Storage, Officers' Mess, Magazine, Training Field, Enlisted Accommodation, Officer Accommodation and so on. The mess building was highlighted in red, and a path from his room to the entrance appeared on the screen, with the distance shown as 350 metres. He tapped the mess building and the screen showed a floor plan and the seating arrangements. Each of the ten long tables held between twenty and thirty diners. The buffet server was against the wall; by zooming in and tapping on any of the various segments he could see what dish would be available at each buffet for the next meal. If he got hungry in the meantime, he could always order something up from his automat.

'This army thing might just be all right,' Necker muttered to himself. There would be no demands on his time until lunch, so he settled into the shiny new Cocoon and flitted from screen to screen and channel to channel in a dissociative blur. Only when all the screens flashed the same message – Mess Open – did he unfold himself from the chamber's caress, stretch and shake his head. Four hours had disappeared. He decided he needed a shower before heading off for lunch.

At the mess hall, Necker easily found Navel, whose bright mop of spindly red hair made him easy to spot. Navel had made the acquaintance of the lofty female sitting next to him, and he was talking volubly, amplifying his words with his hands.

Necker sat across from Navel, who introduced him to the girl, Dirndl. She had substantial girth to go with her height, but she was not fat. To the contrary, she looked very healthy. Her shoulders and arms were well toned and powerful, as though she'd been bred for physical labour. Necker could not picture her at a screen conducting surveillance, and he wondered if she had trouble getting into a Cocoon.

She told him she came from a soldiering family, but she had not planned to join up. None of her family members had come home from the war. She had been recommended to work as a delivery driver for her local Synthetron, and was happy with that plan. 'My father went off to the war, so did my brother, and my cousin and my aunt, and that's the last I heard of any of them. So I wasn't interested in joining up. But just a couple of days ago I saw Joe talking about the War in the East, and I just knew I had to go and fight for Freedom.'

Necker immediately liked Dirndl. She had power and a dazzling white-toothed smile, and he assumed she would be a good person to have at his side in battle. If Navel was his new best friend, being the first fellow recruit he'd encountered, he was more than happy to allow Dirndl to join their group.

A fourth newcomer joined them and introduced herself as Bloat. Like the others, she'd never entertained the idea of enlisting, but had been instantly and immovably persuaded to do so by Joe's stirring speech. She was eager to make friends, and she picked Navel, Necker and Dirndl because they 'Look nice, and new like me'. Bloat wanted to lead men into battle without actually fighting herself. She felt that she had strategic and leadership skills, 'Almost like a Sharp', and that it was just a matter of time before these were recognised.

It didn't take the other three long to figure out that this was not at all true, but they listened politely and nodded, because she was mildly amusing. By the time the kitchen staff had cleared away the lunch dishes and started preparing for dinner, and almost all of the rest of the diners had long since gone, the four of them were firm friends. They agreed to meet again at 1830 to make the most of the evening mealtime together, which they did.

After that good-humoured and light-filled meal, Necker returned to his room to find the next day's schedule posted on his digital bulletin. There was a parade at 0615, but after that nothing except breakfast and the other meals were showing. Another day off! It was all very civilised. InterFace time, socialising, and nothing too taxing planned for the foreseeable future. He furled himself into his Cocoon and slept there through the night. When the sensors detected that his eyes had closed and his breathing had become shallow and even, the screens dimmed and the sound turned down. He slept in bliss, dreaming of a heroic homecoming, during which Bock, who had left Biz's side to be with him, feted him most of all. The next morning all fifteen new recruits gathered at the parade ground, where Mandrill delivered the standard, scripted introduction.

'Soldiers and Gobblers! You are our next generation of Freedom warriors. Your job is to defend our nation and our Freedom by invading a nation of Freedom haters. We do this because we believe in peace enough to fight for it. We love our Freedom so deeply that we are willing to give up its many pleasures and live among dirty Sandrags, taking them on and beating them in battle. We haven't a minute to lose. We have to get out there and win Freedom for Joe!'

The recruits whooped and hollered and awkwardly hugged each other. Mandrill spread his arms out, calling for quiet.

'Alright, settle down,' he said. 'Today you'll be fitted for uniforms, but we can't begin training until the fourteen recruits needed to complete your unit arrive. Once you have your uniforms you may spend the day at leisure in your rooms.'

Robe, the sullen, pouting adjutant, guided the recruits to the uniform store. They were fitted and issued with combat, drill and dress uniforms, as well as shorts, singlets and t-shirts for training, and regulation socks, underwear, hats and shoes. Finally, they were sized for a curious pair of boots with ten short hexagonal studs spaced around on the soles. They looked uncomfortable, and none of them had a clue how they might be used. Like his new mates, Necker looked at the boots, shrugged and put them into his regulation duffle bag.

Robe then told them that they were required to spend their free time watching the InterFace in their own apartments. The recruits found this perfectly reasonable; they were rather pleased to think that defending Freedoms meant enjoying them.

Navel and Necker walked back to their barracks with Dirndl and Bloat. They all thought that, so far, this army life had been just about perfect.

'Fren, if I'd known about this I would have joined up years ago,' said Navel.

'Amen, fren,' Necker agreed. 'Amen.'

In his apartment, Necker ordered up a coffee – Flurient would not be available from his automat until after sunset – and slid into his Cocoon. An hour later, he was enjoying a heated, sexually charged argument between two of his favourite Famers, which he was sure would end in some frenzied lovemaking. But the scene cut. The screens all switched to a single image, that of a decorated officer staring down the barrel of the lens. Perhaps fighting for Freedom wouldn't be quite so perfect after all.

'Hello recruits,' the officer began. 'My name is General Remnant. I am the Commander of this base, Fort Manning. Your training begins here and now. Each day you'll be required to watch three hours of training Eduvids. These will cover a range of topics: the nature of your enemy, map-reading, tending wounds, firing your weapons. Where required, you will also be provided with physical instruction. However, we find that the InterFace education program is highly effective. You will be monitored during these video education sessions; sleeping is a punishable offence, and attempting to bypass the education videos and access the public channels is both punishable and a waste of time.'

General Remnant twisted his round, ragged face itself into

what Necker guessed was supposed to be a smile but looked grotesque and somewhat frightening. 'I am sure you'll find, as I do, that the polished production values and fascinating subject matter of the programs we have scheduled for you will keep you glued to your 'coons.'

'What a fucking Gobbler,' Necker whispered to himself.

Remnant's face was replaced by a title graphic: *Freedom: The Fight That Never Ends.'* Necker rubbed his eyes and steeled himself for an education he'd really rather not have.

A disembodied voice asked, 'What is Freedom?', while the screen played images of citiburb life: people boarding levtrans buses, rows of surveillance workers staring at their screens, shoppers walking away from Synthetron counters with bags of new clothes, happy teens with broad grins filing into TeenStar Cocooneries, quick-moving shoppers filling carts with fresh provisions as fast as they could, and relaxed viewers enjoying the InterFace.

'Freedom is the fortress we built for ourselves, and your job is to defend it. It is liberation from the afflictions of thinking and planning, and knowing that Joe will take care of those awful responsibilities. It is Joe giving us the ability to awaken each morning and do whatever we want – work, indulge in YouStar Fame, consume Flurient – and the divine right to use our Cocoon whenever we wish.

'Yet Freedom is not free. We must live up to its ideals, commit to its rules and abide by its constraints. We must devote ourselves to protecting our Freedom from those who would steal it from us because they can't bear to see us exercise it as we do.

'The heathens in the East have been trying to wrest our Freedoms from us for over three hundred years. Our fight began centuries ago, when those who hate our Freedom held the black, tarry keys to it and we reluctantly, but resolutely, fought the Religoil wars.

'As every schoolchild knows, the Freedom haters were so

intransigent that we had to pre-empt upon them the destruction that tragically ravaged broad swathes of our world with radiation. Since then, not one day has passed on which we were not driven to defend sweet liberty. It has been a hard, cruel and expensive struggle. And yet we have been fortunate. Our defensive aggression against our enemies has ensured that the fight has never encroached on our soil. No, not once in all those centuries.

'We have taken the fight to our enemies on their own grounds, and over the centuries we have fought to forcibly persuade many people into accepting the Freedoms we take for granted. Once habituated to the ways of Freedom, relieved of the dreadful responsibilities that weighed down upon them so much before we liberated them, these people have become not just our allies but our very compatriots, living with us under the benevolent, Freedom loving dictates of Joe.

'Today, our small world holds but minor pockets of resistance to Freedom's overpowering ideals, thanks to the potency of our logic and the technology of our arms. But these few holdouts are the most dangerous enemies we have ever faced. Their desperate and misguided rejection of Freedom makes them especially vicious, notoriously unpredictable and violent beyond even any known standards, forcing us to use, against our peaceful nature, the darkest weapons and tactics against them.'

This speech was accompanied by images of the eras and actions being described: mushroom clouds and monstrous walls of orange flame bursting forth from burning lakes and reservoirs of oil; filthy, unkempt and ugly exotics, chained and bloodied; well-fed and self-satisfied enjoyers of Freedom.

The harangue continued in the same vein for quite a while. It ended with another pre-recorded message from Remnant.

'Should you die in the commission of your duties,' he

reminded them, 'die happy in the knowledge that you are, or at least once were, Free. And that,' he again twisted his face into the frightening smile, 'is an order!'

Necker was dazed, but also felt enthused, or even empowered, by this instruction. He was the last line of defence against those who had the temerity to resist Freedom, and he promised himself that if could not make them surrender to liberation, they would be eliminated from the Freedom loving world. No matter what happened, the enemy could not continue in this heresy that directly violated the ideal of Freedom.

But he was also relieved when Remnant faded from the screen and YouStar returned to the screen. He passed a few hours with the bickering Famers before sitting through another bout of instructive video.

This pattern repeated over the next few days. Following a short address by a senior officer each morning, usually Mandrill or Robe, the recruits were ordered to their apartments until lunch. They enjoyed periods of YouStar, interrupted by lengthy training videos, which demonstrated how to pilot several kinds of levtrans vehicles, how to read digital maps, how to operate communications equipment, and so on, with the purpose of each step and skill explained over and over again. Necker was bored by it, but also more and more excited to get his hands on the real thing.

Then, on the fifth day – the very day that Bock went into the Fame House – the digital bulletin showed a variation in the routine. The recruits were to assemble after breakfast on the grassy training field for 'Skills Assessment and Task Assignment'.

7.

Biz awoke with a start. Knead was piloting the vehicle down a gentle slope towards the gaping darkness of a giant tunnel. The Sharp's fine, Roman profile dimmed as they came into the tunnel, which was lit only by two lines of artificial light high above them in the curved ceiling and reflected on the road. Biz sensed a light behind him being turned off – it was the tunnel door closing, blotting out the last of the daylight outside. With the end of the light came a powerful sense of anticipation, a twinge of apprehension, and a very mild headache, a hangover from the sedating beverage that Knead had given him. They drove on in silence, with the only indication of motion coming from alterations in the bright strips of light. More than once, Biz had the sensation that the vehicle was still and the lights were moving.

A small light appeared ahead, growing quickly until the vehicle shot out into a huge, bright cavern perhaps a thousand metres wide and deep, carved into virgin rock. A weird, dappled rainbow glittered and danced across the shiny black floor, as though they were immersed in some clear, viscous liquid that twisted, broke and fragmented the light around them into a swirling kaleidoscope of colour.

Knead's expression was smug and self-satisfied as he drove into the cavern, extending the silence and drawing out the tension. He stopped beside a square, black structure that was dwarfed by the chamber. When they got out, Biz could only stand in awe of the cavern's scale and beauty. The light came from the vast, flat ceiling; looking up at it was like staring at the sun through a glass of water, only it was the most mystical, refractive water he had ever seen, and instead of a simple glass he was looking up through a giant, flat bottomed lake.

'Black diamond floor,' said Knead tapping it with his foot. The sound was crisp and hard. 'Diamond ceiling too,' he added with a grin. 'A clear one. Holding up an immense reservoir of carbon dioxide. Do you have any idea of the kind of pressure we need to keep it under to maintain that liquid state?'

Biz just stood, gawking. He had never been anywhere so dazzling and impossible. Beneath a lake of liquid carbon dioxide! Knead looked at him and gave a soft chuckle.

'This way,' he said, indicating the black square beside them. Biz followed Knead around the vehicle, his heels clicking acutely on the floor's polished blackness. Inside, they walked along a short hallway and got into an elevator. Knead punched in a code, and the elevator took off – from the feel of it, down, and very quickly. The older man stared at the doors in front of him and rocked back a little on his heels.

Biz was nauseous from the unexpected motion, and knew that the questions streaming through his mind would remain unanswered if he gave them voice, so he held his tongue.

When at last the elevator stopped, they stepped out into a broad, gleaming black corridor lit by recessed lights. Matte black doors offered exits every ten metres or so. Knead took off to the left, with Biz following, their footfalls ticking like speedy metronomes on the seamless diamond flooring. Knead stopped at a door labelled 1419 – the number set into the wall in clear diamond, barely visible. He waved a palm at the door and it opened, then closed soundlessly behind them.

To Biz's great disappointment, they were in rather ordinary, if spacious, quarters – a king bed, kitchenette, bathroom to one side, a small InterTab workstation and a lounge area, but no Cocoon. He turned to Knead with a quizzical look. The older man held up a palm, as if to shut Biz's mouth before it opened.

'No, no Cocoons. We make the reality here, we don't consume it. And the last thing we need is for our people to get sidetracked watching it. Don't worry, you'll have plenty to occupy your time.'

Biz looked blankly at his new boss.

'I know. You're tired, still suffering the effects of the sedative, and nowhere near as sharp as I need you to be. Don't fret, fren, the edge will come, but right now you're still three parts Gobbler and that's no good to me. At your workstation, you'll find an induction manual. Read it, get familiar with the safety procedures and so on, and then get some sleep. I'll come by tomorrow and we'll start the real work.' Without waiting for an answer, Knead waved airily and swept out of the door.

Biz looked after him dumbly for a minute, then took a quick tour of the room. It was airy and comfortable but not extravagant in its appointments. The lounge area offered a long three-seater couch facing two padded armchairs across an ebony coffee table. The kitchenette was compact, and the automat was new. Packets of ready-made dry snacks lined the cupboards and the mid-sized fridge held fresh fruit and soft drinks.

The workstation comprised a simple desk and chair, an InterTab hooked into the Bastion's intranet, and a printed copy of the induction manual, which he leafed through without interest. He opened the wardrobe, which was full of black hemp clothing, all his size. He took a shower in the sparkling, brightly lit bathroom, then lay on his bed to read the induction manual. But he only got through a page and a half before sleep overtook him.

Very early the next morning, Knead breezed in without knocking to wake Biz, who was surprised. It seemed he'd only just fallen asleep, but in fact he had been out for eighteen hours – the sedative must have been extraordinarily strong – but now he felt incredibly fresh. He watched Knead race around on his long, slim legs while he blustered at his new pupil.

'Come on fren, up you get!' he said, grinning hard so the muscles in his neck grew even tighter. 'You've been out of it for long enough, it's time to get into it. Time to get out there and tech some spin!' He turned the lights up to full intensity. In the bright glare, he looked like he had been chiselled from particularly hard rock, his nose long and narrow, his forehead high, round and shiny. His lips were thin and stretched over perfect white teeth, his eyes deep and impenetrable. Knead's hair was dark and cut well above his large, crenelated ears. In less harsh light, he might even have been handsome. But there was also that inevitable Sharpness, that crystalline angularity that would keep him from ever looking pleasant.

Biz hurried to shower and dress in a black suit identical to Knead's while his mentor ordered breakfast from the automat – a thin, coal-dark coffee that shocked Biz's brain into a higher gear at the very first sip. The second he was ready, they left and followed an incomprehensible maze of corridors and hallways, going down several floors and up several more, emerging into yet more lengthy corridors until finally Knead ushered him into another plain but well-appointed room. They sat at a vast topaz-topped table, with only two glasses of carbonated water between them.

'So, tell me what you think you're going to do here.'

'I, er, I guess I'm here to become a Sharp.'

Knead nodded, although he didn't look convinced. He rolled his head in a sideways motion, which Biz took as a sign to continue.

'I feel like I've been invited to join some sort of power elite.' He glanced up uncertainly, almost coyly, but Knead revealed no thought or emotion other than irritation. That might have been the harsh overhead lighting, though.

'I think our job here is to provide leadership, direction and entertainment for the people. The, um, Gobblers,' he corrected himself. He was speaking with as much conviction as he could, but still his voiced wavered.

'So, you think you're Joe?' asked Knead with a chilly sneer.

'No, of course not,' said Biz with a hasty stammer. 'I think we're here to help Joe provide those things. We're, um, facilitators, I guess.' He knew Knead was goading him, but he was confused and nervous.

'Well, that's a little closer to the truth. And what do you think your job will be?'

'I've no idea. I'm not even sure what you do here, so it's hard to say what my job will be. Something to do with the InterFace?'

'At least you're an honest Gobbler,' observed Knead. 'And you're reasonably correct. Given your test results in comprehension and composition, and the analytical capabilities I'm told you have, you will begin as a Spin Tech, spinning news to shape it the way we want. As you progress, you'll become a Psyman, a Psychological Manipulator. When you're a Psyman, you'll be determining what shape the information should be rather than just shaping it under direction. Do you know what that means?'

'No.'

'Well, you'll start in Conflict Spin, but the main task of a Psyman is to maintain the delicate hierarchy of emotions we've instilled in our friends and clients, the Gobblers. To sustain a low level of fear and intimidation through the dissemination of war propaganda, to propagate a powerful and unshakeable belief that they are wonderfully free, and to keep the InterFace attractive by endlessly promoting and carefully stage-managing the YouStar channels. It's essential that we do all that without exciting any appetite for further enquiry or creating any desires that might stimulate actual activity. In other words, our job is to keep the Gobblers feeling comfortably free, constantly distracted and just a little bit afraid, without stirring them up too much or encouraging them to fixate too closely on any one thing. For their part, the Gobblers will assist us by being feckless, disinterested, unfocused, egocentric and endearingly dim.

'But don't let that dimness fool you. At any time, they could latch onto some small snippet of information carelessly placed before them, and start to bring the whole edifice down. They may be Gobblers, but they're still vulnerable to passions, and it's our job to occupy those passions and to divert them into harmless topics. Never forget that every Gobbler is capable of anger and disgust as much as they are of happiness and complacency. If they should ever for any reason get really riled up, they are also capable of protest. We work to ensure that never happens.

'We must be on guard at all times, carefully crafting everything they're told, especially on those occasions when what we tell them contains a grain of truth. And remember, the most effective deceit always contains at least a tiny, wisely twisted element of truth.'

Biz swallowed and nodded.

'So how do you think you came to be here?' Knead asked, changing the subject before Biz could think through that last piece of information and get mired in its implications. He saw that the pupil had been appropriately distracted; in time he would learn to wield the distraction rather than be overcome by it.

'Doctor Psyllium examined me and found that I carry the Leadership Gene.'

Knead stared at him with pity. 'You poor, deluded boy. You're still much more Gobbler than Sharp, aren't you? Still, that will change quickly now that you're here.'

'Because I'll be taught to be a Sharp?' Biz asked, with more hope than conviction.

'Being a Sharp isn't something you can learn, it's some-thing you become – it's a physical, chemical process that drives your intellectual development. You're only here because you appear to have the underlying mental capacity to cope with the physical change. Please tell me you've felt the physical change?'

'I have, for sure. But it's hard to tell if I'm just growing up, or if my Leadership Gene is asserting itself, or if something else is happening. It's been happening so slowly…'

Knead sighed. 'I can see I'm going to have to start at the very beginning with you.'

Biz avoided the older man's eyes, and stared instead at his own hands, crossed demurely in his lap. He was on the verge of tears.

'Let's go back to the beginning of the twenty-first century,' Knead said. 'You're aware of the discovery of Higgs Energy in the early years of that century?'

Biz nodded.

'That's when the seismic changes to our society really began. The true potential of the Higgs Boson was just being explored when the final acts of the Religoil wars played out, spreading radiation across what was then known as the Middle East. We had achieved our aim of suppressing the native populations so they could never challenge us again. But the precious oil beneath those now glowing sands was suddenly inaccessible. So typical of the idiots of those centuries. They were just beginning to realise the enormity of their folly when the much greater calamity struck.

'Our sun, in complete disobedience to what was known of physics at the time, burped out a monstrous coronal mass ejection, consisting primarily of caesium-134. This CME was directed straight at the earth, and it pretty much annihilated most of the remaining population, especially in the northern hemisphere. Our sun wasn't supposed to push out heavy elements like caesium. Even now we're not quite sure how it happened; maybe there was a comet or asteroid composed primarily of caesium, or something we don't know about, that flew into the sun, and the sun then regurgitated it, it just so happened, at us. Who knows, but at least it hasn't happened again.

'Anyway, although there was precious little notice, just a few hours really, the space based SOHO observatory did alert its science team to the composition of the ejecta. So there was enough time to get many of the best and brightest of the scientific and political communities to a safe place, where they rode out the storm of destruction. The great unwashed, who weren't even given the courtesy of a warning, were exposed to a lethal dose of caesium, causing severe burns, painful, gross and incapacitating illness, and finally a mercilessly painful death. The radiation from our bombs combined with the radiation from the Surge to shrink the world's population from almost eight billion to around fifty million.

'This was in fact a stroke of good fortune for the planet, as the exponential growth of the human population, coupled with the ruinous practices of energy generation, had placed its future in serious jeopardy. For a time, it had seemed certain that humans would drive not just themselves but every other species on the globe to extinction.

'The Surge itself led to extinctions and near-extinctions, but it was reasonably short-lived, and because caesium-134 has a two year half-life, in twenty years it was effectively gone. A lot of the survivors died of cancer, but the human race survived, and the world's other species celebrated this annihilation of the annihilators with an astonishing outbreak of growth and evolution. Many of the species we see now arose during that time, filling niches left by the extinct species.

'Of course, it didn't seem serendipitous at the time, but even the dimmest people still alive then realised it was a turning point. And when the leaders, the scientists and the thinkers emerged into the daylight, they vowed never again to fall victim to the myth of perpetual growth that had driven society for the preceding two hundred years or more. They committed to finding a less deleterious means of generating energy. It was just at that moment that our perception changed – we would no longer generate energy at all, but simply capture it.

'At the same time, the survivors agreed that if *Homo superstans* was to continue on this planet, it must rid itself of a number of addictions and temper some of its other habits and customs. The first to go were the twin, allied evils of war and religion. It was hard to have one without the other, anyway. But then we discovered that we'd need war, even if in a much-altered form, and we brought it back. Communication was another issue of major importance, but we'll get to that later. In fact, I'm getting way ahead of myself. Let's concentrate on how you came to be, allegedly, a Sharp.' Knead sipped his carbonated water.

Biz wondered how long this would take. He suspected that Knead was the kind of person who, if you asked him about his new vehicle, would start with the invention of the wheel. Still, he should have been grateful. At last he was getting information of some kind, even if it was tedious – and still only by way of background.

'It was fortunate that among those preserved for the benefit of posterity were men and women who had, only a few years prior, isolated the Higgs Boson. Using nanotechnology, also fortuitously developed in the decades before the Turning, they engaged with the Higgs Field at a quantum level. The Field gives what we think of as mass to ordinary particles, and when it interacts with those particles, it releases almost infinitesimal amounts of energy. The challenge was to harness that energy.

'Almost everything we now make is coated with lithicarb, a compound of lithium and carbon only a few atoms thick, which interacts with the Field just as ordinary matter does – but lithicarb harvests the energy that the interaction releases. This energy is transmitted to storage units via simple electron streams.

'Once this system was in place, it was practically a foregone conclusion that *Homo superstans* would take his next steps into the age of carbon. It had long been known that carbon has the interesting property of being able to bond with a huge array of other elements, or to be reconfigured or constructed at an atomic level to produce an astonishing range of materials. Creating carbon and carbon-based materials for all sorts of purposes then became just a matter of design, calculation and instructions at an atomic level. Simple, really.

'The billions of tonnes of carbon dioxide that had been pumped, billowed, burned and hurled into the atmosphere were still up there, altering weather patterns, creating breathing difficulties and so on. So they – we – *Homo superstans* – began mining carbon dioxide. Dirty air was trapped and separated into its constituents, and the carbon dioxide isolated. It takes a serious amount of energy to separate the carbon from the oxygen in a CO_2 molecule, but the discovery of Higgs Energy made that an engineering problem rather than an insurmountable barrier. The oxygen was kept for recombination with hydrogen to make water, which was getting scarce, or just released back into the atmosphere. The carbon was used for almost everything – light, strong construction materials, fabrics, wires, strings, meshes, surfaces, substrates, cables, containers, dispensers, seals and sealants, conductors, transmitters, resistors, protectors, motors, chips a dozen atoms wide, giant superchips, medicines, ointments, foods, cleaners, heaters, coolers, warmers, magnets, repellers and a million other things besides. Depending on the purpose, carbon could be combined with just about anything, whether naturally occurring or designed, to do anything at all. There was no longer any need to cut things down or dig them up, except for the things we choose to grow rather than make, to eat, or wear, or just enjoy.' Knead paused again and sipped his water.

He stretched his arms out in front of him, clasped his hands together and cracked his knuckles, and ploughed on. 'Smog and haze became historical curiosities. The skies cleared and the climate stabilised. A sense of balance was restored, and our planet slowly returned from ash grey to blue and green. Animals – those that were left and the new species that had arisen – slowly but surely got bigger as the amount of oxygen in the air grew. Plants got smaller, or disappeared. But giant greenhouses with wafer thin diamond windows were kept full of carbon dioxide, so our grown food supplies were more plentiful, nutritious and tasty than ever before.'

'This was lucky, because as the oxygen content in the atmosphere increased, we got bigger as well. A man was once considered tall if he was just two metres – imagine that! Domestic cows once weighed a third of what they do now, chickens were a quarter as tall, and their whales, as they called them, were the size of a large tuna. They had barely any coral, even the largest seaweed was like a bunch of chives, the crustaceans no bigger than walnuts, the bivalves than almonds. Now all of these and more revel in their environment, the environment we created for them.

'There was just one tiny downside to all of this glorious, flourishing growth and happiness: the effect of all that oxygen on people's brains. To be perfectly candid, they went soft in the head. Initially, a higher concentration of oxygen helped people become calmer, less aggressive and more inclined to seek harmony with their fellows. It toned down the carbon dioxide psychosis that had so very clearly affected the peoples of the war centuries. But then, as the atmosphere reached levels of twenty-five and thirty percent oxygen – which kept climbing – that pleasantness turned into hyperoxia. There is no nice way to say this: people became more stupid. Their ability to focus and to retain information dissipated. Their capacity to care for or about things other than themselves waned, and they became more interested in life's simple pleasures: getting high, being entertained, and not having to think for themselves.

'From the perspective of the governors, this had its benefits.

The people became more malleable, more open to suggestion, less excitable. We owe a debt to the quick thinking government officials who banned those things that were likely to inflame people's passions, such as organised sports, democratic elections, concerts and most other forms of music, and other artistic performances.

'Over time, communication and entertainment systems were reformed and refined into the single channel structure we have today, and the old distractions were replaced by Fame, Freedom and Fear. Everything we do is centred around those two carrots and that one stick, those three *F*'s. Fame is the new opium; it helps keep things calm and gives everyone something to talk about in place of the banned distractions and activities. The remaining two *F*'s are used more sparingly. Fear and Freedom go hand in hand, and they are extremely effective in small doses. Whenever the citizenry appears to be getting bored or complacent, or a little too comfortable or interested in something, we throw in a little Fear. Not much, generally, just a few well-chosen words about our treacherous enemies in the East, about how we all need to support our brave troops, and how our foes have made recent gains or technological advances that threaten our way of life. Then we pump up the Freedom balloon and fly it high. If necessary, Joe-casts remind people that what we are fighting for is our Freedom, that nothing is more important, and that only their unqualified support for the war can preserve their Freedom. In extreme cases, where people are in danger of not just thinking for themselves but acting, he hints that we might even be losing. That works every time.' He stopped and scratched just behind his ears, then shook his head like a meerkat.

Biz listened obediently and tried to assimilate everything. He was somewhat shocked by his mentor's cynicism, but he guessed that was just part of being a Sharp, and that he would grow more sceptical himself over time. Who knew, becoming completely dismissive of the Gobblers might just signal his final transition into total Sharpness.

Knead smiled with cheerful insouciance, and said, as though he were talking about a cake recipe, 'Anyway, to return to your own life. You see, as folks out there kept on gobbling up oxygen like there was no tomorrow, and consequently became less discerning and more, ah, innocent, the leadership realised that they should take steps to safeguard their own mental acuity. They looked again to the good people of the war centuries, particularly the last decades. They were angry, greedy and selfish, and they were terrifically focused on getting what they wanted. All exceptional leadership qualities, as I'm sure you'll agree.'

Biz nodded reflexively.

'So the leaders of the new society took a long look at what drove their predecessors. On the surface, it seemed that they derived their motivation from the system itself – the notion that economic growth could be continuous and exponential. Maybe there was something in that. Would the promise of a lot of stuff be enough to motivate and reward the new generation of leaders? Deeper digging showed this to be anything but the case. In fact, it would have led to anarchy. Look at what happened in the twentieth and twenty-first centuries, when that belief was most prevalent. Everyone accumulated and consumed and thought they were buying happiness, harmony and community, when really they were becoming less and less attached to each other and more and more attached to things. And when their knick-knacks and gadgets and baubles didn't make them happy, they became even more frenzied in their efforts to accumulate more, because they were so convinced that the only reason they weren't happy was because they didn't have enough things. So they attacked one another to try and get more stuff from each other, and society dissolved into a morass of violence and greed. Their excellent leadership qualities couldn't shield people from the all-consuming appetites nurtured by the idea of perpetual growth. Instead, they made the drive to satiate those appetites more deadly.

'Unfettered growth did inspire innovation and promote the management tools we so admire now – cunning, secretiveness and cold, level-headed calculation – but it also sowed the seeds of its own destruction, because ultimately it was never controllable. It stimulated unwanted emotional responses, and the actual acquisition of all that crap was very distracting. In the end, the leaders determined that although the previous system celebrated and fostered leadership qualities, those qualities had not originated in that system.

'Then one day a bright young scientist by the name of Phase managed to unravel the mystery. It wasn't what the people of the war centuries did – the system that they worked in – that made them so deliciously devious and so dedicated to acquiring power over one another, it was where they did it: in an ever-growing cloud of carbon dioxide.

'Ever since the late nineteenth century, when colossal amounts of CO_2 had first been poured into the atmosphere, the people of the world, especially those in cities, had been suffering from an overdose. Changing the chemistry of the air they breathed changed the chemistry of their brains, distorting their judgement so that they believed that salvation lay in amassing the trinkets they thought of as treasure. They were sick and getting sicker, and that sickness informed and inflamed their thinking and actions. It was a vicious circle – or rather spiral – in which the sicker they became, the more they tried to accumulate stuff, the more energy they consumed and the more CO_2 they pumped into the air, which further fuelled their carbon psychosis.

'Phase's revelation gave us an insight into how our world had come so close to obliteration, and it meant that we now had a mechanism for separating the leaders and the led – a physical means of attaining an edge over ordinary people. So our predecessors in government did the intelligent thing: they started to dose themselves up with carbon dioxide, to regain that cruel, cold focus so indispensable to leaders everywhere. As the general populace became more intoxicated with oxygen and less affected by carbon dioxide, the leadership cohort learned more about CO_2 poisoning and how to control it so they – and we – could use it to endow ourselves with the best qualities of the people of the war centuries without falling victim to their many excesses. We learned how to change our brain chemistry without unduly damaging our brains.

'After centuries of being essentially identical to the people they ruled, the power elite found a way to physiological superiority. The more CO_2 the leadership cohort took, the Sharper they became. Conversely, as they became more oxygen affected, the general public became dimmer and dimmer. Their growing oxygen narcosis gave them the wonderful insulation of not knowing, the divine gift of not caring about anything beyond themselves and their screens. As Joe says – and we keep repeating – they enjoy unlimited Freedom. What they don't understand, and don't have to, is that their greatest Freedom is being free from awareness.

'But you and I have had that Freedom taken away from us. We're not free; we're leaders. Sharps. We are not gifted with ignorance; we are burdened with the capacity to control. We're compelled to direct what happens to those who are ignorant and free. We're responsible. And the primary tool of our responsibility, what keeps us sharp and gives us the clarity we need to lead and control, is carbon dioxide.'

Biz stared at the table as if he was trying not to look into the light of understanding.

'Oh, come on!' said Knead with a hint of exasperation. 'Surely you'd already guessed. Consider the way you've changed in the last few years. Become harder, smarter, clearer. Less inclined to tolerate, let alone enjoy those activities and pastimes so beloved of your former peers. Your so-called Leadership Gene treatment is nothing but regular doses of carbon dioxide. It's changed the way your brain works. You've become more like the people of the war centuries – more controlling, more avid, more grasping.

'All that time, all those people thought that what they wanted was things, but what they really wanted – needed – was control over their lives and power over the lives of others. What they did not recognise but we do, is that consumerism is a poor substitute for power.

'And now you possess that magical combination of clarity and power – or rather, it possesses you. Your mind is becoming ever more cunning, devious and ambitious, like the minds of the war century people, but you won't share their delusion about what's driving you. You'll have full knowledge of how and why you act the way you do. Like them, you will lust for power, secretly loathe the people you control, and disdain the weak, or you won't survive here. But unlike them, you won't be a victim of the mindless, stupid avarice that clouded their judgement and undermined their focus. And, of course, you won't have the same competitive environment. You'll work with your peers instead of against them, to accumulate collective power rather than create individual dominions. And the people you rule over are much more malleable than the subjects of the war centuries' leaders.'

So this was what it is to be a Sharp, thought Biz. This is how I *became* a Sharp. But that was impossible – he retreated to his long-held delusion. 'But Doctor Psyllium took my blood. He said I have a degenerative disease. Was that just not true?'

'Straight out bullshit.' Knead smirked. 'We threw the blood out. It was a cover story, and one that only a Gobbler would buy. As if there could be a disease, degenerative or other-wise, that your nanomat and nanostream couldn't deal with instantly. Your test results over a period of years indicated that your mind was developing faster and more acutely than your peers. Psyllium visited your home to examine your mind, not your health. You passed his interview, barely, and as soon as you were approved, your CO_2 treatment started. I won't lie to you: you haven't progressed as much as we'd hoped.

'But now, you don't need external treatment. The atmosphere in the Bastion is set at around late mid-twentieth century levels. We've been slowly increasing your CO_2 levels for three years so that you wouldn't get sick when you arrived. Now that you're here, your CO_2 concentrations will keep elevating until they're in the ideal range. You'll gain greater clarity and become – I hope – a lot sharper than you are now. You'd better, because we have high expectations of you in the near future.

'Anyway, that's probably enough one-on-one for now. Consider what I've said, and study up on Conflict Spin and Psyman. You'll have to learn how to promote Fear through insinuation and fabrication without ever having to provide a shred of hard evidence. The trick is to conjure up a shadowy, tense background, so the Gobblers don't become actively terrified but do stay anxious enough to keep them from having ideas of their own.' With that, Knead left the room.

Biz closed his eyes, rubbed his temples, and tried to overcome his disbelief. He assumed that greater acceptance would come with greater clarity, and turned to the Conflict Spin primer on his InterTab screen.

8.

Bock woke the next morning with the world's nastiest Flurient hangover. All motivation, all animation had been drained from her. She opened her eyes and saw the flaking eggshell coloured paint on the ceiling of her room, then shut them tight again. She really was at home. Before her lay an abyss. She would be sucked into the InterFace workforce, to be progressively drained until, old and desiccated, her prune of a body would be spat out to be burned unmourned.

Her left Manacle throbbed lightly; she had to be at the Surveillance Centre in three hours for induction into the work-force. The Centre was at the Hub, just a few hundred metres from her front door. She didn't know if she could make the walk that would end in the InterFace, in mind-numbing days, weeks, months and years monitoring the same set of fixed cameras, watching thousands of uneventful Gobbler lives and searching for the slightest deviation from the norm. She opened her eyes again to stare at the too familiar ceiling. Her mind was blank. She felt old. Something was missing. She forced herself out of bed, her movements slow and heavy.

The house was quiet except for a low hum of voices in the main room. Caper and Trinket must have been in their Cocoons already, watching the new Famers going through orientation. Soon Bock would be just like her parents, watching Famers in the morning, then going to work at the Surveillance Centre to watch the fameless. Perhaps their Manacles were throbbing, too, and they could go to the Centre together, as

94

a family – that was usually how it worked out. It was better that way: they could all watch YouStar at the same time. Then, when Bock was given her own home at twenty – or when she moved in with a partner – her schedule would change and, unless she made an effort, she wouldn't see her parents at all. And she wouldn't make that effort, because it would just irritate them if she turned up and dragged them away from their Cocoons.

Bock moved with listless determination into the kitchen, resisting the force dragging her back into her room and her bed. As she ordered up a coffee and waited for the automat to put it together, she thought back to the month just past. Her memories were already incoherent, chaotic. She could only muster flashes: an image of herself sweeping with imperious confidence along a swarming red carpet, a snippet of lewd conversation with Swain over a sumptuous dinner, the echo of Arena loudly expelling a hearty laugh, the feel of silk against her skin. Soon those memories would be lost forever.

She shook her head as if to hasten their loss, and tried to focus on her future, but it was difficult. Holding thoughts in her mind and tracking them as they wound to a conclusion was trickier than it had ever been, as if the thoughts were chasing each other round her mind, refusing to be marshalled and put in the proper order. Funnily enough, this wasn't entirely distressing. In some ways, it was amusing and diverting.

Her Manacle throbbed three times. She found herself sitting at the breakfast bar, nursing a three-quarters-empty, cold cup of coffee, and she had no idea how long she had been sitting there. The time had simply been swallowed up with inconsequential meanderings. She had to be at work within the hour. She ate breakfast and then walked down the road to the Hub with her parents. They told her where to go for induction.

A leery Gobbler called Taint, a surprisingly young man with a bad habit of invading his female co-workers' personal space, introduced Bock to her work. But before he began he pushed his face close to hers, breathing stale Flurient fumes all over her. 'You're the one that was on YouStar last night, aren't you? Buck, is it?'

'Bock,' she said. She tried to move her head away from his, but he kept coming closer.

'So you and that fellow Swan, you do it or what?'

'His name was Swain.' Although she knew that they had been caught in the act, she added, 'And no, we did not "do it".'

'Oh yeah? I seen you. Maybe you and me will do it some time, eh, fren?' His chin was unshaven, his hair looked like matted straw, and his body, like his breath, was rancid. He was the last person Bock would consider as a partner, but she knew she couldn't afford to get him off side at this point. He could easily report her to the Liberty Guard as an unwilling worker.

'You never know, Taunt,' she said, as coyly as she could. 'If you do a good job of teaching me what I have to do here, who knows what might happen later?'

'That's Taint, love, and it'll be my pleasure. Come with me.'

She followed him to a vacant workstation: a simple desk facing twelve small surveillance screens. The station controlled the zoom on each camera, the ambient light and contrast, and the volume of the microphones. She could also call up a display of the personal information of any subject on the screen if she pointed the cursor at them. There was an intercom microphone connected directly to the Centre's Liberty Guard squad room, should any person need to be arrested and removed. Finally, she was given an InterTab on which she could make reports of suspicious activities not deserving of immediate intervention. Taint showed her how to bring up the menu of report templates, which covered littering, loitering, talking too long with one person, inappropriate language or refrences, property damage, and making rude or defiant gestures at the cameras.

There were ten more, similar desks in the big room, with a toilet and a coffee-only automat a few paces away. The people around her didn't take much notice of her. They were working, staring glumly at their screens, occasionally zooming in on someone or bringing up information, just to look busy.

Bock only had to concentrate on her screens for three hours, with a five-minute break every hour. She watched a bare citiburbian street that could have been the one she lived in; it looked familiar and yet so strange from the cameras' high vantage points.

As Taint left her workstation, he said, 'I'll be the one watching you to make sure you do what you're supposed to, so don't make me come down here and give you a spanking.' He waited for her to nod. 'And maybe I'll message you later, so we can hook up.' He ambled off scratching his crotch.

9.

Necker was excited but apprehensive, and just a bit annoyed. He'd grown accustomed to spending sixteen or more hours a day lounging in his Cocoon, paying minimal attention to the educational programs while waiting for YouStar to resume. But he was also keen on enacting some of the things he'd seen. He longed to get his hands on powerful weapons, to develop the combat strength and skills he would need to overcome his enemy and somehow find the bravery he hoped was hidden within him. Today they would finally get on the training field for skills assessment, which hopefully meant some deadly armaments would be involved.

His conversation with Navel and Bloat at breakfast was taut and filled with false bravado. They were jumpy with anticipation, brimming with expectation.

'Shit's about to get real, Gobblers,' Navel announced. He wore a broad grin, but Necker detected a tremor in his voice.

At last the recruits in Necker's unit – now a full complement of twenty-five – gathered on the training ground. Mandrill and Robe were waiting for them. The sergeant was businesslike, brisk but not unduly brusque. Together, with much pushing and shouting and directing, Mandrill and Robe arranged the recruits into five straight, evenly spaced ranks, and Mandrill ordered them to remember their row and number, as they would be required to fall in to this formation whenever the order was given.

'Just like real soldiers,' said Navel, sucking in his guts and thrusting back his shoulders after Mandrill's manner.

Once everyone in the unit had assumed the correct position and stance, they did indeed resemble a parade of genuine, professional soldiers standing at attention. Mandrill then taught them a new order: 'at ease.' Standing with the hands clasped behind their back and their feet shoulder-width apart came naturally to them, and they stood in this position for some time as Mandrill addressed them in grave and conspiratorial tones, as though he was letting them in on a deep, dark secret. Which turned out to be true, as they gathered from his opening words.

'Soldiers, you have all signed the official Secrecy Act. This means that if you impart any of what you learn, see or do while in the army to your friends, family, acquaintances, associates or random strangers out there in Gobbler land, you will be deemed guilty of treason and incarcerated, executed, or both. So will the unfortunate recipient of the information. Do I make myself clear?' There was general nodding and murmurs.

'What's a recipient?' Navel whispered loudly to Necker.

The hitherto silent, sullen looking Robe, who appeared to be thinking about something upsetting, sprang into life and showed off her fine pair of lungs. 'You will answer yes sir in loud, clear voices and you will do it together. Now!'

The startled brigade yelled in a higgledy-piggledy, undisciplined way, and Robe made them do it again. And again. And several times more, until it came as a chorus rather than a cacophony, and the recruits' faces were all as red as the adjutant's. Shooting an admiring glance at his pugnacious deputy, Mandrill continued his address.

'Now, being the ignorant Gobblers you are, you will not know that for almost three hundred years a certain concept has been disallowed within the general community. It occurs quite naturally in certain working situations, but acknowledgement of the concept or attempts to analyse its potential and put it into practice privately are strictly forbidden.

'This concept is teamwork, and it operates on the premise that a group of people acting in a coordinated, co-operative fashion can achieve much more than they could if they were operating independently of each other. This concept has been expunged from the collective consciousness for a very good reason, namely, that anything that encourages people to collude with each other, to develop shared thought patterns and complementary actions, allows those people to become more attuned to one another and to develop a group mentality. This inevitably leads to the generation of shared ideals, which can easily mutate into shared *independent ideas*, which may then lead to dissatisfaction with the current situation, exacerbated by the discussion and dissemination of said dissatisfaction, until genuine dissent is born. Even if the shared, independent ideas are stupid and wrong. From there it is but a short step to conspiring to change things, by which time we have strayed dangerously from Freedom into disobedience. Do I make myself clear?'

'Yes sir!' the bewildered unit shouted.

Mandrill had developed an incomprehensible idiom over many years, through listening to the Sharps who regularly visited and delivered his instructions, and he deployed it in order to seem intelligent, although usually the effect was just to confuse his listeners, as on this occasion.

'I tell you this not because I think you enjoy abstract conversations, but because you have signed the Secrecy Act, and because as defenders of Freedom it will greatly assist you in your mission if you attain a high level of cooperation. That is, I expect you – Joe expects you – to become a team. A team that thinks and does what it is told to think and do, but a team nevertheless. Do I make myself clear?'

'Yes, sir!' In spite of their enthusiastic response, this revolutionary thinking was not clear to the recruits at all. The idea of consciously cooperating with their peers to create a whole greater than the sum of its parts was so new and radical that most of them would have had trouble grasping it even if it had been explained in straightforward language. Mandrill's mangled prolixity cloaked the concept in language so dense that not one of them could penetrate its meaning.

But Mandrill got the affirmation he had expected. He could see by the looks on their faces that his intake group didn't get it, but that didn't faze him. Once they had experienced the fluidity and cohesion of teamwork they would internalise its values so well they would never forget its implications.

'Now, given that you are sworn defenders of Freedom, you will not of course fall victim to the negative aspects of teamwork. That is, if you are ever tempted to entertain ideas of your own – which I doubt, given the fact that you are all irremediable Gobblers – you will not under any circumstances share or nurture them with your teammates, as you will come to know them. Being in close cooperation with your teammates, learning to rely on them and being trained to act so that they can rely on you, may lead you to think that you share some special bond, and hopefully that will be true. But that bond is only good for following orders, not for collaborating on ideas that may not be acceptable. In other words, just because you can trust your teammates on the field, does not mean that you can allow them into your minds. I will do the thinking, you will do the doing. Do I make myself clear?'

'Yes sir!' they screamed. They had only really understood the last part, but they were more than ready to comply with that. The stuff that went before that was probably important, but since they couldn't comprehend it they figured they couldn't contravene it. Several, including Necker, were relieved that they would not be required to exercise any independent thought during this new enterprise called teamwork.

'Okay, to matters practical, then.' Mandrill knew he'd gotten through to them on the important point, that obedience was the key to success. The recruits didn't notice the self-satisfied look on the sergeant's face, as Robe had captured their attention. She had opened a large bag of round balls, each about thirty centimetres in diameter, and was placing them in a straight line on the grass, spaced about two metres apart. About fifteen metres behind them there was a rectangular frame some seven metres wide and two and half metres high, and a net was attached to the frame and the ground behind it. Having placed the balls, Robe stood in the mouth of the frame, facing the recruits and the line of balls. She went into a semi-crouch that showed she was ready to spring at any time, held her hands in front of her as though she was pretending to hold one of the balls, and took on an alert, eagle-eyed bearing.

The recruits had no idea of what to make of this. They had never seen balls like this, nor the frame, nor the net. But perhaps it had something to do with teamwork?

'Your task,' Mandrill told them, 'is to take turns at the following. You will approach one of the balls on the ground before you, and kick it with your foot as hard and as directly as you can into the back of the net. Robe will try to obstruct and intercept the ball – the challenge is not just to kick it straight and far enough so that it passes beyond the frame and into the back of the net, but also to avoid Robe, who will be doing all she can to stop the ball reaching the back of the net. Should you succeed in kicking the ball past Robe and into the back of the net, you will be said to have kicked a goal. Do I make myself clear?'

It all sounded easy enough, and the recruits were keen to give it a shot. Mandrill took three paces up to the nearest ball, gave it a swift kick, and it flew straight into Robe's waiting hands. The recruits all laughed and clapped, and jostled forward so that they could be next to try. For the next two hours, the unit had an immensely enjoyable time at this marvellous sport of "goal kicking", with varying degrees of endeavour and success. It took most of them quite a number of attempts before they could even kick the ball close to the goal mouth, let alone past the surprisingly quick Robe. Some kicked with the side of their foot, some kicked with their toes; some developed their kicking skills quite quickly while others laboured without achieving anything at all.

They were also all given an opportunity to take Robe's place in the goal mouth and try to intercept the incoming ball. Most lost their nerve at the sight of the fast-moving ball, and dodged more balls than they saved. But for some, it was as if they had been doing it all their lives after just a few minutes.

Necker and Dirndl were strong, naturally gifted kickers, while Bloat displayed exceptional agility in the frame. The ball did not frighten her in the least; on the contrary, she heaved herself into its path without hesitation every time it came close enough for her to do so.

Navel spent a lot of time toying with the ball with his feet, and in a short space of time was able to flip it up over his head, bounce it off either his forehead or his knee as it fell, and use his other foot to kick it aloft again – this, Mandrill told them, was like 'having the ball on a string.' The exercise was tiring and challenging, but they loved it nonetheless, and retired to lunch happy and excited. None could tell with any certainty whether they had actually experienced any teamwork, but they were not fussed about that in any way, and it was agreed over lunch that if teamwork was anything like goal kicking, it would be a lot of fun.

Over the following days and weeks, Necker and his colleagues learned a lot about teamwork. Based on the abilities they had shown in the first few days, kicking the ball into the net and to one another, running while keeping the ball just ahead of them by giving it little toe-taps, and taking the ball from others, Mandrill organised them into a squad of fifteen players and ten non-players. In a contest, he explained, just eleven of the playing group could be on field at any one time, and the remainder would be on the bench – as he called it – or warming up to take part.

Those who had shown little to no ability – and there were a few of those – were assigned support and administrative tasks. Empath was a masseur; his unnaturally long, strong fingers and austere, asexual manner fitted the role perfectly. Kettle organised the beverages and refreshments. Grabe managed the equipment. Torose, who demonstrated a crafty sense of strategy, but whose bulbous body and knobby limbs kept her from executing anything at all, became assistant coach to Mandrill. The other non-competitors were given other jobs, and the unit settled into its new designation as a team.

They were instructed in the rules and objectives of the sport, which was called battle. They trained for three hours every morning, and after lunch spent the afternoons in their Cocoons. Then one day, Necker's team was given an opportunity to put their skills into action, taking part in a genuine battle. The strenuous, competitive physical encounter was incredibly fulfilling for Necker and his friends, even though they lost – even Bloat's goalkeeping couldn't keep them in the battle. They had a chance to see real teamwork in action (that of the opponents, who were nearing the end of their training) and to experience first-hand the value of the essential elements of team play: strategy, planning and mutual trust.

Occasionally the routine of skills training or morning scratch battles was interrupted by other training programs. These were cursory introductions to the kind of skills Necker had thought they would be concentrating on all the time: operating and firing small weapons, handling hazardous materials and general radiation safety, marching, health and safety instruction, and uniform maintenance. But by and large their time away from the Cocoon, which continued to interrupt InterFace programming with propaganda and instructive videos, was spent in honing or applying their skills on the battlefield. At mealtimes, they gathered to discuss the day's contest, or the tactics devised by Mandrill and Torose for taking on opposing teams, and to enjoy the camaraderie their teamwork had awoken in them. Every now and then someone, usually Dirndl, would raise the question at the back of everyone's mind: when would they begin training for actual warfare?

'Don't get me wrong,' Dirndl said, in a typical diatribe. 'I'm loving this so far. The contest is great, I feel energised and healthy, and I'm sure my nanostream has never had so little to do, but playing battle isn't any way to defend Freedom, is it? Now that we know all about strategy and teamwork, we need to know the nitty-gritty. We need to learn how to kill and maim, and if those things aren't achievable, how to capture and interrogate our enemies. I want to love my weapon, to sleep with it and carry it everywhere. As it is I've barely touched a weapon, and the one I got my hands on was, well, small and gentle. I want firepower. I want action and blood and noise and smoke and death!'

'Chill, fren,' Navel said. 'I'm sure we'll all get enough of those things. And if you're lucky the Eduvids will cover some larger weapons soon. In fact, I'm sure I've seen some heavy weaponry videos. But I kind of doze through a lot of it.'

'Bullshit. Unless all this is leading to a new phase, and one that starts soon, we'll all be going to war with nothing more than ball-boots and a game plan.'

Even Necker, who was attracted to Dirndl, was inclined to think that she was overthinking things. 'Fren, Mandrill isn't going to lead us into combat until he's sure we're ready. He may be a Gobbler, but even he isn't as stupid as that.' And they all laughed, and someone mentioned the vomiting Famer from last night, and the discussion drifted away from war and training. Even Dirndl couldn't dwell on things that irked her for too long.

10.

It didn't take long for Biz to slip into the routine of life in the Bastion. There were many areas he was not yet allowed to enter, and many activities he knew nothing about, but for the time being it was a full-time job to learn his role and become accustomed to his new life. He was part of a small group of new Bastion inductees who had just finished school. Although they were all assigned different tasks, they lived in the same part of the citadel, saw each other in the junior mess, and passed each other in the black diamond hallways or riding the elevators between their designated go levels.

They were also required to attend lectures during which Knead or one of his Cabinet colleagues would expound on what the inductees were to do and how, with occasional forays into the why. Biz usually sat with his new friends, Psyman tyros like himself: Globe, Lintel and Bias. Globe worked with Biz in Conflict Spin. Despite her charming freckled face and soft, clear, cobalt eyes, she was a tiger, a tower of rage against the enemy housed in a compact, pneumatic body. Slender, spicy and sensual Bias revelled in her gossipy, voyeuristic work in YouStar Spin, while Lintel, narrow, dark, deep voiced and deep of understanding, was a Freedom Specialist. He worked to demonstrate to the Gobblers just how much Freedom they had, often by creating new regulations or restrictions around an apparently new aspect of liberty.

'My job is to build a bridge between Fame and Fear on the one hand, and Freedom on the other,' he said. 'Everything you lot do must be traceable back to the expansion of Freedom, or its protection.' Lintel seemed to have become much sharper more rapidly than Biz and his other close colleagues, even though they were the same age and had been receiving the same dosage of CO_2 treatment for the same amount of time. He hated Gobblers with a passion. To him, they didn't recognise their Freedom, or celebrate it enough. 'Ungrateful bastards with their noses stuck in their fucking Cocoons,' he would boom in his basso profundo.

For a time in his early days in the Bastion, Biz missed Bock terribly. His ability to focus, concentrate and remember grew, along with an appetite for constancy and routine, and he wanted to share that routine with her. Particularly in the long and difficult weeks immediately following induction, he spent lengthy periods wondering where she was and what she was doing, certain that, whatever it was, she would have enjoyed the Bastion more.

Every few days, most of the citizens of the Bastion – Bastionados, as they called themselves – would gather in the giant atrium beneath the CO_2 reservoir, to socialise in the dappled diamond rainbow light. Talking about work at these events was prohibited, or at least discouraged, since cross-conversations between Sharps of different strata and security levels could be dangerous. But there was so little else in their lives that they were left with nothing to discuss other than the food (uniformly excellent) and their health (also universally excellent). They couldn't even talk about what was going on in the outside world, because every bit of it was under the control of someone in the room. As a result, these events were generally considered to be a mild form of torture. Biz and his friends went, of course, and imbibed a little beer or scotch – which seemed to be the preferred poison of Sharps – ruthlessly maligned Gobblers in general, non-specific terms for a while, then gratefully retired to their own apartments.

The only exceptions to this rule were the meetings that Joe came along to. Then, everyone did their best to appear cheerful and enthusiastic, talking and laughing perhaps a shade too loudly in the hope that their exuberance would tempt Joe to join their conversation, perhaps offer a few words of wisdom, and maybe even remember their names. But these visits were very rare, and he almost never had the time to talk to juniors or even regular Sharps – like most of the Bastionados, Biz and his friends had never seen Joe up close.

The tedium of the social evenings aside, life fell into an agreeable pattern. Biz was absorbed in his work: editing and rewriting information about the War in the East, which Knead sent to him in a private stream. These were usually reports of threats, or of stolen plans detailing the enemy's destructive designs: a plot to blow up the Fame House, for instance, or to destroy the InterFace, or assassinate Joe, or simply to invade and lay waste to Freedom itself. Biz's task was to spin these threats – he often suspected that Knead made them up on the spot – into credible menace. He would reveal the plot, detail its potentially catastrophic consequences, and conclude by claiming that, thanks to the admirable strategic direction of Joe and the vigilance and courage of the defence forces, the citizenry would remain safe and free.

As Knead explained it, the people needed to feel that their Freedom was hanging by a thread, and that only Joe, with the help of the armed forces, could ensure the thread remained unbroken.

'It's all about the suspense, the tension,' Knead repeated. Having seen one of these Face-casts, the populace could embrace and enjoy their Freedom while remaining vaguely concerned for its future and eternally in debt to the man that stood guard over it for them. 'We don't want to arouse their disquiet too much lest they start believing that the man in charge isn't doing a wonderful job,' Knead said. 'The Gobblers' overwhelming emotion, the takeaway if you like, must be relief. We knock them over the head with the harsh truth a couple of times, then stop and apply the comfort that Joe will keep the truth from hurting them too much. They start out feeling frightened, they finish feeling soothed and reassured, and they understand that it's all due to Joe. Everything is in order, but it will only remain that way if they put their trust in Joe and obey him without question.'

In the early days, Knead rejected much of Biz's work. It was too fearful. There wasn't enough Freedom. The threat was resolved without enough of Joe's involvement. 'Where was Joe at the time? Standing sentinel over liberty and the pursuit of happiness of course. And I'm not seeing that here; bring it back when I can.'

But after a few months, Biz became more adept at creating an undertone of Fear, laying over it a veneer of confidence, and sealing the whole with a liberal coating of compliance and conformity. His work frequently passed the first review, or required only a few very minor revisions. As he became better at it, he started to enjoy creating and then dispelling anxiety. If he stopped and concentrated, he could almost feel the clarity descending upon him as his body chemistry adapted to the high levels of CO^2 in the air he breathed. And the same thing was happening to his friends.

At this point, Knead started to explain why the young Spin Techs were doing what they were doing.

'The system is built on anonymity,' he explained to Biz and Lintel during a short break. 'But the belief must be that it's built on Fame.'

'Surely it *is* built on Fame,' said Lintel. The young man sat ramrod straight and at the ready. His venom for Gobblers was already legendary, and that, along with his dark, long, straight hair and raw-boned pincer looks drew not a few admiring glances from the other anti-Gobbler Bastionados.

Knead looked at him quizzically; he had thought the young man quite advanced. 'No, it is *believed* to be, but it only appears that way. Our Gobblers' brief dalliances with public life are the masquerades of Fame. They arise from and fall back into the pit of anonymity, and as they fall back they're convinced that they've been famous. How could they have been famous when, less than a day after they've vacated the Fame House the audience can't even remember their names?

'If anyone other than Joe was allowed to achieve real, lasting Fame, people may look to that person for advice and guidance on all sorts of things not even remotely related to the source or origin of their Fame. What if a famous person – a civilian who was adored by the masses – started to believe in their own infallibility, and started to entertain treasonous ideas? What if they actually criticised the leadership and encouraged dissent? It would create confusion, impinge on people's Freedom to do whatever they're told without thinking, and it could end up with that second famous person challenging Joe's status. What possible good could come of that?

'Back in the war centuries, all sorts of unqualified people had their views aired to millions of people, and sometimes they were taken far too seriously. People who had occupations and lives that have since disappeared – musicians and people who acted in films, people who could kick a ball or bat one over a net, basic Gobblers with no background in leadership but great prowess in front of a camera or behind a golf bat, felt compelled to run around telling people that their leaders were wrong, their wars unjust, their Freedoms illusory. Only chaos and anarchy can ensue in a society that allows such rabble-rousing.

'That's why the possibility of real fame was dismantled. The sports, music and entertainment industries were eradicated.

We eliminated any and all activities in which an individual might publicly excel and thus stand out from his or her peers. The objective was that only Joe would ever again occupy a position of influence due to popularity. Now, before the public warms to anyone enough to take their opinions seriously, that person's moment in the spotlight is over, they're gone, replaced by a new, anonymous Famer. It works beautifully.' He smiled expansively.

'And doing away with sporting and cultural performances had the happy side-effect of eliminating large gatherings of like-minded people. The power of the mob, the potential for the transmission of ideas and sharing of beliefs, was denied in one fell swoop. It was a glorious day for the people.

'It wasn't such a bad day for those in charge either. Power no longer requires the odious accompaniment of Fame. We control the masses in absolute anonymity (with the notable exception of Joe of course). Hell, the Gobblers don't even know where we are, let alone who we are.' Knead's knowing, cynical cackle startled Biz, and elicited a conspiratorial chuckle from Lintel.

'Our anonymity absolves us from the further burden of explaining ourselves to Gobblers, who are obviously incapable of following any reasoning whatsoever. They can barely talk to each other, let alone understand matters of state. They wouldn't know a reasonable decision if it jumped into the Cocoon with them and started twiddling their knobs. Trying to explain ourselves to them would take millennia; our anonymity means we don't have to waste our time.

'In any case, it's better for them, too. All that thinking, all that weighing up options, considering consequences, evaluating policies and then monitoring, managing and assimilating events – it would ruin their insular, facile little lives. It would be like hoisting a goldfish out of its tank and telling it, now's your chance to go ahead and breathe. The stress alone would kill them.

'Better that we are left to pull the levers of power beyond the glare of the public spotlight. Without the need to justify everything we do to a mob that hardly cares either way, with no need to pander to pressure groups or bow to the demands of lobbies and factions, we can apply our decision-making skills evenly. We can dispassionately observe, consider and respond in the most beneficial way for all.'

Biz could tell just by looking at him that Knead really did revel in his power. He clearly needed to accumulate and consume responsibility the way the people of the war centuries accumulated and hoarded useless bits of metal and glass. And it seemed that there was a weird sort of equilibrium at work: the Sharps, poisoned by CO_2, were sick but talented; the Gobblers, healthy but fools, enjoyed their oxygen delirium. It occurred to Biz that one day Knead would be the new Joe. He had the skills and the ambition, if not exactly the look. But, of course, that applied to everyone else in Joe's Cabinet. When Joe did eventually die, it wouldn't be an easy choice and would most likely spark a bloody fight.

Biz didn't give voice to these thoughts. Instead he asked a question. He thought he already knew the answer, but he was willing to risk facing Knead's scorn to be sure.

'Every day I write stories about the heroic exploits of our troops in the Eastern theatre,' he said. 'Why don't we ever name these brave soldiers? Hold them up as examples and shower them with praise and gratitude? Some of the deeds I'm writing about seem extraordinary, but even I never know who carried them off. And I want to know them so badly! I want to see and meet them and learn what real bravery is all about. I want to parade these guardians of our Freedoms through the streets and have the world share in their glory. And I know that even the most addled Gobbler would feel the same. So, why don't we?'

Knead looked at Biz with exactly the scorn he had expected, but he also managed to speak with diplomacy.

'You've answered your own question. The Gobblers would adore it. They'd lionise these soldiers. Revere and *remember* them. And that's no good. We need our real heroes – the people who actually do worthwhile things – to be anonymous, and our Famers – who are famous for precisely nothing – to be excruciatingly, if momentarily, familiar. The people who matter the least should be at the forefront of the Gobbler consciousness, filling their thoughts with useless prettiness. The people on whom we actually depend need to be faceless, whether it's the courageous scrappers in that harsh land, or us, the unknown soldiers of superintendence. Just like us, the soldiers need anonymity to do their job.'

He brightened up a little, tried to sound brisk. 'Besides, imagine if we did make one or more of our brave boys and girls actual living heroes – made them really famous. Not the kind of Fame that endures for a month, but genuine renown, so people got interested in their thoughts and their actions outside the narrow confines of their heroism. How could we allow that sort of competition with Joe? What if this new hero didn't corroborate what we say about the war? How would the people react if we sent this hero, to whom they have opened their hearts and minds, and for whom they've cried tears of gratitude, back to the front? Supposing this hero disappeared in the desert or was killed? We'd have a riot on our hands. Heroes arouse passions and create memories, and that's how you get people thinking, and that, above all else, is what we want to avoid.'

His mentor regarded Biz with a look that may have been intended as avuncular and empathetic. 'Look. Once upon a time, the world was full of real heroes. Everyone knew who they were because there were pictures of them – yes, real hard-copy images called photographs or prints – all over the place. People even had the capacity, through mobile communications devices called phones, to share these pictures, among other things, with each other. Every single person had the opportunity and the means to communicate with any and every other person on the planet, sharing their thoughts, pictures, movies and much more through these phones and through computers they kept at home and at work.

'Using these devices, they communicated feverishly almost every moment of the day: with friends and family, with strangers who shared their interests and beliefs, with co-conspirators and confederates. Think of the chaos that caused. Competing cults sprang up all over the place. Ideas were spawned, flourished and spread around the globe like a virus. Eventually it became impossible to tell the heroes from the villains because anyone and everyone had the means to promote themselves and their ideas quickly, slickly and convincingly.

'Not only that, but the volume of information being disseminated around the world became so vast as to be almost unimaginable. It was a snowstorm of digital data, every flake containing at least one idea of some nature, many of which were not conducive to the smooth running of society. So, the government of the day bravely undertook to collect it all. They created computer storehouses to record every word spoken into a phone, to copy every word transmitted electroncially, to gather, examine and store every pixel of every picture sent by anyone to anyone else. The idea was to use algorithms to sift through every single piece of information to find out what people were thinking and planning and telling each other. Anyone with any ideas or beliefs that might lead them to act against what their government had decreed was the common good could be identified and silenced before they had a chance to act.

'But the snowstorm of data quickly became a blizzard, and the poor government was buried under an avalanche of useless facts. It turned out that it was pretty much all just mindless drivel, petty arguments, mundane chatter and worthless banter. Even the most committed of observers couldn't find the genuinely worthwhile or the truly sinister among the masses of stupidity and silliness. The government had to find another way to gain control of the communication channels.

'The Religoil wars and the Surge made it possible. The creators of the new world stripped away the means of communication. The InterFace, or internet as it was known then, was shut down, because, they said, terrorists were using it to organise a revolution in the disorder and confusion after the Turning. Communication infrastructure was destroyed by spectacular explosions that were blamed on terrorists.

'The true genius of the leadership was in how far they went. They banned the production, possession and trafficking of images. They destroyed any existing images, ostensibly to stop our enemies communicating through cleverly crafted visuals that contained seditious allegories and hid messages. People used to adorn their walls with pictures of people, places and ideas. The pointlessness of it! The new generations would have none of these. Have you ever seen a still picture hanging anywhere? Of course not. To have such a thing would invite prolonged examination and contemplation of its significance and meaning. No, they all had to go, from the most puerile stick-figure to elaborate paintings containing layers of meaning and symbolism, which people called art and studied and endowed with ridiculous power. The government allowed people to experience only the moving image, created, controlled and fed to them via the newly resurrected internet, now called the InterFace.

'Unlike the internet, the InterFace didn't link people together. It was and is a one-way flow of information, with many channels, all controlled by the government. In fact, it was more like the old television, only differently delivered. At first people complained: they wanted their old internet back. But it was explained that things had to remain this way for a while longer, as they said, to thwart those who would use the internet for nefarious purposes.

'Well, the mob got used to it, and slowly the topics covered were whittled down to the three *F*'s. Interestingly, the fan mail feature was introduced later, mainly to feed the government's addiction to hoarding information about people. It doesn't do any harm, I guess, but only because the Gobblers are too stupid to communicate about anything other than YouStar.

'The point is this: we have a system that is almost ideally balanced. Putting genuine heroes – if they actually existed – into the works would gum things up pretty badly.' Knead looked at Biz condescendingly. 'One day, you'll truly understand all this. But until you do, you're not going to get to the next level. So, work harder, breathe deeply and, for heaven's sake, Sharpen up, man.'

Once Knead had left, Biz and Lintel leaned back in their chairs. Biz sipped his coffee. 'I just don't know if I'll ever get it,' he said.

'Fren,' Lintel sighed, 'You've got to stop being a Gobbler. You seem to be hanging on to what you were and trying to make sense of it from that perspective, when instead you ought to be embracing your power. Accept your clarity and be grateful for it and enjoy the unique position you're in. You've been invited into the palace, and you're wondering how that might sit with the morons in the ghetto. Fuck 'em!' He was gleeful. 'Don't ask why, ask why not? Or better yet, just ask how? How can I make this work for me? How can I attain mastery over those miserable oxygen whores? How can I expand my power and deepen my influence? How can I be the next Joe?' This startled Biz, but Lintel was not in the frame of mind to be the least bit circumspect. He was energised after Knead's speech, which had obviously affirmed his self-belief. 'I'm serious,' he said, having noticed the look on Biz's face. 'If you don't want to be top man, why are you here at all?'

'I was brought here.' Biz stared glumly at his hands.

'You're here because you belong here,' Lintel corrected him. 'You'd hate it out there in Cocoon-land, devouring scraps of other people's illusory Fame. You'd be bored. Mindless. Powerless. You just don't seem to have recognised that yet. The sooner you do, the happier you'll be. You're not between two worlds, you're *in* one. So, turn your back on the other one and start to live.'

Lintel was right. Biz had been acting like a Gobbler who'd been transplanted into the world of Sharps, when in truth he was a Sharp himself. Born to power, self-awareness, and insensitivity. He had to shake the idea that he didn't belong, divest himself of the guilt he was carrying because somewhere deep inside he felt it was wrong to deceive and manipulate people. How could it be wrong when they lapped it up? When they begged to be relieved of the anxiety of thought? It wasn't. It couldn't be. Could it? He felt a little better. From that day on, Biz vowed that he would not apologise for his presence in the Bastion, would no longer be unsure of what he was doing, or why. He was there to give the fatuous crowd what it wanted, and he would lay it on with a trowel.

'You're right, fren!' He slapped his thigh and stood up, thumping Lintel on the shoulder. 'What have I got to be afraid of? I'm positively dangerous!'

'That's the spirit! Let's get out there and spin something special for those ignorant, undeserving suckers.'

Biz strove to be more like Lintel. He stopped worrying about the effect his work was having on people and started celebrating the depth and breadth of his influence. He focused on how to work, not why he was working, and became a much more valuable colleague. Knead made it clear that the new Biz pleased him. He was much chummier during the weekly gatherings and much less critical of Biz's work. Biz and Lintel became close friends, hanging out with each other whenever they could, swapping techniques and ideas for new stories they could spin, and sometimes enjoying too many scotches together. So, life went on, and went on improving. Although he still had moments of self-doubt, his clarity grew, his sense of entitlement expanded and his empathy for the Gobblers troubled him less and less until it almost wasn't there.

In fact, Knead had to remind Biz that he needed to retain some vestiges of common identity with Gobblerdom lest he become so Sharp that he could no longer communicate with the masses. To help him with this, Knead promised the young Spin Tech that sometime soon he would be sent out into the community to become reacquainted with his audience. But he was pleased with the young man's progress, and said he would give Biz more interesting, challenging assignments to broaden his education within the Bastion. Biz would need a greater understanding of the big picture as he worked towards his promotion as a Psyman – a Psychological Manipulator.

11.

Gneiss had knocked back a few too many Flurients on Friday night, and the next morning he did something very unusual for him: he inhaled pure oxygen in an attempt to rid his brain of the cursed swelling and throbbing. It had been another tough week with his new class – a pack of undisciplined, unwilling first graders who he would have to guide through to adolescence. He knew it would get better, in a year or two (or three), but for now it was still painful. He had drained his coffee and was putting another on to brew when – again, un-usually – there was a knock at the door. He rolled his eyes and ran his hands through his hair. He knew he was bleary-eyed and dishevelled but he didn't care; he wasn't expecting anyone.

He was surprised to see Bock at the door. He broke into a welcoming smile, his white teeth showing brightly against the dark halo of beard and moustache. He bowed low and ushered her towards the interior of the house, a gesture he used to great, if sarcastic, effect in the classroom. Bock giggled and swept past him with an imperious sneer, holding her hemp shirt as though it was a floor length dress.

They went out to the broad, carbo-timber deck that over-looked his backyard, a twenty-square-metre patch of grass and surprisingly healthy plants surrounded by carbo-timber fencing. All around were houses almost identical to Gneiss's, with solar-steel roofing and coal-brick walls held together with carbcrete. Nobody else was on their deck; they were sleeping, working or InterFacing; most likely the latter. He handed Bock the freshly brewed coffee, and went back to the kitchen to order one for himself. When it was done, he joined her in the cool morning sunshine.

'I saw you on YouStar.'

'Really? I didn't think you ever watched.' Gneiss had always rubbished YouStar and the InterFace in general as a meaningless distraction and a waste of time.

'I make an effort when a student is on. Especially someone like you.'

Bock blushed, and her teacher smiled. But still, she found nothing to say, and took a deep draught of coffee instead.

'I imagine it's a bit of a shock coming back to reality.'

'Oh yes, yes it is. It's weird,' Bock said. 'And to make it worse, ever since I left school I've been feeling more and more strange.'

'Strange how?'

'Like, lightheaded, even giddy sometimes.'

'Ah.' Gneiss nodded and sipped. 'Do you have trouble remembering things? Trouble concentrating?'

Bock's emerald eyes widened. How well he knew her! 'Yes!' She blushed again, at herself this time. 'I know it sounds silly, but I feel as if I am getting dumber. I don't even think that's possible, but it really feels that way.'

Gneiss chuckled softly. 'I'm going to give you something.' He got up and walked into the house, returning with a small, tube-like instrument and a little box. There was a fine metal screen on either end of the tube. Box and tube together fit easily in the palm of his hand.

'Recognise this?' He passed it to Bock.

'Of course. It's like the little thing that was attached to the inside of my Educoon.'

'Correct,' said Gneiss, lapsing into teacher-speak. 'In fact, it's the same one. It's a carbon distiller. It stopped you from getting dumber, as you say. Now you've been away from it for a while, the effect is wearing off. Your brain chemistry is changing.'

Bock looked at the little instrument in her hand in disbelief, then looked back at Gneiss to see if he was joking. He wasn't. 'How?'

'It's a long story. I'll tell you some time. Just put it in your bedroom and it will help.'

'Oh. Okay.' She put the unit in her pocket and concentrated on her coffee.

Gneiss changed the subject back to YouStar, and Bock relaxed and told him all about it from beginning to end. She didn't notice that he wasn't terribly interested in her co-Famers, or what they got up to and with whom, let alone what she had worn and where; she was too rapt in the story herself.

'So, while you were in the Fame House, you didn't get a chance to InterFace at all?' asked Gneiss.

'No, there are no Cocoons in the house.'

'So you wouldn't have seen the Joe-cast that came on after you'd been in the house for a few days.'

'No,' she said, with concern. 'Was it important? If it was I'm sure they would have showed it to us.'

'It was. Joe was talking about the need for people to volunteer to become teachers. He asked that young people who have just left school, like yourself, and who enjoyed their schooling, think about going into teacher training.' He looked at her nervously. 'I thought you might have come here to talk about that.'

'Oh. No. I didn't see it. I've just started working in surveillance. I don't think I'm really cut out for teaching.'

'It's not hard. Most teachers just learn how to operate the control panel, and let the Educoon do all the work. All that stuff I did, the extra reading on the history and teaching channels that almost nobody even knows about, let alone accesses, isn't really supposed to be a part of it. I really wish you'd consider it. I think you'd be a great teacher.'

Bock blushed again. 'I, er, I guess I will think about it. Thank you.'

'So, if you didn't come over to talk about teaching, why did you?'

'I was just… I suppose I was just a bit lonely and lost, and you know, I feel like I'm getting dumber all the time, and I kind of thought, well when I was with you and Biz I felt smart, so maybe I could visit you and maybe get some of that back. I know it sounds silly.'

'Not at all. In fact, that distiller might be exactly what you wanted. As to your being lost and lonely, I know how you feel. I feel the same way a lot of the time.'

'Really?' There was a hope in Bock's voice. Perhaps if they both felt the same way, they could spend more time together and that would help both of them.

'Yes, really. I've missed you and Biz.' He kept silent for a few moments, then forced himself to speak. 'My new class isn't going too well.' Silence fell between them again as he tried to find a way to explain what he was feeling.

'You and Biz, your class, was my first class,' he eventually said. 'I was straight out of training and you … you were just babies. We grew up together. Teaching you, I learned to be a teacher.' He stopped, not sure if he was clarifying the situation or making it even more difficult for Bock to understand.

'I got into teaching because I had a plan. I wanted to make a difference.' He looked distractedly over Bock's shoulder at the house next door. 'I put my plan into action with your class … well, specifically with you and Biz. I'd never met a child like you, and Biz was a good foil. You had so much natural intelligence, and you were so little like the others.' He'd stopped looking at Bock at all, as if he was talking to himself. 'I taught you what I thought was important, and I watched you grow up and change. It was amazing.'

Bock affected to understand, but she was struggling to see where Gneiss was going. It had started to sound a bit like some of his lessons.

He stopped again, and thought for a while. 'There's something,' he hesitated, 'There's something I should tell you.'

Bock peered at him, not knowing what to say.

'You and Biz,' he said, looking into her eyes, 'you're special. You were born special. And by that I mean you,' he pointed at her, 'you were born special. Not Biz. I … made him that way. You, I just helped. Him, I changed. But you were always different. You,' he swallowed, 'you are the only born Sharp I ever met.'

There was a sorrow or a longing in his voice, and Bock didn't know which, or why it was there. She still didn't understand what he was talking about, but she could see the emotion in his eyes and she felt it too. She wanted to hug him.

Gneiss concentrated on his coffee cup for a few seconds, then began again. 'There's no Bock or Biz in my new class,' he said. 'No plan. Just a bunch of little kids. Gobblers. Horrible, mean, stupid, difficult little Gobblers. Not one of them wants to learn, and to be honest with you I don't think I want to teach them. The only way I can get them to concentrate on the fundamentals like reading and writing, even for a few minutes, is to remind them that without these skills they won't be able to send or understand fan mail on YouStar. Without that, I doubt I could teach them anything. I certainly don't take the side-tracks I did with you. I just work the knobs and monitor their Educoon. It's easy and it's empty. If it wasn't for the gardening, I'd have nothing.'

He looked terribly sad. Bock got out of her chair and sat next to him on the couch. She leaned over to give him an awkward hug from the side.

'But you're an amazing teacher. I know you'll connect with these kids, it'll just take time. Look how well you connected with us.'

'With you and Biz,' he said, with bitter self-contempt. 'The rest of those little shits I never gave a toss about.' He looked suddenly bashful. He obviously thought he'd said too much. Bock leaned over to give him another hug, and this time he turned in his seat to face her and return the embrace. She tightened her grip to let him know she understood. He laid his head on her shoulder and closed his eyes. They stayed that way for a long time. When at last he moved, he only moved his head to look up at her face. As he did so, she leaned down to kiss him.

12.

Knead interrupted Lintel and Biz's morning beverage break. They were discussing the unrelentingly affirmative Freedom Spin, and how it differed from the Conflict Spin, which trod a fine line between Fear and Freedom.

'The art of Conflict Spin is…'

'You're going to like this,' Knead announced.

'Oh?' Biz lifted an eyebrow. When Knead interrupted a conversation like this, he had something important to say.

'A research scientist has developed a new superfluid that can be manipulated to any level of viscosity. It has all sorts of applications for weaponry, transport, even the mechanics of science itself. I need you to meet with this fellow and get the gist of what this stuff can do. He's actually something of a phenomenon, this young fellow. Came across the fluid as part of his atmospheric engineering research,' he sniffed. 'In another time, he might have been what they called a rock-star scientist. Instead, he's actually doing some good in the Bastillion.'

The Bastillion. Without ever having been there, Biz knew all about it: a high security area cut off from the rest of the Bastion, where batteries of researchers worked on physics, chemistry, medicine, mathematics, computing, robotics and other hard sciences. Until now he'd been restricted from entry into the Bastillion, and he was thrilled to be going there at last. He stood up and, beaming, bowed to Lintel, who was open mouthed. 'Be seeing you later, fren.' He fell into step with Knead, as the latter made for the door with a sharp click of his heels. They stopped at a directagon, and Knead punched in their destination: 'Bastillion: Particle Laboratory'. A strobing red light appeared within the fathomless depths of the black diamond floor. They followed it on the circuitous route to the Bastillion, past security barriers that demanded their biosigs. Biz was almost dizzy by the time they stepped into an elevator for the fourth time. It plunged through the levels, occasionally slipping one way or another – forward, back, left or right – for a few seconds before resuming its downward trajectory. When at last they alighted from the little box, he was breathless.

He was also quite unprepared for the appearance of the place when the elevator doors finally opened. For months and months – was it over a year? or two? – he'd been encased in black diamond walls, floors and ceilings. They absorbed the sparse light and reflected only pale shadows and precise sound waves. But the corridor into which they stepped was the exact opposite – every surface matte white, as clean and soft and bright as freshly fallen snow. The perfectly featureless walls, floors and ceilings seemed to move with waves of light, but if Biz stopped to stare at any one section he could see nothing and hear nothing – it was deadly quiet. The only sign that they were in the same world they had just left was the directional light embedded in the floor, strobing away from them.

'Every surface is a specially developed nanomat that absorbs sound, bacteria, viruses and any stray molecules that might escape from our laboratories,' Knead explained. 'It reflects light at such obtuse angles that you can only perceive it on your periphery. It can be a little disconcerting at first, but you'll get used to it.'

Biz darted his eyes up and down the blinding corridor, hoping that one of the many doors, flush with the walls and barely distinguishable, would open. But Knead seemed anxious to avoid his student seeing what went on in these rooms. He hustled Biz down the hallway to the right of the elevator.

A hundred or so metres along, they turned into a corridor on their left, which featured the same resolutely closed doors, before one on the right noiselessly opened. Knead stepped in and Biz followed him, and the door closed again.

The room was bathed in thick silence. Snowy white benches and desks bristled with esoteric electronics, flasks, tubes, filters, cubes filled with weird matter or perhaps antimatter, and diamond cylinders holding exotic gases under pressure. Amid all this a slender lad was working; he was perhaps a year younger than Biz, but seemed to have vastly more responsibility. His coat was covered or made of the white nanomat. His InterTab held who knows what secrets. When he finally looked up, his expression said that he had been expecting his visitors, but was startled anyway, as he'd been deeply engrossed in his work.

'Particle, meet Biz.'

The scientist shyly held out a white, hairless hand, which felt as fragile as his face looked. Biz gently gripped the cold, nearly fleshless hand and worked it up and down once as delicately as he could.

'Pleased to meet you,' the scientist said in a soft, low voice.

But they had met before. Biz had been just a child, perhaps four years old, when his playmate Particle had disappeared, along with his parents. Biz had been devastated – Particle was his chief source of entertainment and companionship whenever he could get out of the house. When he'd asked his parents about Particle's disappearance, they'd shrugged and changed the subject. When he persisted, his mother told him it wasn't polite to ask questions, and that when people disappeared they would not be coming back, and unless he wanted to disappear too he would keep quiet about it.

Could this pallid, hairless young spectre be that Particle?

He let go of the bony hand. He stared into the grey eyes, seeking an answer, but Particle did not return the recognition. But surely this was the boy – he was the right age. He had the right name. He had been disappeared. And yet the fog of years stood between him and the Particle he'd seen fifteen years ago. He couldn't be sure, but he couldn't shake the feeling of familiarity either.

Knead either did not notice or did not care about the look on Biz's face. 'Biz is a level six Spin Tech from Psyman, working on the war. He'll be writing an InterFace factule about your latest development. Give him the scientific background, but more importantly fill him in on why it's a significant discovery, what it does and how we'll be using it in a practical sense. That way he can spin it out to the Gobblers as a new weapon in our armoury of Freedom.'

For the next hour, Particle expounded in the simplest possible terms how he'd created the product, and how it would revolutionise transport and materials fabrication. Biz was absorbed and forgot his feeling of connection with the prodigy. His task was interesting and challenging, and the acquisition of such fascinating new information was a tonic to his mental strength and clarity. He looked forward to turning this wondrous new substance into a fearsome weapon that would strike fear into the hearts of the bad folks of the East, while at the same time offering another layer of solid protection for the people.

After an hour of explanation and questioning, Particle fell silent. Knead stood up to leave. Never one to stand on ceremony, he asked Biz, 'Got enough?'

'Oh, absolutely.' He knew he was on the verge of gushing. 'I am genuinely galvanised by this discovery of yours, Particle, and I can't wait to share the relevant parts of it with the world.'

A flash of memory seared his mind: he saw a blank, round face, an older, plumper, dimmer version of Particle, and without wanting to, without any act of will on his behalf at all, he said, 'In fact I think I have the perfect name for your slippery new substance: Flaunch.' As he spoke, he looked into Particle's eyes, but nothing registered on the young scientist's face.

What he couldn't see was Knead's face, its narrow nostrils flaring and eyes growing hard. The mentor left the room with stiff, terse motion and strode down the hall, inflamed, in under a second. When Biz caught up and the laboratory door was closed safely behind them, Knead wheeled on him.

'What the fuck was that about?'

Biz knew he'd stepped over a line, but he didn't know why. It had just come out – he guessed he'd been trying to make a connection with Particle, but without thinking that while the young scientist may have forgotten his parents, Knead certainly would remember them.

'I've no idea why I said that,' said Biz. 'It just popped into my head.' Knead looked disbelieving. 'I swear! I… I'm not even sure what I said,' he lied. He was trying desperately to look innocent, and wondered if in fact it just made him look more guilty.

'So, you just happened to mention Particle's father's name as the name of his new superfluid?'

'Really?' Biz stammered. 'Flaunch is Particle's father's name?'

'Yes. Yes, it is.' Knead gripped Biz by the shoulders so that he had to face him. 'Now, answer my question carefully. And remember, I know where you lived when you were a child. Did you really not know that the name Flaunch is connected to Particle, and were you not trying to send him some kind of message?'

'I swear to you, I had no idea what I was saying.' Fear and stress made his voice quake and his eyes widen. For a moment, it looked as though Knead did not believe him. But ultimately the older man relaxed his grip.

'I suppose it's plausible. You were just a baby at the time, no more than four or five, and a Gobbler at that. It may be some kind of ghost memory, a shard that's found its way to the surface at a very inopportune time.'

Knead walked ahead of him, quickly, and Biz took long steps to catch up, until the older man stopped and turned on him suddenly. 'Either that or you're a sly, opportunistic Sharp with a streak of rebellion in you. And if you are, well played.'

They walked on in silence following the red light in the floor. If Knead's mind was filled with doubt, Biz's was alive with fear and wondering.

Once again, he felt that he shouldn't be here, that he didn't have the arrogance and hide necessary to become a full Sharp. Then again, he had crossed a line and gotten away with it. Maybe he was sharper than he thought? Or was Knead giving him enough rope to hang himself?

Their footfalls echoed sharply in the glistening corridor, and nothing more was said until they reached Biz's workstation. As Biz turned to go in, Knead held his shoulder again, for a moment.

'You can see why we discourage the creation of memories. People hang onto them long after they think they have let go of them. It's dangerous.'

13.

After that trip, Biz was free to go to the Bastillion whenever he wanted, provided he had a good, work-related reason. He started to find those reasons so he could visit Particle, while also not going so often that he attracted suspicion.

The young scientist was friendly enough, but diffident and shy, lacking confidence in any conversation not centred on his work. He was totally immersed in his science and indifferent to everything else. He was so much sharper than Biz, the latter concluded. But then, Particle had been living in this CO_2 atmosphere for much longer. *My god, what sort of potential had he shown to have been brought here at such a young age?* Biz asked himself.

All this made Particle quite difficult to get to know. Still, Biz kept visiting, being careful without mentioning Flaunch or any other element of his own former life. He knew they were being watched, and he was circumspect to the point of obtuseness. He gently probed the young scientist for any details that he might remember about his past. This delivered slim pickings indeed. As far as Particle knew, he'd always lived in the Bastillion. His earliest concrete memories were of white nano-mat walls, teachers vigorously instructing him in the sciences, and other young Bastillionaires. He had no memories of his parents, and assumed that they lived somewhere outside the Bastion. In any case, they didn't matter to him.

'They're Gobblers,' he said, simply. 'They wouldn't understand what I do, and they wouldn't care.'

131

'But surely even Gobblers can be proud?'

'If they are, it doesn't affect me.' Particle shrugged. 'What's important is my work. My discoveries. I will make their world a better place, but I don't need them to thank me for it.'

After a few encounters like these, Biz became confused and disheartened. He was almost certain that Particle's parents had disappeared when Particle himself had, so where the hell were they? What could have happened to them? If only his own memories were clearer.

If he was to find an answer, he would have to coax it out of Knead, which would be no easy matter. It could be dangerous, even fatal to his career. After his lapse in Particle's lab during that first visit, Knead had been watching him carefully, monitoring his work and keeping tabs on his movements. Now was not the time to be asking controversial questions. Even pursuing his relationship with Particle was potentially damaging. He resolved to walk away from this nagging connection to his past.

The antidote was to throw himself back into his work. Although he enjoyed digressions like Particle's superfluid, his first love was Conflict Spin. It so perfectly captured and embodied the two most important *F*'s, Freedom and Fear. These were the controlling emotions. Fame was a mere distraction, a trifle used to divert the Gobblers and scramble their brains, to stop them pondering larger questions and to fill their minds with empty facts.

Fear and Freedom, on the other hand, were the blocks upon which true allegiance could be built. The Psyman wielding these two *F's* had to be subtle and careful – the message had to stick, but not so fast that it became an encumbrance on the Gobbler's mind. But they were the key to true emotional control and dependence.

'Fame is the basis for happy Gobblerdom,' Bias had disagreed one night as they were arguing about it again over a scotch. 'Fear and Freedom are too visceral, too stressful to maintain the whole time. They require vigilance. Fame, on the other hand, is delightfully devoid of anything but fluffy happiness. It teaches inattention, changeability, transience and forgetfulness. Concentrate too much on Fear and Freedom and sooner or later you'll have people seeking information on their own, sharing opinions with their neighbours, talking about things that matter. Smother them with celebrity and bedazzle them with Fame and you've occupied their tiny little minds for them. Arouse them with Fear and incite them with Freedom and you're more likely to stimulate than pacify them.'

'Bias is right,' Globe agreed, bobbing up to make her point, her round face framed by a jiggling cloud of curls. Her interjection surprised her friends, not just because it was unlike her to butt in, but because she was so committed to Conflict Spin Tech. The only criticism that could be made against her was that she sometimes took it too seriously. She was regularly outraged by the devious schemes and unrelenting evil of the enemy, and consequently sometimes weighted her spin with too much Fear. She often had to be forced to leaven her work with references to Freedom.

Given her consummate attachment to the job, and the powerful analyses she applied to conflict, Globe was another colleague who looked, to Biz, to have become much sharper than he had in the time they'd been in the Bastion. Then again, she also appeared to have much to learn, and for that Biz was grateful.

'He's right, because the hard work of generating Fear and venerating Freedom would exhaust the Gobbler mind if that was all we had to serve up to them. Keeping their minds soft and pliable with all that Fame crap is a wonderful narcotic. Load them up with a generous helping of the trivial comings and goings of idiots like themselves until they're full and it puts them into a satisfied sleep. And just when they're at their doziest, we sneak up and BAM, hit them with a solid jolt of Fear. It doesn't just startle them, it panics them. They don't know what to do. It's beyond their ability to assimilate the detail, let alone figure out a response. But we follow up straight away with the soothing balm of Freedom, applied liberally by Joe, and they feel comforted. Cared for. But if we hit them again with more Fear, or even more Freedom, it would revive that agitation. They might even experience some real emotion. So instead we lull them back to la-la land with stars and glamour until we need to shock them awake again.'

Biz was impressed by this bit of logic. It showed him, again, why there must be a flow of sorts to Psyman. A balance. He would have to strive to achieve this balance better himself. He'd always thought that Bias, so thin, so highly strung, was kept in Fame Spin because that was where she could do the least damage. But obviously he had been wrong. He saw that Bias understood the magnetic allure of Fame, and knew how and when to serve it up. He clinked glasses with his friends and sat back in his divan, affecting to be content with himself and his role. But still, in the deep recesses of his own over-active mind there lurked the unsettling idea that they were all doing better than he was, and that he didn't really belong. He chugged a full tumbler of scotch, eager to become a Gobbler again, if only for the night.

Time passed. Biz's clarity sharpened slowly. He remained conscientious in his work and became more adept and confident in it. To Knead's relief, Biz also spent less time with Particle and eventually, having no valid reason to be there, stopped going to the scientist's laboratory altogether. An agreeable pattern settled in their part of the vast hidden edifice of the Bastion.

One afternoon Biz was at his workstation editing an interesting Conflict Spin development. On his screen, bright showers of varicoloured lights bursting in the sky flickered and flashed against a soundtrack of deep, booming cracks. He had written the script the day before and supervised the recording of the voice-over that morning. Now he was editing the footage supplied from the East, cut to a dramatic pace that emphasised the report's urgency. Lintel had done the voice work; it turned out that his rich, mellifluous voice perfectly conveyed the gravity of news reports, and he was able to simulate the requisite sense of drama.

'These may appear to be ordinary fireworks of the kind banned over two hundred years ago. But they celebrate nothing more than death. For these attractive starbursts are PhosPods, a lethal new weapon in the enemy's arsenal. Every droplet, every tiny pinpoint of pretty colour consists of jellied phosphorous that attaches quickly and irremovably to any surface. It burns at over twenty-five hundred degrees. It is almost impossible to extinguish. Should one of these droplets land on you, it will burn through you with an agonising pain that you can't stop or treat. If you are lucky, it will be lethal. The enemy has devised this cruel new weapon of destruction for no other reason than to help them curtail your Freedoms, destroy your happiness and see you weep with pain and loss. If not for the strategic brilliance of Joe and the brave armies at his command, our enemies could be dropping these eye-catching pods of death on your citiburbs tomorrow. Fortunately for all of us, our brave, highly trained soldiers, under Joe's direction, are defending us in the enemy's land itself so that we can live in Freedom and celebrate the decimation of the Sandrags, who welcome death as the key to a martyr's paradise. We know where paradise is, Sandrags, and it isn't in your burnt-out hellhole of a country. It's here in our own glorious streets and Hubs, in the Cocoons that bring us such wonderful entertainment, and of course in the palace of Freedom and joy itself, the Fame House.' He had paused, triumphantly. 'We now return you to that home of Fame, glitter, fun and Freedom.'

Biz was downloading library vision of soaring oxygen vents gleaming in the sun, and quietly clean streets where people courteously went about their business; this was about to dissolve into a wide shot of the Fame House when Knead knocked and entered. Biz looked up, and his mentor indicated that he should finish his editing.

Knead's expression was a strange one. Usually, Biz could tell if he brought good tidings or bad, whether he was to be congratulated or castigated. But on this occasion, he couldn't tell what the older man's docile mask indicated. He seemed grave, but also had an air of good news. Unusually, he fidgeted as he stood waiting, which was disconcerting. Biz had intended to insert another shot of a buzzing TeenStar Cocoonery, and shave a few frames off the oxygen vent shot, but figured he could come back to it later.

Knead gestured that Biz should follow, and moved towards the door. 'I have something important to tell you. It's a significant new assignment. But before I do, come and take a walk with me.'

As they clicked down the hallway following the direct-agon's red light, Knead spoke in kindly and encouraging tones. 'Your apprenticeship is to all intents and purposes finished.' He almost smiled. 'You've been working hard and effectively, you get on well with your colleagues, and you can be trusted to behave autonomously. I don't mind telling you, that business with Particle almost cost you very dearly indeed, but you seem to have moved past that, and I'm pleased to see that you don't spend too much time down there with him. Incidentally, you were wasting your time. It's not that he doesn't remember, it's that he doesn't know what happened to his parents. But I can tell you, and I am sure you will respect my confidence in this matter. As protocol dictates, we were obliged to give Flaunch and Pound the Freedom Ride.' He looked sideways at Biz; the younger man wouldn't allow himself a visible reaction even though he'd felt a momentary shock of dismay. He kept his eyes straight staring ahead.

'Now, you're different from your peers, Biz. There is something about you that doesn't quite fit the standard mould, and yet in so many ways you outperform your colleagues from the same intake. You're not as sharp, perhaps, but you're more devious. You're not immune to emotion, as they are, but you don't let it overtake you either. I am quite sure you don't know yourself the scope of your potential, but you will learn it, and possibly sooner than any of us think.'

They stepped into an elevator, and Knead kept talking about Biz's work and prospects, finishing with the uplifting statement, as they exited the elevator, that he felt, and his colleagues agreed with him, that Biz was the kind of person who could one day join Joe's Cabinet. This time, Biz could not keep his elation under control; Knead noted it with a curt smile. 'There is only one part of the Bastion you've not yet been introduced to.' They stopped. 'I'm sure probably heard of it, but I very much doubt that you know what its function really is. I'm here to show you.'

The door swished open and they walked into a darkened foyer, clearly a reception area of some kind. They were met by Clamp, a roundish figure with pleasant features and huge, powerful hands, which was all offset by his sharp, iced-indigo eyes. He was not threatening, but charismatic – perhaps even magnetic. Biz had seen him before, but never taken much notice of him. Clamp was in the stratosphere of the Cabinet, while Biz and his friends were on the ground. Now he felt a formidable power emanating from Clamp, like a light.

The Cabinet member stepped forward and held out a hand. 'Welcome to Psymorph.' As Biz shook Clamp's hand, Knead took his leave with a smile.

Of course, Biz had heard of Psymorph – Psychological Morphology. It was said that the real work of the Bastion was done here. Minds were shaped and personalities were altered, but few outside the department knew how, or why, or when. Part of Clamp's job, it turned out, was to explain it all.

Over the next hour and a half, he gave Biz chapter and verse regarding Psymorph. 'We are here to create the outcomes we wish for in people's lives, by taking an interest in their early development and nurturing it in the direction that we choose. We utilise a broad array of tools, from repetition and propaganda, some of which you create, to more direct methods. These include simple coercion, but also hypnosis, most often with post-hypnotic suggestion.'

When Biz was being considered for the Leadership Gene project, Clamp explained, Psymorph teams were also scouting children of lesser intellectual abilities and preparing them for other tasks. Sharps like Biz were fed the Leadership Gene story in order to boost their egos and make it seem as if entering the Bastion was an honour as well as a necessity for their long-term health, but when it came to things like military recruitment, cruder methods could be employed. Strong, athletic children were visited by Clamp or one of his lieutenants, and hypnotised. After they'd finished school, when they heard Joe utter the words 'Say yes to the War in the East,' it would trigger an irresistible desire to join the army.

'We implant other triggers in other children of course,' Clamp expanded. 'In those chosen for the so-called caring professions, for instance. If a child appears particularly empathetic – a rare trait in a Gobbler child, I can tell you – we hypnotise them and implant the suggestion that they become computer medico assistants or teachers. Kids at the other end of the spectrum, those who completely lack compassion – the sociopaths, if you will – we groom for the Liberty Guard. Provided they're not too bright.'

Clamp was cheerful in his elucidation of the important work of the Psymorph team, and Biz took in what he was saying with as much equanimity as he could, although it was hard to avoid thinking about Necker's fate.

'We use many other methods and techniques. If we insert a pregnant woman in the Fame House, for instance, we can initiate a mini baby boom. We can also subtly compel people to spy on their neighbours outside of their regular surveillance work. We can constrain them to walk to their local Hub rather than catch a levtrans, if we decide that the general populace needs more exercise. It's a constant battle to keep them all doing exactly what we want, but making them think it's their choice.'

At the end of the tour, they sat facing each other. 'As a senior Psyman, you'll be expected to work with your Psymorph colleagues to develop propaganda and spin directions, to gain a greater understanding of the work we do, and make use of our findings. Do you think you can do that?'

Feeling slightly overwhelmed, but excited and energised, Biz pumped Clamp's giant hand enthusiastically. He was eager to begin. He followed the directagon back to his own area, feeling as fulfilled as he ever had. He was now a Psyman. His mentor had high hopes for him. And he had something to look forward to: further instruction in the mysteries and magic of Psymorph. It helped make sense of a lot of things that he'd seen or heard about, and he could see a vast array of uses for Psymorph techniques. Clearly, much of what he'd done previously complemented Psymorph's work. He just wished he'd been introduced to it earlier.

True, he'd briefly felt bad about Necker. Knowing that Necker had gone off to war not out of any deep-seated belief in the cause but because of a suggestion implanted in him, was troubling. But, he told himself, Necker was not suited to much beyond a physical life anyway, and who knew – the army may have been good for him. Besides, whether it was an implanted suggestion or not, Necker had believed that he wanted to fight in the war, so he got what he thought he wanted.

Knead was waiting for him at his workstation, idly flicking through the Spin archive, rereading some old stories, clucking to himself as he did so. With overstated courtesy, he stood and invited Biz to take his own seat, then folded his lengthy limbs into a visitor's chair.

'It sometimes happens,' he said with a smirk that he tried to purl into a frown, 'that one among the incoming Famers gets an odd idea in his head. Usually he's the type of person who has almost nothing to offer, an insignificant little person whose personality, even in the heady spotlights of YouStar, is so unremittingly bleak that virtually nothing will break the tedium of it. Naturally, unless the rest of the YouStar intake is equally lacking in grace, beauty, liveliness, conversation or interest – a practical impossibility – this person will rate very lowly indeed. After a short time in Fame House, his channel will be completely unwatched except by a few poor souls who share the nonentity's dearth of character and watch in the hope that they will learn how to make themselves less unappealing to the public. He will have become a Fame wraith.

'So, he convinces himself that what he needs to do to maximise his YouStar rating, even if only for a brief shining moment, is to commit some kind of heinous act. Something that will turn the public stomach enough that he will capture the viewers' attention for a little while, and everyone will know his name. To turn a ratings dust mote into a flaming meteorite of Fame and notoriety, a charmless Gobbler hatches a plan for violence and catastrophe, something that will keep our avid public from slipping out to the automat to order up a Flurient whenever his mug appears on the main channels. This highly, ahem, impactful behaviour will rivet the viewers to their screens, craning forward in their abominable armchairs and licking their lips in anticipation of delicious shock and horror.

'Of course, such an act carried out by an otherwise undistinguished Famer serves a purpose. It allows us, the producers and Psymans, to express and encourage the public expression of vehement disapproval. It gives us the opportunity to get our rather malleable population of Gobblers collectively clicking their tongues, joining in the chorus of disapprobation and despair at the egregiousness of the act, and enjoying the subsequent feeling of moral superiority over the perpetrator that floods their dim consciousness.

'It also allows us to editorialise on the inherent danger of life in our volatile world, to instil a dollop of localised Fear which is even more potent than the geographically removed threat the traditional enemy poses. It keeps the citizenry in line, reminding them that we are there to protect them and their Freedoms – one or two of which we may judiciously curtail during times of heightened threat – and reinforcing the idea that certain death awaits the less than eternally vigilant. If we have a new restriction ready to go and implement it in the wake of a tragedy like this, the people applaud, rather than oppose our decisive action. If there is resistance, we can always implant the story that the berserk Famer was in fact an agent of the enemy who has infiltrated our own society – a terrorist – and that deals with that. Objection quickly turns to embrace of the new restrictions.

'We recognise that providing Gobblers with an unalloyed stream of sweetness, light, love and Freedom on YouStar gets cloying, even for them, which is why we occasionally insert your Conflict factules into their programming. But when the nastiness intrudes into YouStar, when one of our under-performing personalities takes it into his head to do something awful in the palace of Fame, we publicly tut-tut but privately approve. Of course, we would never actually incite or encourage violence of this nature; that would not only be distasteful, it may result in an episode of blowback, which we try to avoid.

'Now, I tell you all of this not out of idle curiosity. I want you to keep it in mind as you execute a most challenging assignment, one that requires equal measures of outrage and grief, in a very public forum.' Knead's left eyebrow raised.

Biz had been listening intently, to be sure, but he was also wondering why Knead would choose to discuss this now. After all, he'd been in the Bastion for some time. He understood the nature of the InterFace and YouStar sufficiently to piece together an analysis of such an event. It was fairly elementary Spin Psychology, which he he had a solid grasp of by then. Still, the reference to an assignment intrigued him. He guessed that some such incident must have occurred and that he would play a role in its exposition and denouement, and in public, no less. In public? This must be the long awaited foray back into the citiburbs.

Like everyone else, he had grown used to working in the Bastion, a long way from the familiar streets and Hubs, out of sight of the coal-brick houses and carbo-timber fences, the oxygen vents, whizzing preon drives and levtrans buses. But the idea of doing some fieldwork in the real world excited him, even as it made him lightly anxious. He did not want to betray any of this to Knead, so he played it cool.

'Okay. Go on.'

'Well, something has happened, something that will allow you to put the theory you've been learning into practice. It will be the most delicate and most challenging assignment you've faced to date. We're sending you because we need the Sharp involved to, at the very least, appear emotionally involved.'

A chill ran up and down Biz's spine, but he kept his air of studied indifference and lukewarm professional interest. 'It sounds interesting,' he said coolly. 'I'm certain I'm ready for it.'

'Excellent. As you've already guessed, some ill begotten miscreant has somehow managed to circumvent our security – a system that's admittedly designed to intimidate and constrain the law-abiding rather than prevent genuinely committed criminals from carrying out their plans. It pains me to tell you, it was in fact one of our own. We often insert Sharps from the Ministry of Education and Information into new groups of

Famers, as you know, to keep an eye on things. Well, one of them, Nib, has completed such assignments numerous times, usually under an assumed name like Traub, Helix or Nubble, but sometimes under his own name. The Gobblers are too stupid to realise they've seen him before. The brief is to remain unobtrusive and observant, and this usually ends up with the insert being a Fame wraith. However, it seems that this time around our Nib took his lowly status a little too much to heart, and snapped. He smuggled a weapon into the Fame House on day one of his YouStar sojourn and there, before the cameras and of course the legions of ardent InterFace viewers, viciously slaughtered his fellow Famers before he could be restrained through the application of several projectiles to the head.

'The ratings are, of course, off the charts. The scene is being endlessly replayed and chewed over in all its gory splendour, along with the requisite condemnation. But we need to move swiftly to capitalise on it. If only we'd known it was coming, we could have prepared some new restriction to impose in response, but we can only utilise it as a general stimulus to Fear, I suppose, rather than attain some specific aim. So, I need you to go back into Gobblerdom for a short while, to lead the mourning and stoke the public indignation, and to suggest that greater vigilance and lesser latitude by the authorities is the only antidote to such poisonous acts.'

Biz was thrilled. This was a truly important mission. His words would carry so much weight! His ratings, if he were subject to them, would be astronomical. And he would have an opportunity to practice the skills he'd been developing in a public arena — to see, out there, the effects of his words on real world Gobblers, to understand how the citiburbians reacted in real time instead of having to rely on dry reports generated by the Bastion's Gobbler Poll division.

What was not clear was why it concerned him personally, and why he was being given this task. He knew other Psyman

Spin Techs who had been in the Bastion for longer but had never taken on such a public role. Although missions like this were exceedingly rare, they did happen; usually they were handed to a Psyman with direct experience in the area affected. So he would have expected the job to go to a YouStar Spin Tech rather than a Conflict Spin Tech.

'I'm not ungrateful,' he said. 'But why me?'

'Oh,' Knead shrugged, a little too airily, 'your mother was one of the slain.'

Biz almost faltered. He had become so adept at playing the Sharp – indeed, at being the Sharp – that he had clearly fooled Knead into believing that he was truly devoid of emotion. But this news stabbed him in the heart. Inside he was bleeding, but he would not allow the blood to drain from his face. He said, simply, 'In that case I'll play the grieving son just as if I were one, and the enraged public official with equal fervour.'

Knead nodded. 'Excellent. It really is too bad, though. Nib was a good man.' He shook his head and left the room.

Biz stared straight ahead for a few moments, swallowing hard. He was determined not to show the emotion that was crushing him. He turned back to his screen, blinked and continued editing the story about explosives that looked like fireworks.

14.

Seven weeks into their training, Mandrill brought battle practice to an early end so he could deliver fresh orders.

'Tomorrow, we ship out for the war. Tonight you pack your kit, polish your boots and prepare yourself to defend Freedom. Do I make myself clear?'

Fear and adrenaline ran through twenty-five rigid, erect bodies: this was it.

'Yes sir!' they called, in thrilled unison. Most of them didn't know if they were ready or not; several were sure that they were not. But the time for not being ready was past.

'We are so underdone,' Dirndl said. 'If that's the training my dad, my brother and my relatives got, it's no wonder none of them have come home.'

Less than twenty-four jittery, jokey, jam-packed hours later, they were piling onto a Suborb for the two-hour sub-orbital parabolic flight to the war zone. The mood was sombre.

They were, after all, travelling halfway around the world to meet an enemy about whom they knew precious little. "They hate our Freedoms," may have been an excellent motivator to fight, but it offered little in the way of useful detail about the enemy. The Eduvids had been marginally informative, but the unit's practical knowledge of the Sandrags, and the country in which they would fight them, remained almost non-existent. In general, the passengers were as quiet as the engines whispering outside the big, wide windows.

'Shit, I still don't even know how to fire a projectile weapon properly,' Necker muttered. 'I mean, I've seen it done plenty of times on the video screen, and we saw Robe fire one once, but is that really enough?'

'You better hope it is, fren.' Dirndl was stern, even hard-faced, but she reached over and squeezed Necker's hand. He gave her a look of gratitude, friendship and solidarity.

'Don't worry,' Navel smirked, 'when some filthy Sandrag is firing at you, you'll learn quick enough how to return fire.' He sounded unconvincing, and he looked unconvinced.

Necker looked out the window. He could see the curvature of the earth and its thin blue ribbon of atmosphere. It looked like a soft, silken cocoon keeping the earth cool and safe in its glowing azure embrace. But despite the beauty, he wished he was back in his Cocoon at the base, or better yet, at home with his parents. He wondered if they ever thought about him, unaware of the irony – this was the first time he'd thought about them in several months. He was aware of the answer, though: unless he were to appear on YouStar, he was gone from their lives. Perhaps not quite as easily forgotten as last month's favourite Famer, but not exactly clear and present in their minds, either.

He shook his head: the horizon seemed to be getting higher, and the ocean that had been below them was now an endless sea of featureless sand. They were coming in to land.

The heat was oppressive. It pushed up in waves from the grey-brown concrete of the apron as they emerged from the cool, steel Suborb. Necker felt his very pores opening up, and the moisture being sucked out of them as if by a vacuum. A fine dust invaded his nose and his mouth and filtered into his lungs, and he was sure he could feel it replacing the moisture he had just lost. After two minutes, the blighted, charmless land felt like hell. Every last one of the recruits was baffled – why would the Sandrags strive so hard to defend *this*? It was easier to see, though, why people would want to leave here and invade someone else's homeland.

'It's not our Freedom they want, it's our air conditioning,' said Navel, to chuckles of dry laughter.

Mandrill and Robe herded the unit into a levtrans bus; they all tried to squeeze through the door at once, their bulky packs shoving into the faces of those behind them, whacking them on the side of the head, scraping across cheeks and bending noses. The pain was irrelevant; the temperature was bearable inside the vehicle, and there was at least a drop of moisture in the artificial air. They crammed into it gratefully. And, once inside, there were more than enough seats for all of them – deeply cushioned plush seats with individual armrests and air vents and lights.

As the bus moved off the airbase and took to the broad strip of black tar that bisected the desert, everyone looked out the windows at the countryside around them. Nothing grew, nothing moved, nothing disturbed the flat line of the horizon. There was nothing but grey sand and rocks that pulsated heat. No one spoke. All eyes searched the featureless plains, seeking something, anything other than the endless carpet of sand stretching out on all sides. When the landscape had not changed after five minutes of travel, they started to lean back in their seats and contemplate the future. After ten minutes, still without turn, curve, dip or rise of any discernible degree, the vehicle started to descend a pronounced slope. Heads jammed against windows to see what was happening.

They were entering an enormous, gaping valley, probably fifteen kilometres or more in length and four or five wide. On the valley floor they could see trees – mostly tall palms bordering green-leafed groves of olive trees, and variegated orchards where fruits of different colours blossomed and hung heavily on crowded branches. Huge, diamond-glassed greenhouses caught the last rays of the sinking sun, and everywhere they could see encouraging signs of life: houses, long, low buildings and a very few taller ones, roadways buzzing with preon drives and buses, and clusters of little buildings that looked a lot like the citiburb Hubs they knew from home.

The valley had opened up out of the flat plain as though it had been gouged into the hard land – which indeed it had – before miraculously filling with all of this life. Necker and his colleagues didn't care how it had come to be there. All that mattered was the change from the mind-numbing sameness of the desert above. They passed through growing fields and busy hamlets, and then headed towards the far side of the valley, where the buildings had a familiar, drab, functional design – it was obviously the military base.

When the vehicle stopped by a long, low coal-brick building, they piled out. They were in the heart of the valley, and the sun was sinking behind the western rim of the ridge. The dry golden light made the dust and air and treetops glow. It was pretty and surreal, but not welcoming. The heat was still leadenly oppressive, and the languor and studied indifference of the people moving around them – mostly Sandrags in flowing robes – disturbed them. They felt foreign and intrusive.

There were no fences, no guards and no weaponry to be seen; the lack of military rigour disconcerted them. The people milling around were the first Sandrags they had seen other than those on their video screens, and they were startled that the enemy wandered so freely within an army compound. They had already forgotten that they were the visitors here – although they felt alien, they also felt that this was a part of their homeland, just in the wrong country.

'We must be a long way from the front,' Bloat said with obvious relief. She instantly started to sweat, and almost choked on the desiccated desert air, although it was marginally cooler on the valley floor than it had been on the desert heights. Necker grunted agreement and looked around. The buildings were all low slung, as though to keep closer to the cool ground air, but they had long, wide footprints, and they were made of top quality carbcrete and lithicarb. The road practically gleamed, as did the pathways, windows and vehicles around them. A lot of effort was being expended on keeping the place neat. The only things that looked dusty and old were the Sandrags, who were clearly charged with the housekeeping. One was even working the road with slow, desultory sweeps of an electric blower, removing the sand and dust swept in by the arriving transport.

Necker shouldered his pack and followed Bloat and the other recruits into the big building before them. The wall of cool air that whooshed out as the automatic doors slid open greeted him like an old friend; its refreshing temperature and humidity calmed and reassured him. Navel whistled and wiped his forehead with the back of his forearm. Behind him, Dirndl shook her dust-laden ringlets vigorously as she stepped over the threshold.

They were in a spacious reception area with a central island surrounded by counters and desks; corridors radiated out of the huge room, three to every wall except for the one behind them, which had only the entry doors and a couple of shallow, glass-fronted offices.

Robe ordered them to fall in, and the unit complied with instant discipline. There was comfort in their unity. Mandrill, who had been swapping papers with the junior officer behind one of the reception desks, walked over and spoke to his charges.

'Team, this is our home for the foreseeable future. We mount our campaign from here; we eat here, sleep here, train here and stick together here. Your accommodation is down corridor two on the south wall. Take your assigned room number.'

They marched in commendable formation across the reception area and on an order from Robe slipped into single file to pass through the designated door. The room entries, Necker saw, were much closer together than they had been back at Fort Manning. They would each have a room of their own, but it didn't look like they would be that spacious.

Necker opened the door to his room, S214. Although narrow, it was long, with a slim bed big enough for the tallest recruit, a kitchenette that really was not much more than an automat with a sink, some storage for implements, a fridge, and a surprisingly generous bathroom. There was also a closet that would easily house everything in his pack. But one thing was obviously missing: there was no Cocoon. Not only was this place hot, dry, distant and deserted, it was cut off from the one source of comfort and companionship that had been with him all his life. He sat, bereft, on his bed, knowing for sure that his colleagues were all doing the same thing. This would be much harder than any of them had ever dreamed.

At 1830 sharp a bell sounded, and his digital bulletin flashed up a message: *Fall in, Reception*. Necker stopped unpacking. In the hallway, he met Bloat and Dirndl, who looked as shell-shocked as he felt. He didn't have to ask to know what had given them such despairing looks.

The unit assembled in Reception and Mandrill and Bloat led them out across forty metres of seething hot tarmac, brightly lit against the deepening night, to the refectory. There they joined a crowd, smaller than Necker had expected. There were maybe four other units, most of whom looked comfortable enough with their surroundings and were amused by the glum looks of the new arrivals. These old hands talked loudly and ate heartily, while Necker's comrades sat quietly and talked in low, disappointed tones.

They couldn't fault the food though – it was delicious, plentiful and dazzlingly fresh. Clearly the valley was much more fertile than the desert that enclosed it. Nor could they have any complaints about the service – for every soldier in the room there seemed to be two Sandrags fetching drinks or food, or cleaning up, or just bustling around.

The entire unit appeared to be overwhelmed by the peaceful presence of the enemy, the newness of the place they were in, and the unknown challenges of the job before them. In addition, they were all dead tired from the journey. Even Navel looked unusually subdued and reflective. He pushed his generous serve of carbosteak and real vegetables around on his plate and sighed a lot. Only Bloat appeared relatively untroubled. As long as they were a long way from the front, she said, she would be more than happy.

Having dined well, if not happily, the weary unit took to its feet almost as one and trudged back to their rooms. Dirndl gave Necker a look as he left her in the corridor, which he took to be supportive but may also have been a silent plea for companionship. He was not in the mood for interpreting glances, meaningful or otherwise, so he nodded and entered his room, closing the door without looking back at her.

He lay on his bed and stared at nothing, his skin drinking in the cool air wafting from the air conditioner. He wondered about this place. How did the valley get here? Where was the war? Why must it be in such a hostile environment? He fell asleep musing on Dirndl's look back at him. He probably could have darted across the hallway and gone into her room, but he wasn't at all certain that was what she wanted. He was surprised to find, besides, that he wasn't really in the mood for sex. As he dropped off he told himself he would jump her bones in a couple of days, when they were both more sure of this new situation and their place in it.

His sleep was filled with sand and screams, and Sandrags running everywhere with wicked grins on faces blasted brown by the sun and covered with bristly hair. He, too, was running, without direction or purpose, around the strewn wreckage of shattered, burnt and broken Cocoons.

He woke, against his will, fifteen or twenty minutes before reveille, with a sense that he was not alone. Someone was moving quietly through the darkness towards him with a soft swish of fabric, an almost imperceptible footfall. He opened his eyes and in the gloom he could make out a dark shape, a large dark shape, advancing towards him. He caught a faint aroma of spice and musk mixed with perspiration, and heard the tiniest clink of ceramic on ceramic.

He sat up quickly, ready to defend himself, aware that he was ill prepared for even a modest attack. A hand emerged from deep within the folds of the robe the figure was wearing, causing it to swish quite loudly. Two fingers clicked crisply together, and the light switched on. A large man, a bearded Sandrag in magnificent flowing mantle, with a red and white checked keffiyeh on his head, stood at the foot of the bed. His skin shone pale brown in the low electric light, and his beard flowed with the same silken smoothness as his robes.

He was carrying a very old fashioned cup on a saucer, and steam from the cup curled into his facial hair. He tilted his head forward in a slight motion, which Necker read as a bow. The dark, moustachioed lips parted to reveal an expanse of perfect white teeth.

'Good morning, sir,' the man said in a deep, soothing voice. 'I am your batman, Saud, and I have your tea.' He pushed the china cup and saucer in Necker's direction.

Necker was confused. He automatically put out his hands to accept the cup and saucer, staring wide-eyed at the man as he did so. 'My what?'

'Your tea, sir.'

'No, the other thing you said.' Necker was no longer afraid of the man – his manner was far too pleasant. But he was concerned about what this Sandrag was doing in his room, other than handing him a cup of tea. He was also aware that the benign expression could turn to one of menace in a moment, so he was alert for any change in demeanour.

'Your batman,' Saud explained, again. Seeing no flicker of recognition of the word, nor any light of understanding on the soldier's face, Saud gave a small sigh and said, 'Your batman, sir. Your orderly. Your valet. Assigned to take care of your room, your uniforms, your equipment and your good self. Hence the cup of tea.'

'But! But you're the enemy,' Necker stuttered. 'We're fighting a war against you.'

The Sandrag regarded him quizzically, then shook his head. 'No, sir,' he said with a gentle lilt.

Necker looked at the cup of tea he was holding, noting that the tremor in his hand caused ripples across its steaming surface, then back at the man. He was at a complete loss. The Sandrag sighed again, properly this time, and sat down on the foot of his master's bed.

'You know, they get so used to not telling you anything, they sometimes forget to disclose important information.' The tail of his keffiyeh swept back and forth across his neck and shoulders. 'This may come as a shock to you sir, but there is no war, only battle.'

'What are you talking about?' said Necker. 'I'm here to fight the war.'

'No, sir, you are here to battle. There is a big difference. Think, sir, about your training. Did you study weaponry? Tactics? First aid? Camouflage?'

'No, we played battle. But that was just to teach us teamwork.' Necker was uncertain, confused. 'We'll learn all that war stuff on the job, surely?'

'Surely not, sir. On the job training in combat would, I'm afraid, result only in your very swift demise. But fortunately for you, combat was replaced by battle over two hundred years ago.'

Necker didn't understand. He felt as though he'd been transported to some other world, some bizarre and frightening place where he could be sure of nothing. He didn't like it. 'No, no, no!' he said. 'Your people hate our Freedoms. You want to take them away from us and make us live unfree, like you do.'

'Do I look like I hate your Freedoms, sir?' the Sandrag asked. 'Do I look as though I am in any position to take anything away from you? Other than your empty tea cup and possibly your laundry?'

He smiled and lay his hands palm upward on his lap. He could see that Necker was not coping well with the news and that a full explanation was in order. Up and down the hallway, similar conversations were taking place between Necker's colleagues and their batmen.

'Sir, consider the world,' Saud began. 'Very soon after the discovery of Higgs Energy, armament and ordinance design escalated to the point where the mildest skirmish would be sufficient to wipe out vast armies and destroy great tracts of earth. War as it had been known became untenable – if the attacks that laid these very lands to waste through radiation and the decimation of the world's population by the Surge had not already achieved that result.

'There was nothing left but to learn to live in peace. We here in the radlands, having suffered the full effects of the nuclear assault, our population reduced to a mere sliver of a fraction of its former size and all our lands withered under the burden of radiation, were only too happy to submit to the terms your government named – your Joe.' Saud smirked a little. 'These turned out to include a continuation of hostilities under much modified terms. Our leaders agreed to provide anti-Freedom rhetoric and to be accused of various provocations, as well as to provide the arena for the conflict. Your Joe, in return, promised to employ every person in the land, to undertake such works as the excavation and establishment of the wonderful valley you see here, and to refrain from killing any more Arabs. Or Sandrags, as you so affectionately call us. For the first hundred years or so your soldiers were actually engaged in remedial and building works, but since that was all completed we have been entertaining your troops and ourselves by staging the sporting contest you call battle. It fits in neatly with your propaganda requirements. Please drink your tea before it becomes too cool.'

'Bullshit!' said Necker. 'That just can't be. You're a threat to our way of life. A danger to our security. My enemy!'

'Sir.' Saud was unflustered and apparently unflappable, maintaining his serenity in spite of Necker's insolent tone. 'I am no threat to anyone. Your government keeps up this war, for want of a better term, not because of our aims but in service of its own. Having an enemy gives your society a purpose, a goal. It also provides a reliable mechanism of persuasion and control. You can be talked or threatened into or out of almost anything if the alternative is framed as a hazard to your security or your much-vaunted Freedom.

'You are, in that respect, much more fortunate than us. We, who have nothing, can have nothing taken away from us, so we are in a sense free to enjoy our own lack of Freedom. Everything we have comes from you, and the only thing you do not give us is the Freedom you so obviously relish at home.'

Necker sipped his tea. It was exquisite. He sipped again. But he was still having trouble understanding. 'Why bother going through this charade? Why not just end it all now, and produce it on a computer in the Bastion?'

'Because, sir, sending you here creates opportunities for authentic visuals that are superior to anything a computer artist could imagine. Could anyone really make up all of this?' He spread his arms wide. Necker saw nothing that could not be imagined.

'Besides, our people, who are so good at hosting your little war, are also experts at creating the kind of anti-Freedom rhetoric that your pundits so much love to despise. Then there is the fact that we need this war for our society to survive. If your armies all went home tomorrow, our *raison d'être* would go with them.

'The good news, for us, is that your government needs this conflict as much as we do. As little as it would impact on the lives of you or your countrymen at home if your government supported us out of sheer altruism and humanitarian good nature, they would lose out in popularity. Although your country is on an avowed mission to share Freedom and Democracy with anyone and everyone, your people are less enthusiastic about sharing your wealth. Even if it is, in the context of inexhaustible energy, carbon building and Synthetron fabrication, limitless and therefore meaningless.'

Necker relaxed a little and lifted the teacup to his lips again. It really was delicious, and the taste, combined with the thought that he would not have to actually fight and quite likely die in a real war, was soothing. 'So, no war. Then what happens next?'

'You battle against your own teams and against ours.' Saud smiled knowingly. 'Every international contest is reported as a genuine conflict – the enemy is engaged, attacks are mounted and courageous defences deployed; but all these are merely metaphors used to describe the contest and the various twists and turns in the actual play, to lend veracity to the description. We celebrate the end of every tournament, and a great many other things, with fireworks, and these are reported in your home country as the explosions of actual armaments. It really is rather shrewd, don't you think?'

Saud got up from the end of the bed to clean up the small mess he had made in the kitchenette. Necker sat back and finished his tea. Minutes later, reveille sounded and he leapt out of bed. Saud helped him into his uniform – the first time anyone had ever done that – and set about making the bed.

Necker walked out the door and up the hall, shaking his head in disbelief. Breakfast in the refectory was an intense, talkative affair. Everyone had been awakened by a batman with a cup of tea and the news that the war was a giant sham. Most were, to at least some degree happy with the news, but some were suspicious.

But Dirndl was downright angry. 'I fucking knew it,' she exploded. 'I knew these fucking Gobblers couldn't run a war to save their lives. Goddam it!' She pounded the table. 'I am a fucking warrior. I didn't come here to battle, I came here to kill Sandrags!' She slammed the table again, and realised that most of the room was staring at her. She blushed. 'In the name of Freedom.'

'Hey, look at the bright side, fren,' Navel said. 'No war means your cousin or your brother or whatever must still be here, right? I mean, how many casualties can there be?'

Dirndl brightened and nodded. Her father and her brother, not to mention a cousin and an aunt, should all be in this country somewhere – maybe even on the base. She set off to enlist Robe's help in finding them. The talk continued through breakfast, interrupted only by Mandrill, who ordered all personnel to be on the battlefield in thirty minutes, in full battle gear. There was to be a practice match against another group of recently arrived recruits.

15.

It had been a long time since he'd driven these streets. Biz couldn't really tell if the citiburbs had changed, or if it was just his perception. So much was the same – tall, tubular oxygen vents standing high over rows and rows of coal-brick and carb-crete houses with solar-steel roofs shining in the clear evening, Hubs bubbling with people picking up fresh food for their evening meals and teens wandering into the Cocoonery for a bit of communal isolation, preon drives and levtrans buses creeping silently on the jet black roads. There was still a camera tree every forty metres, wreathed in a tangle of long and short range cameras to record every movement and action for examination and analysis. And the Gobblers still seemed goofy and carefree, but were still no doubt as careful as ever not to be seen doing anything unusual.

Yes, he had changed, there was no denying it. The last time he had been here, he'd been a young, green Gobbler. Now, piloting his preon drive through the well-ordered streets, he was a Sharp. He was no longer one of the people: he was above their petty concerns and hopeless addictions. Now he was one of the privileged few who told these people what to think and how to feel. It was no surprise that for the first time ever he felt a sense of ownership. He knew these people much, much better than they knew themselves, and that gave him a great deal of power over them. He loved that feeling.

He turned into his parents' driveway and emerged from the vehicle: an official, an important man. The neighbours would be surprised to see him here like this. Impressed, even. Or they would, except that they'd never take their eyes off the InterFace for long enough to see what was going on outside their own front doors, and if they were to see him in passing, perhaps on their way back from a toilet break, they would probably look blankly and wonder who the hell he was. He'd been gone for more than two years, after all. A lot of fake famous personalities had been paraded before them since then. They probably didn't even remember that Arbeit and Viand had a son, once.

Happily watching the screens, typing comments and switching views, Arbeit didn't hear Biz come in, and seemed startled to find his son standing next the Cocoon and watching him.

'Oh, hello,' he said uncertainly, when he noticed that he had a visitor. When he realised that his visitor was Biz, he climbed out of the comfortable seat and stood looking at his son. But he didn't seem to know what to say.

'You've grown taller.'

'I suppose I have.'

'You're here about your mother?'

'Yes, father. I am sorry for your loss. What a horrible, horrible thing to happen.' Biz made an awkward movement that could have been the initiation of a hug, but he was thwarted when Arbeit leaned back to take a quick look at the screens on his Cocoon.

'Yes, yes, awful,' said Arbeit, nodding. His eyes kept darting back at the flickering screens. Foozle, his favourite, was seducing yet another willing victim in pursuit of ratings and orgasm. 'Still, it's been very exciting. Cameras and so on around here. I've been on the InterFace once or twice, even though it was Viand's turn to be famous, not mine.' He smiled.

Biz looked around the room, which was strewn with debris and musty with dust. His parents had never been too fastidious, but this was worse than he'd remembered. The dust was everywhere, in spite of the automatic vacuum and cleaning machines. Pieces of dirty crockery and greasy cutlery lay in odd places like under chairs and nestled in corners. Only the cocoon was clean, shiny and unsullied by abandoned dishes, dropped clothing and assorted other unidentifiable detritus. Biz found small comfort in the knowledge that his father was, at least, eating.

'You'll miss her, I expect?'

'Oh, I expect,' his father said. 'Horrible business. Horrible.' he said, shaking his head.

'I'm here to officially lead the mourning.'

'Oh, yes?' His father stopped looking at the screen for a few moments. 'You'll be making an appearance on the InterFace then?'

'Yes. In fact, I need to Face-cast from here.'

Arbeit nodded and smiled; Biz could see, behind the new gleam in his father's eye, some slow calculations about whether the husband might get his face on the screen as well as the son.

'Oh, splendid,' Arbeit sighed. 'Tip top. You'll be bringing cameras and so on then?'

'Yes.'

'I am sure that will be very interesting. The other cameras only came to the door. I guess I should clean up a bit.' He looked around at the mess and sniggered.

'No need. Someone will attend to that, I'll see to it.' Biz stood straighter, with authority and not a little pride.

'Oh, really? Wonderful.'

'Anyway, I should be going,' Biz said. 'I've got a room in the local Hub's Surveillance Centre, where visiting Sharps stay. I just thought I should drop in and offer my condolences.'

'Very decent of you, boy,' said Arbeit. 'Your mother would like that. And she'd be very proud of you, being on the Inter-Face and all. This is all so horrible, just horrible.'

'Bye, Dad.'

'Yes, yes, bye son. See you on the screen then.'

Biz checked into the Surveillance Centre, and lay on the bed collecting his thoughts. He hadn't thought about his parents much of late. He'd been absorbed in his work, and in the expanding sense of control that went with it. That his parents had fallen out of his thoughts was to be expected, given the massive changes in his life and the pressure, the immense density of expectations that he was now struggling to fulfil. It was natural that something would have to give. But he had always assumed that his parents would still be thinking of him, that every day they would wonder aloud to each other how he was and what he was doing and express their pride in him. But, like everyone else, his parents were so consumed by their box that they could barely spare a thought for him – unless he floated back into their view on the InterFace.

The thought was both awakening and appalling. This was the source of his power, the Cocoon's capacity to obscure or remove any thoughts or actions not related to YouStar. It was power purchased at the expense of people's ability to determine the difference between manufactured and actual reality – or even to want to make that determination. The minds of the Gobblers were wholly the property of Biz and his Bastion colleagues.

They could still feel, and even think, of course, and that's why the InterFace was so important. If they had absolutely no minds left, Joe could dispense with the InterFace and not lose control. But this remnant capacity for emotion and the need to occupy it was what made the InterFace so necessary. Biz's own father, in treating him with such distance and unfamiliarity, and in dealing with the violent death of his wife with such detachment, was showing him what the Cocoon could do to a man. He felt the power. It saddened him. And yet he revelled in it.

The Cocoon in his room dominated the space as they always do: curved black glass and carbon, sheer and inviting with hard, arcing edges but a soft, pneumatic recliner within; a semicircular bank of screens facing the occupant; controls in easy arm's reach; a floating keyboard projected on web-fine, invisible carbon mist, so the keys could be found wherever the viewer needed them. He hadn't been in a Cocoon since he'd left for the Bastion, and couldn't even remember what it felt like. But he did know that once inside, it so completely occupied the senses and mind that the viewer was left with no capacity to do much more than accept and try to assimilate the overwhelming stimulus. No wonder so little was retained.

He knew that in the past he'd spent many thousands of hours in various Cocoons, and he could generalise to himself the nature of his experience based on his objective knowledge of it, but he could not recall a single specific fact from a single one of those sessions. The great power of the Cocoon was in its efficacy as an amnestic. He knew this, and yet, brooding in the middle of the room the thing looked sexy, curvy, smoky and dark, and he was tempted to get into it, for just a moment, to see what he had been missing. And he had good reasons for doing so. If he was to communicate effectively with the Gobblers, it would pay to think like one and act like one. All he had to do was release himself to the Cocoon's captive powers for a little while.

But he couldn't do it. He knew it would subjugate his whole mind and body; it would feed him the candy of inconsequential activities, the fodder of unthinking Gobblers, and deprive him of the nourishment of real information and the exercise of genuine thought. His mind would become a moribund, sclerotic and inactive blob, again.

He didn't want that. He wanted to be on the other side of the screen, making the candy, spinning the fairy floss in different colours and flavours and doling it out to the Gobblers, watching them eat it up and queue for more. Instead of sleeping in the Cocoon, he slept on the bed, thinking about how deep and how high his power might reach, now that he knew the power of the InterFace. He slept well.

It was only much later that he discovered it was a good thing he didn't climb into the Cocoon. Its sole purpose was to test the Sharps who stayed there, and if they fell into watching YouStar, they failed. Biz had unwittingly passed another of Knead's tests.

The next morning, Biz got up early and hurried to his father's house to prepare for the Face-cast. He had to marshal the Gobbler camera crews and make-up artists and all the other flotsam of a Face-cast. He had to choose camera angles and arrange cameo appearances. He had to coach his father, who was to be the public face of loss. His appearance was to be as short as possible, preferably visual only, and if not, then to limit the old man's utterances as much as possible. Arbeit was an unknown, and Biz wanted to keep his father's tendency to be star-struck under wraps. The last thing he needed was for the chief mourner to look thrilled by his own Fame. Biz would follow Arbeit's short appearance with a presentation of his own in order to make political capital from the tragedy. He would read his own stirring narration as the inconsolable son of one of the victims. Then the viewers could get back to YouStar, and the new cohort of Famers who'd been hastily drafted and put into place within hours of the massacre.

By early afternoon they were ready for the live cross. Biz signalled the technical director and, across the country, to the aggrieved grunts of viewers everywhere, a graphic cut into the regularly scheduled YouStar programming:

In Honour of the Fallen
We Forget, not Forgive.

This cut to a close-up of Arbeit sitting in his living room, staring at the camera as it zoomed in slowly and tracked around him.

Despite Biz's stern admonitions, Arbeit wore a shy, sly smile. He'd so enjoyed the action around him that morning that he had quite forgotten to enter his own Cocoon, and it was clear that he was relishing the opportunity to flutter into the spotlight. It had been years since he had been on YouStar, and the attention he had received following Viand's death reminded him of how much he craved even the merest fragment of Fame. He understood that this might be his last shot at notoriety. Even if he made it onto YouStar once more, he was too old and ugly and slow to garner ratings. This was his last glowing moment. He was determined to make the most of it.

Biz began his voice-over. 'This is Arbeit. Three days ago, his wife Viand was brutally slain in the worst YouStar atrocity of the decade.'

The lights in front of Arbeit switched off – his moment had ended – and the picture changed to a brief tracking shot around the inert body of Viand lying in a pool of blood. Biz would have preferred a static shot of his mother, but understood that there must never be a static image – if the subject does not move, the camera must. The shot of Viand was followed by the other victims of the massacre, in various poses of agony. The camera zoomed in on their wounds or craned around their bodies.

Biz continued his homily in soft but firm tones, with gravity and emotion. 'Viand was one of ten victims of this tragedy, including the perpetrator, who did not survive the arrest process. We shall not name the evildoer, but we will remember his victims: Crucible. Dervish. Slue. Minish. Claque. Omen. Gad. Redox. Viand. Their stars shall shine forever.'

The scene cut back to Biz. He sat in a formal pose behind the desk he had set up in his old bedroom.

'You don't know me, and you don't need to. But you should know that one of the victims was my mother. I come from the Bastion, but I want you to know that we Sharps feel the tragic loss of these victims as keenly and profoundly as you citiburbians, perhaps even more so. Joe sent me, and today Joe is speaking to you through me. He asked me to tell you that the deaths of these wonderful humans shall remind us always that the price of Freedom is eternal vigilance, and that in this case, with heartbreaking consequences, our vigilance failed. Despite the surveillance that you so graciously allow us to conduct into every aspect of your lives, we overlooked the actions of this desperate villain leading up to his heinous act. If our observation had been more thorough, if we'd been more suspicious in our analysis, we would have determined before the event that the perpetrator was planning to carry it out. Rest assured that we will never again be so lax, and Joe is sure that each and every one of you will welcome closer, deeper scrutiny of every moment and movement of your lives in the name of Freedom, to prevent such a thing happening again.

'This murderer was not acting alone, and there are others like him. He was part of a sleeper cell, a homegrown terrorist group whose sympathies lie in the East, where an unrelenting cadre of Sandrags awaits the signal that our guard is down. They need only get a hint that our attention is elsewhere, and they will carry out another shocking attack, or possibly even an invasion. Their mission is to snatch our Freedom from us, and they will die to achieve it. The acts of evil men like this Fame House killer are but a prelude to the horrors that await us should we ever relax our iron grip on Freedom. We will not.

'Now I would like to talk about how we – you, my frens here in the citiburbs, and those of us locked away in the Bastion toiling to protect your lives and lifestyle – how we should react to this terrible catastrophe. YouStar is about celebrating the ordinary. Taking the anonymous and giving them the moment of recognition that they so richly deserve, and then allowing them to sink back into obscurity before Fame becomes a burden. By taking the lives of these innocent victims, the proxy Sandrag in our midst has broken the rules of the game. These casualties could become immortal in our eyes through this tragedy. We could hold them up as unforgettable symbols of our Freedom. As the son of one of the dead, nothing would please me more.'

He looked with moist-eyed sincerity at the camera in front of him, and in homes and Cocooneries everywhere, hearts melted. This was a beautiful moment in Face-casting.

'But that would be wrong. It is the solemn duty of each and every one of us to do all we can to honour their memories by forgetting these people. Let them become the nameless martyrs to Freedom they deserve to be. As I have already told you, one of the slain was my mother. Her name is no longer important, and henceforth I will not recall her either in life or death. I shall simply turn my attention to the new Famers now delighting our screens, and enjoy the Freedoms so dearly bought by these victims. Were I to equate the life and loss of my mother with the reality of our Freedom, I would be honouring her person, not Freedom itself. And that would be so, so wrong.'

Biz changed his expression from grief stricken son to that of an upstanding authority delivering difficult but necessary news, as if he himself was struggling to accept what he had to say. His resolve fed down the line into the hearts and minds of his audience.

'Now, some of you, co-workers and relatives of the victims, may seek to remember them in ways that could impinge upon your Freedom to move on from this gross occurrence. I would therefore remind you that possession of any images, be they pictures, drawings, sketches, sculptures or masks – in short, possession of images in any format whatsoever is absolutely forbidden. Only by consciously rejecting the past to live in the now can we truly enjoy the Freedom with which we are blessed, and keeping images of people or places we think we are fond of endangers that Freedom. Accordingly, any citiburbians found harbouring such images, whether related to this event or not, will be detained until their death of natural causes. This is to protect your Freedom, and mine, and that of us all. Stay Free, frens, stay in the present and stay vigilant. In the name of Joe, I thank you.'

YouStar returned to the screens of the people, and Biz let out a sigh of relief. It seemed to have gone well. Around him, the crew was already dismantling the Face-cast.

Biz had hours before he had to head back to the Bastion. It didn't look like he could fill them by spending time with his father: Arbeit was already back in his Cocoon, looking for Foozle. This was the first free time Biz had been given in a couple of years and he didn't know what to do. He wasn't in the mood to grieve quietly for his mother.

Should he visit Bock? He wouldn't know where to find her – he assumed that she would have moved out of her parents' house – and he was unsure if she would remember him as well and warmly as he remembered her. Without any carbon dioxide, she was probably a Cocoon-bound Gobbler by now. No, better to remember her as she was, his lithe and lovely high school friend, than to see her as a vapid automaton glued to a screen. He did wonder if she'd seen his Face-cast, and maybe had a flash of recognition.

He decided to drop in on Gneiss. He'd be easy enough to find, and he would no doubt remember his star pupil. And even if he didn't remember, he would be polite enough to cover his lack of recall, and have something interesting to say in any case. He walked the short distance to Gneiss's house. Nothing much had changed; perhaps the paint was a bit flakier in spots, but the garden still looked healthy to the point of luxuriance. He knocked on the door.

16.

A week after arriving in the East, Necker's unit played their first competitive battle. The heat was torturous: there was so much blazing white light from the sun that the westerners felt they were carrying an excess weight of photons on their shoulders. The light blasted their eyes and fried their brains. Sweat ran off them in torrents and water boys were run off their feet trying to slake unquenchable thirsts. After just a few minutes on field, running was nigh on impossible; just lifting one's legs to walk seemed a colossal effort. So, the Sandrags thrashed them. Bloat was beet red within minutes of kick-off, and by half-time she was half-dead of exhaustion and exposure. The two training contests they'd had against other new arrivals had been hard, but they were a stroll in the park compared to the battle against these fit, highly skilled and merciless Sandrags. By the end, most of them were seriously dehydrated, and one had died of heart failure. They limped off the field, shattered. Their spirits, like their bodies, were broken. They looked like ghosts. Bloat was taken off on a stretcher and placed on a drip.

Saud met Necker's spectre on the boundary line with an iced towel for his head and a five-litre container of barely cooled water.

'It doesn't do to drink it too cold, sir,' he said, as he wound the towel, turban-style, around Necker's throbbing head. Half carrying his boss, Saud led him to the barracks and ran a cool shower. As they walked, Necker vaguely noted that his team-mates were either on stretchers, or being given similar assistance by their batmen. In his delirium, he thought it incredibly funny that, with their turbanish towels, his surviving teammates now looked a bit like their nominal enemies. The Sandrag who had been the valet to the dead man, Pyle, had taken charge of removing his master's body. He looked mortified, as if the loss of his master's life had somehow been his fault, or perhaps just thought that he would be blamed for it. Glancing back one last time as they left the field, Necker was humiliated to see that the opposing team still looked relatively fresh.

Once out of a cool shower and properly rehydrated – the water made from pure hydrogen and oxygen is quite invigorating – Necker lay on a massage table so Saud could give him a thorough rub-down. The man's hands were magic, and the stress eased out of Necker's traumatised muscles.

Elsewhere in the camp, Mandrill was dutifully composing a report on the battle. An expeditionary force had, with conspicuous gallantry and against a formidably armed and trained opponent, taken the battlefield in conditions of extreme difficulty. In spite of a series of spirited offensive sallies and an even greater number of determined defensive manoeuvres characterised by desperation and the power of solid effort, the unit had been routed. The pitiless enemy had extracted one fatal casualty and several serious injuries, attaining several of their goals before the battle had ended and the Freedom fighters had left the field with dignity. His report was communicated to a Psyman named Biz, and broadcast on the InterFace by him with a few further embellishments. The cause of Freedom had been fractionally advanced, but at a cost.

That first incursion was the worst. It played havoc with the team's morale, and replacing the skilful though fatally fragile Pyle wasn't easy. But within a few days the grit and determination, for which the unit was now renowned, had resurfaced. They fought harder practice battles in the week that followed, in the heat of the day rather than the cool of the morning, and felt themselves more ready to meet the enemy. They were better prepared and better understood the challenges that the conditions of battle would present. They acquitted themselves more honourably, and although they were still beaten, it was by a less degrading margin and with no fatalities or serious injuries.

As they became more and more acclimatised and battle-hardened, the team clawed back the margins. They learned to sustain their attacks and when to be more aggressive. Saud, who had watched every battle along with all the other batmen and a thronging, vocal crowd of locals, turned out to be an astute observer and critic. He gave Necker pointers on kicking, tackling in defense and offense, and strategic placement of his body on the field. He attended to Necker's every need before, during and after battle, and quickly became a reliable, if over-obsequious friend. He knew when to discreetly absent himself so Necker and Dirndl could, as he put it, "couple," and when to reappear with a steaming-hot or ice-cold beverage. He knew when to bow, and when to offer a neck-rub.

Necker began to enjoy himself, especially when his side started to win occasional battles against the local teams. The Sandrags fought hard, their tactics were well-honed and at times deviously clever, but they were scrupulously fair on the field, and gracious in defeat. Necker and his comrades stopped thinking of them as enemies in any way, and started to respect them as opponents, admiring their skill in battle.

The months flew by. Every eight weeks or so they would fly to other bases to compete in tournaments, except when their base was the host. Their win/loss record improved. There were no more on field fatalities, just injuries – a blown knee or torn hamstring. If the injury would never heal sufficiently to allow the soldier to take the battlefield again, and if the soldier could not offer skills in a support position, they would be sent home. Saud and his fellow batmen would celebrate the soldier's departure raucously. It was quite touching.

None of the soldiers, curiously, said much about going home. The memory of it had faded, and if they did think about it – as Necker did, for one – their life at home seemed disconnected, compared to their life here in the war zone. The heat, the sky, the vast valleys of green gouged out of the radio-active earth: all seemed much more real and less contrived than their existence at home, which they could vaguely remember as a series of disjointed scenes interposed by soporific interludes in Cocoons. Of those interludes themselves, no specific memories remained. Indeed, Necker had a feeling, which he could neither swear was true nor write off as false, that some-how this environment, this life, was helping him to *grow* a memory. The land was barren and there were no oxygen vents, Hubs, Cocoons or any of the other familiar accoutrements of home, but somehow this place felt richer. Where before there had been nothing much worth remembering – although he did dimly recall his intense friendship with Bock and Biz as a batch of adolescent longings strung together by a series of Communal-coon and Flurient binges – there was little he wanted to forget in the theatre of war. He hung on, even to the bad things. And the good things were much more alive in his mind than they ever had been before.

Chief among these was Dirndl. They had grown ever closer during their time together on the team, and, particularly before he had learned to trust Saud, he'd drawn much on her strength and determination. She'd repeatedly told him that, if her father and brother and assorted other relatives had all survived here for so long (as they must have done, because none of them had ever come home either dead or alive) then she must too. And that meant that Necker also had to survive, she said, because she needed him there as her companion and lover. That made sense, and he wanted it to, though not because of any inherent logic. Together they'd pushed through the dark days when heat, loss on the field and the gruelling training schedule had threatened to bring their minds undone.

It was all the harder, then, when he lost her.

Whenever they flew to a different base for a tourney, Dirndl's first thought was always to find someone who had been there for a while and ask whether her father, her brother, her aunt or her aunt's boy were there or had been there, or whether anyone had met them elsewhere. Sometimes someone would claim to have known one or more of them, or to have known someone who had maybe mentioned one of them.

'Cuff?' they'd say, when she mentioned her brother. 'There was a masseur by that name in Japhet, I think. Or was it Cough?' Elsewhere, someone would say, 'Floccus? Big girl like yourself? I think I slept with her at a fiesta one night in Addin. But I'm pretty sure she was just passing through.'

Dirndl never actually found one of them, but in Japhet she had a breakthrough. A thin, young lieutenant told Dirndl that she had been very friendly with Cuff, 'If you know what I mean.' He had been stationed there, but a few months ago he had been moved to Javan, some three hundred kilometres to the east. Dirndl talked to her batman, who said that she knew how to get to Javan.

So, on a rest day, ignoring Necker's pleas and Robe's warnings, Dirndl and Faisal took a preon drive and left the valley. They never returned. They never arrived in Javan. It was as though the desert had swallowed them up.

Necker's lifetime of committing nothing to memory came to his rescue. At first, for a few moments, usually on the field, Dirndl would disappear entirely from his thoughts. In the heat of battle, his eyes fixed on the ball and his heart on the goal, his mind would clear of the sorrow and wondering, the certainty that she was dead but the painful hope that she might still live, somewhere. Then the same thing happened at practice, while he was being massaged, or in the mess. In the end, he only remembered Dirndl at rare moments, when thoughts of her came unbidden and then disappeared just as quickly.

So much had happened in the two years since he'd joined up, and at times he saw it all with great clarity. Sitting with a Flurient, watching the fireworks and hearing the excited shouts of the Sandrags mix with the boom of the explosions and the laughter of his teammates, he thought again of every step and turn. His path from the Citiburbs to the desert amazed him. And although when he thought of Dirndl he was sad, even that was okay. What was the use of having a memory if you only remembered the good bits?

He took a large swallow of Flurient, emptying his cup. In an instant, Saud was there at his elbow, swapping the drained cup for a full one.

The unit was moving to Dimanah. This was a good thing. They'd visited the teeming, festive city – alive with colour and the hubbub of the Sandrags' good-natured arguments with each other – before. The surrounding valley was as fertile as the town was lively, and the produce available enjoyed a wide reputation for excellence.

The Major Offensive tournament had been scheduled there in preparation for the annual Decisive Battle, also to be held in Dimanah. Many forces were marshalling, and the battles promised to be exciting and hard fought affairs. Necker's unit was in fine form and he personally was at the peak of his.

But he was also the only one of his little coterie left. Bloat had suffered a complete mental breakdown brought on by the unending heat, and had been sent home; Navel had been drafted as a coaching assistant for another team back in Rakem – his cheery good humour, natural loquacity and superb ball skills made him a natural for the job. Necker saw him occasionally, and when he did they shared many more Flurients than was appropriate for a senior athlete of Necker's standing. Luckily, Mandrill and Robe could overlook his indiscretions because

Necker had become so important, between his on field experience and his natural talent. Anyway, his nanostream would clear up any stray cannabis molecules left floating around in his system after these little binges. He looked forward to similar fun at Dimanah, where the redheaded joker would be based until the Decisive Battle.

Saud leapt up to gather their gear as soon as their transport landed, then rushed ahead to set up their quarters and locate the all-important wet mess. As the others made for the exit in their usual disciplined fashion, Necker looked out the door at the blazing tarmac, hoping that Navel would be there to greet him. He couldn't see the notable red hair anywhere until he got to the bottom of the stairs – and then he grew excited, missed the bottom step and pitched forward. His left knee crashed into the carbcrete apron, and his head whipped down so he smashed into the hard surface face first. He couldn't even put out a hand to break his fall.

He regained consciousness in a hospital bed, drowsy, woozy and unsure of where he might be. His face hurt and his head banged like one of the drums the Sandrags beat on the side-lines of a battle. Saud, who had been sitting meditatively in a chair by the bed, jumped up.

'Oh, sir, I am so sorry I was not there to catch you.' His voice exuded soothing sincerity, as did his self-deprecating smile, and Necker was comforted, as if by an unguent. But he couldn't understand a word the man was saying, and he looked at him dumbly.

'You fell from the transport, sir. Your face was lacerated, several of your teeth dislodged and your nose broken. These are now fixed, although there will be some residual bruising, and you will require a period of recovery.'

Necker put his hand to his face and felt the soft gauze covering his cheek. He nodded slowly but said nothing.

'There is another injury sir.' Saud cast his eyes down and

lowered his voice almost to a whisper. 'Your knee took your full weight as you fell, and although this damage too has been ameliorated, even your nanostream is not up to the task of fully repairing the insult to the bone, cartilage and ligaments in the knee. I am afraid you will never take the field of battle again.'

Necker continued to stare at Saud with minimal comprehension, not, this time, of the words themselves, but of the scope of the statement and its implications. Never take the field of battle again? How could this be? What would he do? Saud filled in the gaps for him.

'You're going home, sir.'

Necker smiled and gazed at his brown skinned friend, then sank back into his pillows. Going home!

The cure was speedy – just a few days as the nanobots rebuilt his broken bones, skin, and blood vessels. He'd never regain the range of mobility that he had had before, but he would be able to walk or even run without any trouble or sign of a limp. There would just be a period of rehabilitation, which Mandrill promised would be better taken care of at home.

Necker had little to do during those days in bed except contemplate the meaning of going home. He didn't have any idea what to expect. His parents would be virtual strangers, even more than they had been before he'd signed up. No doubt they would be polite, even pleasant. But he doubted they would be able to tear themselves away from their Cocoons long enough to get to know him. Well, he'd make them. He'd drag them out of their InterFace induced fog and make them listen, and talk.

Those blasted Cocoons! He hadn't thought about them for what seemed like forever, and now that he did he vowed that he would never get into one again. He'd be aware of what was really going on in his world, and not get sucked into the fantasy realm created by the InterFace and YouStar. He thought of all those hours – years really – lost lying on his back watching ordinary people living elaborately confected lives, only to disappear so they could sink back into comatose oblivion watching other ordinary people pretending to enjoy their briefly manufactured unreality. He would have no part of that.

Of course, if he could get onto YouStar, that would be different. What a story he'd have to tell then! He would make them all sit up and take notice. He may even use his YouStar Fame to shake up the whole world. But first things first. Just to go home and get his parents back. Not even back. Meet them for the first time, get them to take an interest in the world outside what they were being fed by the InterFace, get them to spread the news, dispel the apathy.

He wondered what Bock and Biz were doing. Bock was probably just another automaton by now, and Biz had gone into the Bastion, so he was part of the machine. Beyond reach. But he was sure he could wake up Bock. She'd be amazed at the change in him, and she would surely buy into his enthusiasm for living, not just watching. All he had to do was get her out of that fucking Cocoon. Who knows, with Biz off the scene, they might even hook up? He couldn't really remember her face but he knew that she was beautiful, and that the second he saw her he'd recognise her. At least he hoped he would. He drifted off, dreaming of himself with a faceless Bock on his arm, destroying Cocoons and liberating the Gobblers.

He woke up to find Saud shaking his shoulder with gentle insistence. 'Wake up, sir'. He opened his eyes to find the batman's big, black-brown orbs staring straight into them. There was a mild smell of onions and garlic on the Sandrag's breath and his bright white teeth were bared in a musty grin. 'It's time for you to go, sir.'

He handed Necker a cup of tea, and Necker sipped it with deep satisfaction. He would miss the tea. He wondered idly whether he could take Saud home with him. Although he took the Easterner's many services for granted, and had often treated him with a brusqueness bordering on disdain, he had, he told himself, developed an inordinate fondness for Saud. He assumed that the batman returned this affection, because never once had his smile faltered and never once had he failed in any one of those thousand little duties.

'It will be hard for me to get used to doing things for myself again, Saud.'

'I am sure it will not be a problem for you, sir,' replied Saud, with an expansive smile. His bristled face seemed a mile wide. He helped Necker out of bed, the latter putting his weight on his shattered knee with ginger apprehension; he was encouraged to find it reasonably sturdy. Saud held out Necker's pants so he could step into them, then held out his shirt so he could slide his arms into the sleeves. Then Necker sat on a chair and sipped his tea while Saud slipped on his socks and shoes, tying the laces with care.

The wounds on Necker's face had almost completely healed, and although he had only taken two steps from bed to chair, he was confident that he could walk without assistance when the time came.

Saud packed Necker's kit bag and hoisted it onto his shoulder. He held out a hand, grasping Necker's elbow to help lift him out of the chair. Necker took a few tentative steps: he was comfortably mobile.

'It's okay, Saud, I can walk without help'.

Saud's hand fell away from the elbow in an instant and he bowed slightly. 'As you wish, sir.'

He could not stop Saud helping him into the preon drive waiting for them outside the first aid post.

They drove to the airfield in silence, Saud beaming in the driver's seat the whole way. Necker assumed that the Sandrag's happiness was due to pride in having done a great job, and at being able to send him home almost unscathed.

At the airstrip, Saud drove onto the apron but straight past the Suborb, and stopped instead at a small structure hidden in the control tower's shadow. There were a few other soldiers lined up there.

'What's this?' Necker asked.

'Just a precaution sir. You need to have a delousing shower before you go home. There are all sorts of parasites here that cannot be allowed back into your country. Just step in there and shower, and then you'll be on your way. Be sure and remember which hook you hung your clothes on.'

Necker hugged the Sandrag warmly and joined the queue.

17.

Gneiss answered the door and was delighted, if surprised, to see who his visitor was.

'Biz!' He held out his hand, then used it to pull his old student into a bear hug before dragging him into the house, peering closely at his face as he did so. 'How are you? What brings you here? How have you been? What have you been doing?' He didn't let Biz answer any of his questions, instead leading him through the house and onto the deck in his backyard. He bade Biz sit down, then disappeared into the house to get a couple of Flurients, exclaiming all the while how thrilled he was to see his young friend.

'How long has it been? Too long,' he answered himself, without waiting for Biz. 'And look at you! All that time in the Bastion. You must be so sharp now. Smart, well-trained, a master of manipulation. It really is marvellous!'

Biz blushed. He hadn't expected Gneiss to be so effusive in his welcome. The teacher was staring at him with open curiosity, as if looking for some physical evidence of his Sharpness aside from his smart black Bastion suit. Biz had been indoctrinated in the need for absolute secrecy around everything to do with the Bastion, so he was wary of answering his teacher's rapid-fire questions, no matter how innocent they seemed. Fortunately, Gneiss had hardly paused to draw breath, and when he did he appeared content to just stare at the boy-wonder. Finally he seemed to relax, gave a short, satisfied sigh and said, 'So, tell me about yourself.'

'Nothing to tell, really. I work in the news department, I keep my head down and I have few other interests. They look after us well. It's really not so different from here.'

Gneiss guffawed. 'An entire city of Sharps, compared to this fleapit of Gobblers. 'It couldn't be any more different.'

Biz chuckled politely. 'I am surprised you remember me.'

'My only Leadership Gene student. How could I ever forget you? Besides,' he winked, with a cheeky, conspiratorial glint in his eye, 'you'd be surprised what I remember.'

He moved closer to Biz, reached out and touched the young man's arm, giving his bicep a little squeeze. He looked as if he wanted to run his hands gently over Biz's reddening face. Biz was embarrassed and suddenly quite shy.

'Your memory – it must be so full, yet so accessible. So…' he seemed lost for words, '…useful. And you, you must be so … passionate. So powerful. So deep.'

'Really, I'm not,' Biz said with affected humility. But his shining cheeks made it plain that he was proud.

'I know you can't tell me anything about the Bastion. But I would give anything to know. To see it with my own eyes. It must be magnificent.'

His old teacher might be fishing. 'Really, it's just a workplace. The facilities are nice, but for all of us there it's just about the work. My friends are just colleagues, really.'

'In such a place of burning ambition and hunger for power it must be hard to form true friendships. Frens, not friends.' Gneiss was decidedly unlike a Gobbler: he had a perspicacity that Biz hadn't noticed in the other people he'd encountered outside the Bastion. It was a little suspicious.

He excused himself and asked where the bathroom was, hoping to buy himself time to have a look around. The dual Cocoon in the living room was covered with dust and discarded clothes hung on it. That at least explained why Gneiss had not known that Biz was in town, or why. The bathroom, by contrast, looked normal. But why was the teacher so interested in him? Why ask him about his memory and his work? Why did this Gobbler have so many Sharp traits? Something was not adding up. He would have to probe his teacher's mind, find out where he got this unexpected acuity.

But then all thoughts were gone, and all of his own acuity deserted him: the front door opened and there stood Bock. As ethereally beautiful as the last time he saw her, as soft and lovely as ever. The years evaporated and he was her closest friend, again. His heart swelled. He loved her.

And then reality intruded. He was long gone from her life and, in all likelihood, long gone from her memory as well. It was not possible that she thought about him or missed him. She wore work clothes; she must be working for the InterFace, no doubt accumulating and categorising data about its users, or surveilling her friends and neighbours without knowing why or how the information she collected would be used, if at all.

'Biz!' The shock of seeing him was all over her face, but he could see that it was a pleasant surprise. Her smile was warm, her eyes dazzling and full of light. She dropped her bags on the Cocoon seat and rushed across the room. They embraced, and he smelled the past in her hair, and felt it as her body pressed against his. She could still wield power over him, Sharp or not.

'Fren!' she said in a strong, happy voice. 'What are you doing here?'

'I came to see Gneiss.' He took his face out from under the cascade of hair and scent. 'What are you doing here?'

'Oh, don't you know? Gneiss and I are together now. He probably should have told you.' She flushed pink and pulled away from him.

He had no right to feel affronted by her relationship with Gneiss, but he could barely disguise his dismay. She stepped back to the Cocoon to pick up the shopping, and he followed her into the kitchen.

She started to put the groceries away. 'After you left and Necker left, and I was dealing with a case of post YouStar depression, Gneiss was the only one I could turn to. You don't … you're okay with that aren't you, fren? I mean, you went off to the Bastion.'

He was as offhand as he could be, although his eyes, he knew, told a different story. 'Oh absolutely, yes. I – that is, it's a bit of an odd match, isn't it? He was our teacher for so long after all. But if you're happy…'

'You know he was so much more than a teacher.' She was surprisingly serious. 'He shaped our lives. Yours especially.'

'What do you mean by that?' He looked into her eyes; she avoided his, wiping up a speck of dust on the kitchen counter.

'Oh nothing. So where is the old man?'

'Out on the deck.'

She tossed her head and gestured at the InterFace logo on her blouse. 'Well, go out and join him, and I'll be out to have a Flurient with you just as soon as I change into something less official.'

Biz nodded and went back to the deck. As he sat down he said, 'Bock's home.'

'Excellent! We can have a nice chat and a few drinks. I'll get a couple of fresh ones.' Gneiss unravelled himself from his chair and got up to go in.

Biz leaned back in his chair and contemplated the afternoon. The sky was clear, deep blue and the sun was slowly falling towards the horizon. It had been a long time since he'd had Flurient – he was by then a committed scotch drinker – so he thought that he'd better take it easy if he was going to get any information out of Gneiss.

18.

Biz guessed that citiburbia hadn't changed much in hundreds of years. In this oxygen-rich environment – there were three oxygen vents visible from where he sat – the neighbours' gardens were filled with spindly, straggly plants, but those in Gneiss and Bock's back yard were lush. Biz wondered if Bock had some special gardening expertise, or Gneiss. It wouldn't surprise him if it was Gneiss, he was such a nurturer – and of course he'd been brought up working in horticulture.

The thought of Bock and Gneiss together troubled him. On an intellectual level, it didn't, or shouldn't have bothered him. After all, he had left to become a Sharp, so he had no reason to be angry or jealous. His bitterness was a throwback to the old Gobbler days, he told himself, and he would have to fight it. He would also try to ignore the feeling that Gneiss had somehow taken advantage of Bock's youth, vulnerability, and her natural affection for the man who had taught her practically everything she knew.

Gneiss and Bock emerged with fresh drinks. They were smiling and affable, but Biz could tell they were a bit on edge, too. Perhaps having a Sharp in their home, no matter who it might be, made them nervous. After all, Biz was from the seat of power, and they were just Gobblers. Not exactly average Gobblers, but Gobblers nonetheless. But they were Gobblers who didn't use their Cocoon at all – and so might they have avoided or reduced their vulnerability to the Bastion's power somehow? It was disconcerting how much more alert they seemed than any of the other Gobblers he'd met on his excursion. He considered how he might bring the subject of the unused Cocoon into the conversation, and possibly work around to their unexpected intelligence, without alarming them.

He also wondered how he might pretend to be cheerful when he was suffering at seeing them together. Their body language and the way they looked at each other were enough to tell him that their relationship was more mature than his own relationship with Bock had been, and that brought him lower. Bock's first question did nothing to lighten his mood.

'I sometimes wonder what became of Necker.' She smiled. 'Do you know when he might be coming home?'

'He's not coming home,' he said softly, sadly. He almost added, 'no one comes home,' but caught himself. Why did she have to ask that question? Even Necker's family would have forgotten about him by now. Why, how, did she and Gneiss have such long memories?

'That's awful,' Bock whispered.

Gneiss stepped in to change the subject. 'Biz has been telling me about the Bastion,' he grinned. 'He's in news.'

'How exciting,' Bock said, with no discernible excitement. 'I'm sure it's a hard job, but I know you'd do it well, my fren.' She looked at Biz with pride.

He just looked into his beverage, lifted it and took another sip. Better be careful, he told himself. But on the other hand he couldn't remember Flurient ever tasting so good. And it wasn't just that he had been used to teen-strength, rather than full-strength. It was easy to drink, smooth, and it warmed him somehow.

'I was just going to ask how you Sharps stay so sharp!' Gneiss said in a merry voice, while his eyes glowed.

Biz was startled: it was another unexpected question. 'What do you mean?'

'You know,' said Gneiss with a sly grin. 'Once upon a time

all Sharps were Gobblers just like the rest of us, but now look at you. You're as sharp as a knife. Much different to us.'

'It's the Leadership Gene,' said Biz stiffly. 'It manifests itself by the time the child is five to eight, and its influence on the brain physiology keeps increasing through adolescence and early adulthood, until the person is fully sharp. So, it seems like we're getting sharper until we get to a plateau at around twenty-five years of age.'

Gneiss laughed, shook his head and raised his glass to take a long swig. 'Come on, you don't really expect me to believe that, do you?' His voice was jolly, but the eyes that had sparkled with humour when he had asked the initial question were suddenly as hard as black diamonds.

'It's the truth,' Biz insisted.

'Honey,' Bock said, with a pointed stare at her partner, 'are you sure you want to be asking silly questions like that?'

'You're right, you're right.' Gneiss took another swallow. 'Let's talk about Necker.'

Bock rolled her eyes and drank. Biz took a gulp from his glass. No one spoke; everyone kept drinking. Eventually, to break the silence, and without knowing precisely why he said it, Biz blurted out, 'Actually, my progress at the Bastion is going more slowly than I or my boss would like. All my friends tell me that they feel sharper and sharper all the time, but I don't.'

The Flurient must have been getting to him.

'I feel the way I've always felt, or maybe a bit sharper – but really not as much as I thought I'd be by now.' He had been looking into his near-empty glass as he spoke; now he looked up at his astonished hosts. 'I am so sorry for blurting that out. The Flurient must be getting to me.'

Gneiss was still smiling, but he wasn't laughing. 'I can tell you why you feel that way. There are three reasons. The first is that you were never born to be a Sharp. You were a boy of average, perhaps slightly above average intelligence, but certainly not born for Sharpness. The second is that you've been slowly turned into a Sharp, in spite of your native intelligence, since you were a little boy. You don't feel very much different because I was giving you regular doses of carbon dioxide long before the government started dosing you with it and telling you that Leadership Gene therapy claptrap. Your friends have been getting exponentially Sharper since they went into the Bastion, because they've only just started getting the carbon. You have been getting only incrementally sharper, if that, because you were approaching your optimum sharpness, if I can put it that way, quite some time ago. The third is that your schooling is showing through. Shining through, I should say.'

Bock looked startled at Gneiss's candour, and Biz had the expression of a man whose head has just been taken to with a large hammer. Only Gneiss was enjoying himself. He pressed on.

'All of the lessons I taught all of your class, every year of your school life, they were aimed at you – specifically at you and only you. The rest of those kids could never learn anything other than the basics anyway. So, everything I taught, I taught to you. And to Bock, of course. She actually was born to be a Sharp, but I always thought she was too clever to end up in the Bastion. She was always going to remain an individual.' He burped and took another swallow.

'But Psyllium…' Biz began.

'Psyllium was fooled. He thought you had a Sharp mind trapped in a Gobbler's body, when in fact you were a Gobbler who'd been sharpened through the covert application of CO_2, so you passed his little tests.'

'But, but, but – what? How? Why? Are you joking?'

'I gave you Sharpness and I taught you conscience. I conditioned you because I need you to help me. I knew that one day you'd come back, or at least I was pretty sure you would, so I could explain it to you. Together we can give everyone the freedom you have. Sharpness. Carbon dioxide frees the mind.

It powers passion and it feeds memory. Oxygen makes us dim and easily enslaved.'

Biz was bewildered. It was all new but it was, he knew, all true.

Gneiss changed tack. 'How was your father when you saw him? Have a nice conversation?'

'Well no, he doesn't say much.'

'Does any adult you've met outside the Bastion ever say much? Do you ever get two words out of any Gobbler you meet, not that you'd meet too many in your line of work, of course? No. They don't understand conversation. They understand facile information in, pathetic criticisms and witticisms out, all mediated by a machine. They have no capacity for endurance in anything, no span of concentration, no thirst for knowledge or any idea what they might do with it if they had it. They're automatons. Now how do you think it is that you and me and Bock can enjoy such a robust and focused conversation? What makes us different?'

'You're Sharps?'

'We're Sharps, sure. But self-made Sharps. Well, I am. I gave Bock a helping hand. She's lucky that she found me when she did – after she left school and her CO_2 doses were cut off completely when she moved into the Fame House, her mind gradually began to decay. But when we got together, I helped her re-Sharpen herself, if you like. There are miniature CO_2 distillers all over this house. We reduce our oxygen intake, and increase our carbon dioxide levels.'

'Wait.' Biz was shaken, now he understood the implications of what he was hearing. 'How do you even know about carbon dioxide dosing? That's the most carefully guarded secret in the whole of government. And why – how did you make me a Sharp? Is that even possible? And if it was, why do it to me?'

Possibilities cannoned around his thoughts. The Flurient wasn't helping, but he was just addled enough to think that having a little more might help. He took a long swallow.

'I've known about CO² for a very long time,' Gneiss said. 'And I'm not the only one. Bock and I aren't the only ones,' he corrected himself. 'Almost as long as the government has been creating this artificial divide between the rulers and the ruled, there have been people on the wrong side of that divide whose goal is to remove it. Only when the people are as smart as their government and they have all the facts at their command can they make their choices.'

'But that's absurd,' Biz railed. 'People don't need to make choices, they need to be told what to do.'

'Spoken like a true ruler!' Gneiss was derisive but not rancorous: he still loved Biz like a son. 'But I disagree. I don't need or want to be told what to do. Bock shouldn't to be told what to do. We don't want to be distracted and diverted, to have our minds softened and our lives ruled. That's not freedom; that's bondage.

'Come on, Biz, think of what I taught you. Remember your history. Those people of the war centuries, they ended up sick and stupid and vicious and greedy, but at least they were free. They could make their own choices and plot their own futures. Sadly, when the CO² sickness overtook them, they made too many of the wrong choices, and they chose to give up their freedom. One by one they divested themselves of what they were told were frivolous liberties, in the name of gaining the only freedom they believed really mattered, freedom from fear. They found out the hard way that fear lives with you all your days. Something bad is always coming, even if it's only your own death.

'But there have always been pockets of people like Bock and me, who understand that freedom is not being secure and safe and coddled and protected, it's being able to make your own mistakes and take the beatings that fate administers. And when we rebel against the government and circumvent its instruments of control, we experience that real freedom. We're scared and we're exposed and vulnerable, but at least we're not hopeless automatons.

'Bock and I want to live in a world where everyone can make their own choices, but your government, through its control of communication, its use of Freedom and Fear as weapons, and most of all through its deliberate policy of making it physically impossible for Gobblers to match the intellects of their masters, is ensuring that that is impossible.'

'Shut up!' Biz stood up and waved his glass around, as if warding off a fly. 'Just shut up. Stop moralising and trying to bullshit me. You lied to me! You manipulated me!'

'Yeah, shocking, isn't it?' said Gneiss with a mocking grin. 'To gain true freedom, I – we – had to beat the government at its own game. And you're the unfortunate victim. The way I see it, if I'd left you a Gobbler when you were a child, you would have been lied to and manipulated by your government all your life and been none the wiser. At least this way you stood a chance of finding out the truth, which you are now doing. And now you have a chance to do something about it. Now you know how it feels to be lied to and manipulated, to have a course set for your life that you probably wouldn't have chosen yourself, and you can see how damaging it is. But you can fix it. You can fix it so no one ever has to live a life of ignorant bondage again.'

'Fuck 'em,' Biz growled, and collapsed back into his seat.

'Come on now, you don't mean that. I taught you better than that.'

'No, you didn't.' Biz wiped tears from his eyes. 'You made me into something that's nothing. I can't live the happy, stupid life of a Gobbler, and I'm not smart enough to be a proper Sharp.' It was all beginning to make sense: why Biz had struggled to be like his peers, and why his introduction to the Bastion hadn't resulted in a quantum leap in his abilities. But then, he'd been winning the struggle of late, hadn't he?

Knead had given him this delicate mission in the matter of his mother's death, and Biz had executed the assignment with assurance and authority. 'No, you didn't,' he said again, this time with ferocity. 'You made me a Sharp and a Sharp is what I am. Fuck you and your stupid plans. You know I could get you on the Freedom Ride tomorrow?'

Gneiss froze. He had counted on Biz reacting positively. He'd assumed that years of inculcating his own values into Biz would help the lad to see the wisdom of his actions, even if he regretted that they were necessary. 'Hold on a minute.' He took a quick glance at Bock – all through this she had been looking shocked and pained by turns, but now she was looking downright horrified. 'There's no need to be rash about this. At least let me tell you what we want to do, and then you can decide whether or not you want to be a part of it. I can't believe you would report us, even if you don't want to be involved.' He looked pointedly at Bock. 'That would mean the Freedom Ride for Bock too.'

Biz looked at her. He didn't want to send her to her death, of course; he wasn't even sure he wanted to send Gneiss to his. He was angry with him, more angry than he had ever been, and betrayed and lost and hurt. But he had loved his time in that classroom, and he loved the man himself. But he was furious – Gneiss had placed him in a dilemma. He had to betray someone: either his teacher and friend, or his mentor, Knead. Unless there was some third way, as a voice in the most devious recesses of his mind had started to whisper. He now possessed some very useful information, and if he played his cards right he could gain even more, and leverage it to his own advantage.

'All right. Talk to me.'

'We know we can change a person's local atmosphere, and the resulting chemistry then affects the brain functions. In your case, for instance, I slipped a tiny carbon dioxide air distillation unit into your Educoon. Twenty-four hours a day it collected CO_2 molecules, and then six hours a day, every day of your school life, it meted them out to you, pushing up the CO_2 content of the air you breathed. I had one, too, and so did Bock. I did this from your very first day of schooling, so from a very young age your brain chemistry was being altered. I also visited your home soon after your schooling began, and I put a distiller in your bedroom as well as one in your Cocoon.

'Psyllium believed that your unusual alertness, perception and sense of inquiry were natural, so the government installed that special air conditioner for you, which was not an air conditioner at all, but an extremely sophisticated CO_2 generator. They slipped another small distiller into your Cocoon, and in your Educoon, too. I can tell you, I was lucky they didn't find any of the distillers I'd installed!' He laughed.

Biz didn't see the humour; his face remained hard-set. The level of deception, from every side, was like a burden on his soul.

'Now!' Gneiss hunched forward. 'You're in the Bastion. Not only are you receiving precisely measured doses of carbon dioxide in the enclosed atmosphere there, they are in all likelihood delivering individually determined doses of oth-er atmospherics into your quarters and your workstation, to refine the balances and imbalances in your bloodstream and your brain. This fine tuning probably has something to do with the marginal improvement you've felt in your Sharpness, but the fact that you'd been receiving CO_2 for so long meant that your brain chemistry was more or less permanently altered before you even got there, whereas your peers had some plasticity left, and they felt the benefits of the change in atmo-sphere more than you did.'

Gneiss smiled helpfully, but Biz did not react.

Bock stood up and, without saying anything, collected the

empty glasses and took them into the kitchen. She hadn't said anything for a long while, but she had looked agitated ever since Gneiss had started speaking so frankly.

Gneiss acknowledged Bock as she took his glass, but kept talking with his eyes on Biz, who was listening quietly, not interrupting and not looking as threatening – or as threatened – as before. 'You've probably guessed already that even when it's carried out on a massive scale, like that of the Bastion, this management of the atmosphere is still just making localised adjustments to the composition of the air that the people in the vicinity are breathing. On a global scale, we are still mining carbon dioxide at a prodigious rate and still producing oxygen from the separation process. Most of that is getting pumped out in the citiburbs, through the bloody great vents you see everywhere. The net result is that your loyal subjects are actually getting more and more stupid.

'We are awash with oxygen and becoming more and more starved of carbon dioxide, and the only way to help the Gobblers rediscover their own minds is to stop and reverse the process. And that's where we need you. You have access to the greatest minds in the world today, the Prods who were taken from their parents in infancy, and sharpened and taught and trained and made to work. I'm sure they could find a way to give people back one important freedom – the freedom to think – by lowering oxygen and raising carbon dioxide levels on a global scale.'

'But you're asking me to change the very basis of our society. Even if there was a way, I couldn't do that.'

'Why not? That is exactly what our government has been doing for the last three hundred years. Robbing people of their freedom and making them more malleable by fixing it so that they think less, remember less, communicate less and even want less.'

'I happen to subscribe to the ancient view that governments are there to serve the people, not the other way around. I believe that people should be free to make their own mistakes, to be as foolish and as dangerous to themselves as they wish, as long as they respect the rights and safety of others. They should be able to communicate with one another as much as they wish, and on whatever subjects they wish.'

'But that's a recipe for chaos!'

Gneiss was warming to his subject. 'That, fren, is a recipe for freedom. Allowing people to have and use their own minds, and allowing them, no – *requiring* them – to make their own decisions, and giving them credit for their capacity to do so. And yes, freedom is at times chaotic, just as at times it's glorious, and confusing, and irritating, and frightening and demanding as well as liberating.'

'But they – the Gobblers,' Biz waved his arms wildly around him to indicate the great mass of passivity beyond Gneiss's walls 'they're not capable of making the right decisions.'

'Because you took their ability to do so away! People like you force-fed them oxygen, and drip fed them Fear and war, and started to offer them banal, forgettable stars. People like you restricted communication and hammered home to them that everything every one of them does is watched and analysed, and that any single act outside of the norm would be met with incarceration or death. And the Gobblers took that on board, and opted for dull conformity until it was bred into their children, who were even dimmer and less prone to episodes of independence, and bred other children who were even more so. So now you don't even need the surveillance and the control over communication, because none of them ever do anything worth watching.

'But still, Biz, they are people, not just oxygen Gobblers who are fodder for your wars and your dreams of power, and I want to help them remember that. I want them to demand the freedom they have always deserved, and if that makes it harder for your government, then fuck your government! In fact, I want these people,' he waved his arms around in the same way that Biz had just done, 'I want these people to tell the government what to do and when and how to do it, because that is the most important freedom of all – taking responsibility for your own destiny.'

Biz's mind was rebelling at Gneiss's terrifying words, but, at the same time, it was all ringing a bell. Gneiss had told him this over and over – not in these direct, seditious words of course, but in more subtle and encouraging terms that had made sense and had even been comforting – throughout his entire school life. All those years drilling into his class all that guff about integrity and honesty, and openness and transparency, without ever mentioning the government, as if those qualities were all about your personal life and not about politics at all. Biz had thought his teacher had been trying to mould his personality, to help him learn how to live the right way.

And he had been. But he had also been giving Biz an understanding of how the world should be run. No wonder he'd been so uncomfortable with the mechanics of Psyman and the deception of so many people on so many levels. His schooling had shown him that there was another, more honest way, and it began with trusting people to handle sometimes difficult information.

Of course, most of the population was so profoundly affected by oxygen overdose and carbon dioxide starvation that they couldn't, at present, be trusted. The only way to let them return to self-determination was to restore their mental capacity. To address the concentration of oxygen in the air they breathed, increase the CO_2 levels, and perhaps even add a few other Sharpening elements into the mix as well.

He needed time to think. 'I ought to be on my way back to the Bastion by now. I should go to a Message Centre and send a message to my supervisor to let him know I'll be delayed.' He was determined not to give away any of the emotions that were roiling within him.

'There's a station just down the street,' Gneiss said. 'It's only a couple hundred metres away. Why don't you walk down there and get a little fresh air.' He sneered.

Biz, in on the joke, smirked back. The citiburb air might help wear off the effects of the Flurient, and, ironically, help him think more clearly.

The second he was safely out of earshot, Bock exploded at Gneiss. 'Are you insane? You'll get us both killed!' She might not have believed that Biz would have them killed, but she was close to panic.

'It was the only way. If we're ever going to actually change the world, we need to trust him – and we need to trust ourselves too. And I trust the years of hard work that I put into making that boy who he is today.'

'He's been in the Bastion for two and a half years. He's obviously become a Sharp. Why would he jeopardise that to help us?'

'Because it's the right thing to do.' A smile played on Gneiss's lips.

'Did you not hear me? He's a Sharp. That's the last reason they ever have for doing anything. Jesus. We're dead.'

Gneiss laughed. 'Well, if it was you in the Bastion, I'd agree. But he's not as smart as you. He'll fall back on the years of training I gave him, you'll see.'

'You're not going to tell him about everyone, are you?'

'Well, I did tell him there are others. Knowing that it isn't just the three of us, that there are people relying on him, that he'll be a hero – that might help him make up his mind. I'm not about to name names.'

'Jesus. So, either we're free, or we're dead.'

19.

When Biz came back, he was much calmer and, Gneiss felt, more approachable. The three of them sat down to talk. They spoke about whether the people could cope with real freedom – the liberty to act as they wished – and whether they warranted it; whether they deserved to live, or *could* live, without constant surveillance; whether their lives would fall apart without rigid, enforced compliance. They agreed that, under current conditions, the populace was not intellectually equipped to handle self-determination; they disagreed as to whether or not they wanted it. Biz said that, as the people were under the impression that they were free, there was no need to disillusion them – it may even be dangerous.

Gneiss countered that regardless of whether or not people believed that they were free, their actions were those of the oppressed, and they recognised that even if they were unable to articulate it. Among other things, he said 'Psychologists established centuries ago that people will act differently if they are aware they are being observed. Like quantum particles, the act of observing them changes their character.

'Now, look at all the video cameras everywhere in our world. Camera trees on every street corner, hives of cameras in every levtrans, Message Centre and Cocoonery, not to mention the drones circling and hovering everywhere all the time. And consider communication. We can't communicate with each other except through official channels, and whatever messages we send or receive are monitored and dissected, analysed for the mildest sign of protest or dissent. We all know we are being watched, and any act that deviates from a strictly specified norm will be examined and may ultimately lead to our disappearance.

'Being so closely watched, knowing that our actions are so minutely examined, encourages us all to act small, even if we don't do it consciously. We avoid notice or scrutiny, and constantly work to prevent any scenario in which we are called upon to explain ourselves. Even the most thoughtless, heedless, torpid Gobbler knows this in their heart.

'They feel that lack of freedom and they know instinctively that they're trapped, that they are under someone else's control. This is where YouStar plays such an important role. It encourages Famers to larger acts than they would ever dream of doing in their real lives, to amplify everything they say and do – to make a caricature of themselves, in fact – because it's the one time they truly want to be watched. It acts as a kind of catharsis for them, even though they're not acting with true freedom, just a sad parody of it. The viewers get to pretend that their Fame House peers are larger than life, and so they must be, too. It presents a false mirror, and we all admire the distorted reflection we see there, even though we can't escape knowing that in truth it's a lie. Look at Joe.'

'He's revered. Adored,' Biz said.

'But only because he has to be. Because if anyone did not adore and revere him, their lack of reverence and adoration would render them suspect. Even if much of the general affection for Joe is genuine, it's just a habit formed through repetition, a toll paid because we know it's due and if we don't pay it, it isn't Joe who will suffer but us. If you were Joe, would you want that to be the basis of your authority and popularity? Respect that is at best automatic, and at worst earned by fear?'

'Power is power,' Biz said, with a hint of defensiveness.

'Is it? Is it?'

Biz's mind was churning and the turbulence was revealed on his face. The conflict between what Gneiss had taught him and what Knead and the Bastion demanded of him was agonising and, for the time being at least, unresolvable.

They broke for dinner, and, as they ate, indulged in the kind of inconsequential chat that eases the mind. They spoke of meals they had eaten, and recipes and tastes, remarked on the changing architecture and scapes of the citiburbs, derided the habits and foibles of the Gobblers, laughed at them, and even spoke of the bond that they shared, careful to skirt the question of Necker, while admitting that they were all special to each other.

Biz smiled politely and nodded when Gneiss and Bock described how they had come together, even though he suspected Gneiss of grooming Bock since she was a little girl, just as he'd been grooming Biz as a partner in revolution. At least he had waited until she was of an appropriate age before seducing her – that is, Biz hoped he had. All of this, of course, he kept to himself.

After dinner, they repaired to the deck and took up glasses of Flurient again. Biz was much less tense now; they all were. It was all out in the open, and they were quickly learning to live with it. It's enormously human, that ability to adapt, thought Biz.

He told himself, again, that he was fine with Bock and Gneiss being in a relationship. She did with Gneiss many of the things that she had done with Biz, pushing away a lock of his unruly hair, laying her hand on his thigh when referring to him, and looking surreptitiously for his approval when telling anecdotes that involved him. She was, if anything, even more beautiful than when they had been together. There was a maturity and a sense of wisdom behind her beauty now. Gneiss had given her that, and, for that, maybe he deserved her love.

As to the business of Gneiss's master-plan to change the world, his mind was not yet made up. It appealed to his ingrained sense of justice, the sense that Gneiss had driven into him. And the idea of being the agent of such fundamental change flattered his ego. But it was dangerous, clearly, mortally so. And more than likely the plan was doomed to catastrophic failure: he would be found out, they would take the Freedom Ride, and they would not even make the news.

He thought of Viand and Arbeit, living out their lives in a dreary haze of YouStar, responding like good laboratory rats to the Psyman and Psymorph they didn't even know they were being subjected to. Two people who barely knew each other, who had joined together in the absence of a better idea, and produced a son who, in turn, they hardly knew. There was a world of people like his parents out there: didn't they deserve to be released from their Cocoons? To be given the tools to make their lives their own, not just a shadow of an ideal planned by a master manipulator deep inside a cloistered elite? Weren't they being denied a genuine right?

But did it really fall to him to restore that right? Would they care if he did? In any case, how could he make it happen? He was hardly in a position to craft tiny policy redirections, let alone induce revolution. Neither, he was certain, could he trust any of his colleagues enough to share the idea with them, let alone enrol them in any direct action. Globe would probably think he had fallen under some enemy spell and expose him. Lintel hated Gobblers. Bias was so wrapped up in YouStar that she would not be interested; she might even see him as trying to destroy her life's work, and expose him on that basis.

Right now, he did not have to make any firm decisions, except whether he would betray his friends – and, sitting on the deck, beverage in hand and starry skies stretched out overhead, he assured them he would not.

'I will never give the two of you away.'

Gneiss raised his glass to his former student, Bock to her former best friend. She looked at Biz, her eyes glittering in the darkness with relief and gratitude. She had never been more beautiful.

The conversation resumed, this time in much more modulated tones, without interjections or exclamations. Rather, Gneiss delivered a narrative, in a low voice, punctuated only by intermittent questions from Biz and irregular asides from Bock, correcting or clarifying some detail.

'You may recall that, a long time ago when you were at school, I mentioned that my father was a greenhouse gardener, and how much I loved helping him,' Gneiss began. 'What I didn't tell you was that all those days in the greenhouse, and all those nights sleeping in there, changed the way my mind worked. I came under the influence of carbon dioxide, and I became a lot sharper than my fellow Gobblers. It wasn't until I was no longer able to spend time in the greenhouse, and I could almost feel my awareness slipping away from me that I realised there must have been something in the environment that was helping me. It didn't take long to work out what it was. So, I started visiting my father at work again, and took to stealing CO_2 distillers. I pretended to help him by inspecting the distillers, and telling him every now and then that one appeared to be broken and removing it. I put them in my own house, and then in my Educoon at teacher training, and later, when I started teaching your class, at my own desk. I became a Sharp. So, I realised, all the Sharps in the Bastion had to be taking carbon dioxide as well.'

Gneiss's story seemed fantastic, but to Biz it also rang true. The teacher had stumbled on the secret and turned it to his own advantage.

'I decided that I had an opportunity to right the wrong that has been perpetrated on people for the last three centuries or more, and I worked out a way to do it. Slowly, carefully, I targeted people around me, and I recruited them into a group I call Gardeners. It sounds so benign, doesn't it?' He smiled.

'Our actions have always been small and localised, on a very low scale, as anything else would attract attention. My fellow Gardeners and I identify potential new members, often just by the way they look, the fact that they work or live near a Gardener, or because they're acquainted with one. Ease of access and trust are the critical factors. We put them on a list, then covertly fit their Cocoon and bedroom, and if possible their workstation with a tiny CO_2 distiller.

'Most times we can only get at one or two of these locations, but that's usually enough to start the long, slow process of changing their brain chemistry. The Gardener-mentor who identified the candidate monitors them for changes in personality, increased perceptiveness, more questioning, and improved memory. When the time is right, the target is very gently introduced to our ideas, and we explain the reasons for the changes they've been noticing. Most of them have already realised that something was happening, and are relieved to discover the source of the changes and excited to hear that others have undergone the same transformation.' He paused and took a very small sip of Flurient; he saw that Biz's eyes were shining with Flurient-inspired openness, and his mind working on wild possibilities.

'Only one or two have rejected the change and demanded to be given back their blissful ignorance. Only one got really angry and suggested that he would be taking the story to the Liberty Guard. I want to be honest, here: we regretfully gave him an overdose of carbon dioxide. But normally it is, as I say, a very slow and stealthy process. It takes a good deal of patience, observation, subtlety and management, but it's working.'

Gneiss went on to describe the group's activities and plans. Their number was growing, but few were up for direct action of the kind that Gneiss and Bock and a small core engaged in, CO$_2$ planting. This involved gathering numerous small cylinders filled with compressed carbon dioxide and releasing the gas in public spaces. Gneiss cheerfully admitted that this had no other result than to perhaps give those unfortunate enough to be in those spaces a mild headache, and they had never met anyone who had enjoyed even a moment or two of clarity from a planting. But it made them feel like revolutionaries, it gave them a sense of purpose and shared responsibility, and it was exciting because it was dangerous and seditious. He and Bock both laughed about it, and Biz tried to share in their mischievous merriment.

'But I don't understand. How do you communicate? Every public communication goes through the InterFace, and every private communication has to be transcribed and transmitted at an official message station. There are algorithms to detect even the most sophisticated of codes, and everyone is under surveillance all the time. It just doesn't seem possible.'

Gneiss laughed again. 'Don't forget, the surveillance is being carried out by Gobblers – thousands of them watching and documenting, but not really knowing or caring what they're looking at, overseen by supervisors who are also Gobblers, and who expect the populace to behave with propriety. Of course, there are computers and some Sharps watching as well, so we are careful not to fall into any patterns that would arouse suspicion.

'As for communication, we do it in a way you'd never suspect. We talk to each other. And if we must, we use paper. We handwrite notes to one another. It's so archaic, it doesn't occur to the powers-that-be that it could be happening. The greatest difficulty is in finding pens and pencils, but that's where being a school teacher helps.'

This time, Biz shared in the conspiratorial laughter, and was amused to see Gneiss clapping his hands together with smug satisfaction. 'What about when you go planting?' he asked. 'Passing notes is difficult enough, let alone smuggling cylinders of gas.'

'Well for a start, a reasonably small cylinder can hold quite a number of carbon dioxide molecules, and we don't place the cylinders all at once. We do it piecemeal, over a period of days or even weeks, and they're equipped with timers set to release the gas over a period of about half an hour on the nominated day.

'The trick is to get the cylinders and fill them with CO_2, and that's another instance in which being a teacher comes in handy. There are other teachers involved, and quite a number of real greenhouse gardeners – we need them, so we have targeted as many of them as we can, and most of them have long loved their CO_2 environments without knowing why. So, we slowly accumulate cylinders until we have enough. When it comes time to place them, we use the blind spots in the camera matrices, which we've mapped – there are not many of them, but enough. We are also very quick and professional in place-ment, as we are in passing notes. Some of us have been doing this for a very long time.

'Of course, sometimes a Gardener is caught placing a CO_2 distiller or carrying a cylinder, but again, even when it's the Liberty Guard we're dealing with Gobblers who can be fobbed off easily enough in most cases. When that's not possible, well… We have weapons of our own. The disappearance of a Liberty Guard or security officer never makes the InterFace, funnily enough.'

Biz nodded. He had heard reports of Liberty Guards mysteriously disappearing, and knew that they were never made public. These events were apparently isolated, so there was little consternation in the Bastion; most people put them down to excessive Flurient intake, or Gobblers taking exception to being stopped and questioned by another Gobbler.

Gneiss didn't know why, but he was glad that Biz hadn't reacted to the mention of murder. 'Although everything done in public is recorded, including conversations, there are places, like busy offices and levtrans buses, where audio is recorded in low fidelity, so computers can't disentangle the voices or reconstruct individual speech patterns.

'We can have quite a lengthy four-way conversation on a packed levtrans, for instance. In fact, we can do that almost anywhere. It's mostly a matter of speaking quietly, with minimal mouth movement, and appearing to ignore the person you're talking to, or maybe bumping into them as the transport turns or stops.'

Biz was shocked but also, if grudgingly, admiring. That such an evolved organisation could exist and grow without raising even the slightest suspicion among his colleagues defied belief. It almost made him believe that he could take part in this tiny revolution and not just survive, but succeed. Then again, if the organisation ever became a genuine threat, it surely would come to the attention of the security Sharps.

By the end of the conversation, Biz at least acted as though he was convinced of the need for the Gardeners. He might even have thrown in his lot with them. He was not entirely convinced, of course, and certainly not as convinced as he appeared, but he didn't want to debate the matter anymore – he needed their trust, and he needed time to think.

He left them in the wee small hours of the morning, with great reluctance and an ostentatious show of emotion and fealty. He aimed his vehicle at the Bastion and put it on autodrive. As it sped across the landscape, his mind buzzed with new information, ideas and plans. He'd left Bock and Gneiss with no promises except that he would think about what he had been told, consider how he might help them should he choose to do so, and that he would not tell any of his colleagues about the Gardeners. He also told them not to expect anything to happen any time soon. If it happened at all, it would take a great deal of time and planning.

'I can wait,' said Gneiss. 'I've been working at this for almost twenty years now, a couple more won't hurt.'

20.

Biz arrived back at the Bastion just after dawn, giving him time for only a couple of hours' sleep before he showered, dressed and reported to his workstation. A large pile of work awaited him, which was to be expected – with each passing month more and more work seemed to be coming his way. He found this encouraging, as it signalled appreciation of his abilities. *Gobbler indeed!* he said to himself as he plunged into the pile.

An hour or so later Knead, who usually burst into Biz's space, materialised beside his pupil with slinky suddenness.

'Welcome back fren,' he said briskly. 'What caused your delay? Not trouble with Arbeit I hope?' His concern appeared genuine.

'No, no, not at all.' Biz looked his leader in the eye. Confidence and clarity would be his allies here. 'I was just visiting an old friend and my former teacher.'

'Oh. Good.' Knead was aware of Biz's movements, of course, and had assumed his young Psyman had been engaged in some physical assignation. 'Well, congratulations on the work you did there. I particularly liked the mention of keeping images. Very timely and appropriate. It's always good to introduce or reinforce a prohibition when you address the populace.'

'You approved it before I delivered it.'

'True, but I didn't realise just how powerful it would be as a live Face-cast.'

'Thank you.' Biz was surprised at Knead's effusiveness. 'It did make me think, though,' he said tentatively, 'it's perfectly reasonable for there to be a restriction on Gobblers having, making or keeping images, but why does that apply to us?'

'How do you mean? You're not thinking of keeping an image of Viand, are you?' Knead tilted his head and smirked. 'Or the girl? This old friend?'

'Good god, no. I don't mean individuals keeping mementos, but we Bastionados using images as tools. Specifically, I think it would help to have images of Joe in the citiburbs. There are so many blank walls and spaces. Posters of Joe would add some colour, and they'd help build Joe's cult of personality. It's been done before, you know.'

'Oh, I know,' Knead said. 'And I'm impressed that you do too. You've obviously done your research. But the answer is no. In part because the mere existence of such things, and the technology to produce them, might inspire the Gobblers to emulate our approach by producing images of their own that don't depict Joe, or worse, show him in an unflattering light or situation. It would be the thin edge of the wedge, as they say. People are used to seeing blank walls now, and nobody has seen a still image of any kind for hundreds of years. To break out of that discipline now would be to court disaster.

'The other reason is that Joe himself is, alas, not eternal. Every now and again, Joe dies and a new Joe takes his place. We choose a younger man and we make him up to look like the old Joe. Over a period of a couple of years, we reduce the make-up so that the old Joe slowly morphs into the new, younger Joe. Even the most astute Gobblers doesn't notice the difference, and the new Joe lasts, with care, another forty years. To have pictures of him around the place would queer that process, and perhaps get the populace thinking. Especially now, given that Joe is no longer a young man. Even if he lives for a few more years, he's getting a little doddery, so we might not be able to trust him in front of the cameras. What happens if we have to rush a new Joe into the process, but your posters of the old Joe are still on the walls? The Gobblers would lose confidence in Joe. They'd work out that he was ill or dead. And that would lead to instability.'

It was confronting for Biz to hear Knead speak this way. He was no different to anyone else: he had been devoted to Joe since he'd first recited the creed, *'Our Father of Freedom is Joe, Joe tells us all we need to know.'* He'd never met the leader, and had seen him only for fleeting moments at the Bastion, but he felt as though he knew him. Every important announcement he had ever seen had been Joe-cast. To hear him spoken of as doddery, as replaceable, like some kind of commodity – it was very difficult. At the same time, he was happy, because the conversation showed how much confidence Knead had in him.

But later, when he replayed the conversation in his mind, it just fed into his growing sense of cynicism and ambition. On the drive back to the Bastion from Gneiss and Bock's, he'd decided that he would overcome his natural shortcomings and become the greatest and most acute Sharp ever. Even if he lacked the native intelligence, he had cunning, born of the lazy Gobbler's desire to find the easy way out of anything, and most of his peers in the Bastion lacked that. And now he also possessed an inner anger, almost a hate, at the way he had been manipulated. That drove him to want to conquer them all, Gobblers and Sharps alike. Never again would he be the puppet, he would be the master. He knew how he had to act, and he knew that even if he didn't share their gifts he could play the part so well that no one would ever consider him anything but a natural born Sharp. And a finely honed one at that.

He attacked his work with renewed vigour. Time passed quickly, he grew into his role further, and his confidence continued to develop and blossom. At the weekly gatherings, he made a point of saying that he felt sharper all the time, and his work bore out his claims. He was now a master Psyman, using his insight into the Gobbler psyche to craft spin of increasing delicacy and refinement, layering every communication with different strata of deceptive and coercive control.

Where, once upon a time, the conscience and integrity that Gneiss had drilled into him was a prickly obstacle to his work, now he could turn it to his own purposes. In any situation, he would assess what the right thing to do would be – and then do the opposite. He didn't struggle with that ingrained morality; he used it to his own advantage, grew detached from it, and in so doing, corrupted it. When he became troubled, when his conscience pricked at him, he told himself that he was only doing what had to be done to achieve a higher purpose.

At the back of his mind, he kept a hidden compartment where he stored Gneiss and Bock's words and the implications of what he'd been told. Since that night, he'd been able to see with increasing clarity just how shamelessly the people were being oppressed, and just how shallow and empty his words were – even as he spewed them out in ever greater volume and made them ever more nuanced. And he kept spewing them, but now that he knew, with terrible exactitude, what he was doing, how he was doing it and the effect it was having, he enjoyed it more than ever. He wielded this raw power with pleasure.

He also started to spend more and more time with Globe. They grew closer, they collaborated, and occasionally slept together, though usually in an impersonal way. He also started to visit Particle again. It helped pass the non-working hours, and gave him an opportunity to covertly extract more information about the atmosphere. The scientist, naively imagining that Biz's questions were due to his admirable natural curiosity, was only too happy to answer.

'It's very simple,' he said. 'The chemical composition of the atmosphere is made up of many different molecules, which are drawn into your lungs and enter your bloodstream in the same way as oxygen. These elements are then distributed throughout the body by the blood, and some naturally end up in the brain. The operations of certain centres in the brain are affected – a little, a lot or catastrophically – depending on the elements involved, their concentrations and the activity they modify.

'The levels of certain gases such as nitrogen, ozone, carbon monoxide and carbon dioxide, ammonia and sulphur, and metals such as zinc, iron, lead and so on, can impact the individual's motivation, concentration, memory and communication skills over the short or long term. The operations of the senses can also be enhanced or impaired. In all of these cases, and again depending on the elements involved, the proportions of them and the physical characteristics of the individual, the effects can be positive, negative or, as I say, catastrophic. It's obvious that too much lead or sulphur in the atmosphere leads to poisoning, but even oxygen, the most critical constituent of the air we breathe, can be incapacitating or deadly in the right doses.'

'So, it isn't just oxygen and carbon dioxide that matter?'

'Oh no, not at all,' Particle chuckled. 'Of course, the levels of those things are crucial to one's health and well-being, and an excess of either or both can have a major impact on your psychopharmacology. But everything matters.'

'Everything?'

'Yes, it's very sophisticated. For instance, we work to create an optimum composition for the Bastion's *general* atmosphere, but we also finely control every Bastionado's local environment. We create whatever local atmospheric composition we want to.'

'How does that work?' Biz was genuinely absorbed, and Particle was thrilled to have an audience eager to learn about the intricacies of his scientific work.

'It's fascinating!' He was practically gushing now in response to Biz's enthusiasm. 'We've looked into the make-up of the atmosphere at various times and various locations across the centuries. It's easy enough to do – we find items the manufacture of which we can reliably date and locate, and examine the air trapped within them. It could be anything – a ceramic made by Wedgwood in the English Midlands in the 1760s, a machine to toast bread made in Berlin in the 1930s, a radiation monitor from Japan in the early twenty-first century, a recepta from your own home in 2305, and so on. We investigate the sociological, psychological, environmental and physical profiles of the population inhabiting that time and location, and draw correlations with the molecular composition of the air.

'We know, of course, that around the time of the Turning, people were sickening from their atmosphere. It was poisoning their bodies, their minds were rotten and their hearts were hard, and all they wanted was money and things and fighting. It was an almost global phenomenon, although it was more pronounced in the great cities. And when you examine what they were breathing in and out, it's no wonder. There was a near-lethal combination of carbon dioxide, methane from the millions of tonnes of excrement from the billions of people and their bovine and ovine agricultural resources, and lithium, which they used to make and power the electronic devices they were convinced they needed. Almost everything they inhaled made them sick, unhappy and angry.

'Likewise, the air from, say, London in 1798 is to be avoided. It was thick and groggy with sulphur dioxide, nitrogen oxides, heavy metals and nasty particulate matter, and it produced lugubrious people. It not only darkened the skies, it darkened the lives of the people living in it, dulling their senses of compassion and empathy so they had no moral qualms about pressing children into hard, dangerous labour, throwing the poor into debtors' prisons, and punishing even the most trivial of offences with death or exile.

'I mentioned Berlin – the atmosphere in that city from 1936 to 1939 in particular was laden with a range of chemicals that compelled people to focus on just a few ideas, discouraged independent thought and fostered an industrious collective work ethic. We've used that combination with some success, but it has the nasty side-effect of making many of the individuals exposed to it suspicious to the point of paranoia, and inflating the egos and ambitions of others. Some suffered bouts of extreme violence, while others become automatons. So we have to be careful who we give that one to, and for how long.' They shared a cheeky chuckle.

'It's clear,' Particle continued, 'that in the last five hundred years or so, the greatest period in terms of atmospheric quality was a short time in the 1960s. The hideous assortment of very dangerous chemicals spewed into the air by the two world wars that dominated the twentieth century up until then, and the radioactive particles emitted by nuclear weapons discharged during and after the second world war, was finally beginning to reduce. Meanwhile, the world population was still small enough to limit the volume and variety of chemicals being pushed out by human activities.

'Sadly, this brief period of real quality in breathable air was short-lived. Soon enough people started to pollute the atmosphere again, particularly with carbon dioxide, and that finally poisoned the people. But for that fleeting, shining moment, the air was conducive to discovery, hope, optimism and cooperation, among other things. My personal favourite is the air from San Francisco, 1968.' He drew a deep, satisfied breath and said 'haaaaa' as he exhaled. 'It is a heady mixture that leads one to ask questions, to probe authority and to contemplate change. It stimulates activity in the parts of the brain that awaken inquiry and promote introspection.'

He was carried away by his devotion to this apparently heavenly air, but he at last opened his eyes, noticed Biz looking at him oddly, and continued in a more businesslike manner.

'There is actually a goodly percentage of that San Francisco air in the personal mix piping into your quarters and your workstation right now. However, we temper the anti-authoritarian side of it with air from Sydney, Australia in 1954. That mix opens the centres in your mind that make you determined but polite, conservative and hard-working. Don't want you turning into a hippy now, do we?'

'Do me a favour,' Biz said, suddenly inspired. 'Add some Washington DC, 1972 into my mix. I think I need more ambition.'

'Sounds like you already have quite enough,' Particle smiled, 'but I'll see what I can do.'

As if the thought had just struck him, and as offhandedly as he could, Biz asked, 'What if we wanted to recreate that atmosphere of San Francisco in '68 on a global scale?'

'Well, there is no way we would ever do that. Joe would never allow the Gobblers to attain that much attentiveness, inquisitiveness or independence of thought, although it would be nice to inject a little more of the energy of that time into their lives.'

'God, can you imagine it?' Biz said, with an exaggerated shudder. 'But what if, say, oxygen levels got too high and even the smartest Gobbler was just too stupid or uninterested, and we decided we needed to rein it back?'

'Interesting problem.' Particle pondered for a short while before making his answer. 'But a relatively simple solution. In the first instance, we could simply stop venting vast quantities of oxygen into the citiburbs and that would help immediately. Over the longer term, we could start making combustion engine machines and either dig up the remaining hydro-carbons and burn them, or make our own and burn them. In one and the same action we would use up oxygen and produce carbon dioxide. It wouldn't be an instant solution by any means, but then nothing that involves an entire continent's air quality ever is. However, it would no doubt be effective in the long term. Depending on the rate of burning, we could accomplish the beginnings of a major shift in as little as a generation.'

'Wouldn't we run the risk of becoming half-crazed like the people of the war centuries?' Biz's eyes had begun to shine.

'Heavens, no. Even when they knew that burning fossil fuels and so on at a furious rate was causing major environmental problems, they not only refused to reduce the rate at which they burned, they accelerated the process. They knew that the methane and heavy metals and other toxins that they were billowing into the atmosphere were killing them, their children and the planet, but they kept on with it.' He shook his head in disbelief. 'But I suppose they were insane. We, on the other hand, would not only strictly monitor and control the process, we would build our machines to generate only those elements we wish to release into the atmosphere, in the correct proportions. Ours would be a rigid, scientific approach. I guess if there is any defending what the people of the war centuries did, we might say that they felt they had to do it to sustain their lifestyles, psychotic and unsustainable as they were. Whereas we would be doing it because of the effects, not in spite of them.'

Being careful not to appear fixated on the subject, Biz changed it, and left a short while later. Whenever he dropped in on Particle, they enjoyed wide-ranging conversations, and Biz was prudent enough not to discuss the issue of atmospheric control on every visit, or even every second or third. Given that the subject was Particle's specialty, however, and given that Particle knew how interested his friend was, the scientist himself often brought it up. Biz learned much, and thought more.

One morning, while Biz was sorting through battle reports and looking for ways to increase the Fear content in an encounter that had actually resulted in a convincing victory, Knead summoned him. Most of the time, he left Biz alone to carry out his assignments, and the two only met at the weekly gatherings or if Biz went to his boss for advice or assistance. Although it was unusual, Biz didn't think he had anything to worry about: his work was of a high standard and his liaison with Globe was discreet. Such associations were not frowned upon in general unless or until they went bad and one of the partners' work deteriorated. But Biz and Globe were going strong.

Walking along the long, black corridors to Knead's office, he tried not to be nervous. Surely his conversations with Particle had not come under scrutiny? He had approached them with exceptional discretion and, as a senior Psyman, he was perfectly entitled to see and talk to whomever he wished. It was possible that Particle had detected a pattern in their discourse and reported concerns to Knead, but it was doubtful. For a start, Particle was a scientist, and his interest and skill in reading and interpreting the motives and agendas of people were negligible. Besides, he enjoyed the conversations and would never take steps to put an end to them, would he?

There was one last, terrifying possibility – that Gneiss or Bock may have been caught carrying out a Gardener mission, and mentioned his name. He tried to dismiss the thought, but the more he tried, the more it swirled around in his mind.

Thank god that, when Biz entered his office, Knead looked up and smiled. Grinned, actually. The meeting was obviously not to discuss a problem.

'I have a problem,' Knead said, sardonically but amicably.

'That's terrible, sir.'

'Yes, awful. My problem is that I am to lead Joe's Cabinet.' Knead could barely contain his glee. He had long been Minister of Psyman, but to lead the Cabinet was a great honour. Cabinet members were perhaps the only people who had influence over Joe, so they were by far the most powerful people in the government. It was said that if they all worked together they could even change Joe's mind. To be acknowledged as leader of the group made Knead almost as powerful as Joe himself.

'I see. That is a huge problem,' Biz said, beaming. 'A great responsibility. But I am sure you will take it in your stride.' They were easy with each other now, more colleagues than superior and subordinate, although Biz knew his place in the hierarchy and would not step out of line.

'I hope you're right, fren. But I can't take on that mighty task and retain my present commitments. The problem that vexes me most is selecting my replacement as Minister of Psyman.' A pleasant light danced in Knead's eyes, and his lip curled as it did when he was toying with someone. 'I need someone with all-round skills, a good grasp of subtlety and the hunter's instinct. Someone who knows what has to be done and is prepared to do it. Know anyone who fits the bill?'

Biz thought he knew where this was going, but played the game anyway. 'Well, what about Gamma?' He was the oldest member of the team and perhaps the natural successor. 'He is a fine practitioner and a genuinely nice fellow. And of course, Glaive is as sharp as anyone on the team – '

'Not Globe?' Knead interrupted.

Biz was thrown. 'Um, er, she's a great operator in Conflict Spin, to be sure, and she loves it. I'm just not sure her, um, sphere of experience, or perhaps her interest in things outside of Spin Conflict is – '

'Correct answer.' Knead laughed. 'You didn't talk her up, you didn't do the gentlemanly thing and sacrifice your own ambition to secure the post for her, or because you thought that was what I wanted. You damned her with faint praise, which I like in a leader, and you were accurate in your appraisal of her abilities. I'd say that makes you the prime candidate for the job. What do you say to that?'

Biz tried to quell his elation, and wore as serious an expression as he could.

'To be quite honest, fren,' he ventured, with calculated familiarity, 'I think that is the most appropriate choice. I mean, certainly, others have their outstanding qualities. Bias, for instance, has a deep understanding of the population through her work on YouStar – '

'You're babbling, man,' Knead said, showing his straight white teeth in another broad grin. He still enjoyed needling Biz when the opportunity arose. 'Do you want the job or not?'

'Of course! Yes, sir, I do, thank you. Excellent choice, sir.'

Knead circled his wide carborundum desk, and shook his replacement's hand with vigour. The transition was swift. Just a couple of days later, Biz was behind the desk himself.

<h1 style="text-align:center">22.</h1>

Following a brief period of coolness between them based on Globe's assessment that it wouldn't be right for her to be fucking the boss, Biz and Globe resumed their close working relationship. This was a necessity, given his position and hers, although Biz didn't see as much of her as he would have liked, thanks to a wider range of responsibilities and a new stable of subordinates to manage. They also resumed their social relationship, and she would often come to him with ideas, concerns or problems.

'Fucking Gobblers,' she raged as she entered his office. 'I've got a report here about some moron trying to build a barbecue or something, and getting killed when the gas cylinder blew up.'

'Oh?' Biz was tickled by Globe's no-nonsense delivery and use of profanity. It was a vivid contrast to her usual diffidence and propriety, and made her seem more human. He could say that about very few people in the Bastion.

'So, I'm thinking of spinning it up into a homegrown terrorist story. You know, Sandrag sympathiser plotting mass murder in the homeland gets what's coming to 'em when their bomb goes off prematurely, that sort of thing.'

'Sounds plausible. Let's have a look.'

Globe gave Biz her InterTab and he started to read. In an instant, the smile vanished from his lips. The blood deserted his face, and felt as though it had left his whole body. It was Bock. She was dead.

'I'll take care of this myself,' he said, maintaining a semblance of composure with some difficulty. 'You can go.'

Globe's look was uncertain, but she knew better than to argue, and left the room quietly, wondering why the hell that story had made Biz so pale.

After she left, Biz let his head crash down on his desk. He didn't need permission, but he sent a message to Knead and the rest of the Cabinet that he was required at home and would be back within a week, perhaps less. He made all the necessary arrangements, including asking Gamma to step in as Acting Director, then signed out a preon drive and sped to the last place he'd seen Bock alive – Gneiss's home.

His old teacher was alone in the quiet house, grieving in dark silence. Tears stained his face and wet his beard. The two embraced.

'Thanks for coming,' Gneiss whispered.

'I had to. She was precious to me. Tell me what happened.'

'It's my fault.' Gneiss was adding unnecessary drama to an already emotional situation. 'If she hadn't been working alone on a Gardener planting, this never would have happened.'

'Just tell me what happened,' Biz repeated, desperate to know about Bock's last minutes.

'There's a storeroom at the school where we keep the large gas cylinders when they're ready for refilling – carbon dioxide, nitrous oxide, methane, natural gas and so on. The school is allowed a certain amount of each gas every year and we have to give back any empty cylinders when we take delivery of the new full ones, but until then we can use the empties.

'We accumulate CO_2 in small cylinders, then take them to school and transfer the gas into the larger cylinders. That way the Gardeners only need to carry one small, full cylinder with them at a time. We had an operation coming up, and Bock was in the storeroom transferring CO_2 from the larger cylinders back into empty, smaller ones that we'd collected and were going to use for the planting. It's not exactly clear how, but we know what happened – the valve on the smaller cylinder was either faulty or improperly secured, or maybe Bock just overfilled it. The valve blew off the cylinder and hit her. Her skull was shattered. It's likely she was dead before she hit the ground.' Gneiss's voice broke and he sobbed into his crossed arms.

Biz was grief-struck too, and didn't know how or whether to comfort Gneiss. Instead, he sat, absorbing his own anguish, while the older man cried.

After a while Gneiss composed himself, although his voice was still shaky and hesitant. 'I knew Bock was down there, and when she didn't show up at home I went looking for her. She was just – lying there. I don't know, I brought her body and the cylinder, a fucking barbecue gas cylinder, I took them home. Then – I don't know how, I don't remember – but I staggered to the Message Centre and sent a message for emergency services. The fact that I was covered in blood at least meant I went to the front of the queue.' He managed a weak smile.

'The emergency team didn't even ask how I found Bock, or where the cylinder was or what she was doing – they were just well-trained Gobblers. But I guess a report ended up in the Bastion?'

Biz nodded.

They were quiet for a long time, remembering Bock. The house became dark. Eventually Biz stirred. 'It's time to act,' he said, in a bland, off-centre voice.

'What?' Gneiss sounded like he'd been shaken out of a dream.

'It's time to act,' Biz repeated. 'Bock's death will not have been for nothing.'

Gneiss peered at Biz through the darkness. No light of understanding illuminated his ruined, red-rimmed eyes.

'Get yourself together, we're going to put an end to this.'

'To what? What do you mean?' Gneiss was waking up fast.

'I've been consulting, since we last met, with our head of

atmospheric engineering. Without explaining my motives or plan, I've spoken to him at great length and I believe I have the solution. I know how we can begin to change the global atmosphere.'

Gneiss was stunned. He had not expected this now, not when his head was filled with the fog of sadness and he could barely bring himself to care about any Gobblers at all. He marvelled at Biz's strength and presence of mind, even if he didn't care much for his timing.

'I don't care anymore,' Gneiss said. 'I don't want to be a Sharp. I want to go back to being a Gobbler, immersed in the comfort and oblivion of the trivial. Ride a train of emotions without roller-coaster highs or wracking lows, just a flat, straight, tedious, track to the end of my life. I've had it.'

'No, you haven't,' Biz said. 'You have work to do. Bock's memory demands it. Or would you rather she died for nothing, alone in that storeroom, filling gas bottles with your ideas?' He clapped slowly twice, and a light switched on.

Gneiss blinked and shook himself, ran his hands through his hair and rubbed his beard so it swayed and shook. He was trying to wake himself up. 'I suppose you're right. You really have the answer?'

'Oh, yes,' Biz nodded. 'I have the answer, all I lack is the power. But I am getting closer to that every day. And you can help me gain it.'

For the first time since finding Bock dead, Gneiss was able to look away from the horror and sadness and towards hope. Biz was right: if he gave up now, Bock would have died for nothing. For less than nothing, in fact, for a bad idea doomed to fail because he didn't have the spirit to make it come true. She would have laughed at his weakness. 'Okay. Tell me about it.'

'No, not yet. It's complex and involved: there is much that needs to be done to make it happen, and it's beyond you or me to do it alone. I propose that we meet with your most trusted and accomplished Gardeners. I'll explain my plan to everyone once and give everyone specific jobs.'

'How can we meet without arousing suspicion?'

'Bock's funeral. Get them there as mourners – I'm sure their grief will be real enough. At the wake, I'll put the thing in motion.'

Gneiss nodded. It was a good idea – the perfect cover for a gathering like this. He regarded Biz with gratitude, and saw tears fill his old student's young, wise eyes. The lessons he had inculcated had held true. Still, his innate reluctance to have all the Gardeners in one place at one time made him ask, 'Do we really all need to be there? Can't you just tell me?'

Biz shook his head. 'It involves the production of combustion engines, the disposition of hydrocarbon and other fuel sources, the coordination of a wide range of covert activities and the recruitment of others – even some within the Bastion. It's a difficult, long-term plan, and one that I dare not record anywhere, not even on paper. I need to meet with your people, determine who would be best for each task, explain their roles to them and satisfy myself that they are trustworthy. One word in the wrong place could bring us all undone. I know it's a risk for us to meet, but we won't get an opportunity like Bock's wake again for a very long time, if ever.'

'You really have become a high-functioning Sharp, haven't you? Well, I respect your judgement. I'll do what I can to get them here.'

'They'll have to act as if they are from Bock's family or workplace.'

Gneiss nodded. 'I'm glad you're on our side.'

'Thanks, I guess. This is the hardest thing I've ever had to do.'

'And the bravest.'

Biz bowed his head. Gneiss couldn't tell if it was humility or grief; either way, he wouldn't intrude on his friend's thoughts.

Biz returned to the Bastion that night to prepare for the funeral in three days. This was to be the most momentous act of his life, and its success or failure would determine the remainder of his life in the Bastion, including perhaps its length. One false move could bring the whole thing crashing down – leaving him exposed and vulnerable.

Above all, he found the secrecy the hardest part. He'd been carrying the secret of the Gardeners around for a very long time, and he was used to that. But now he was taking action, the suspense within him was mounting. He thought about Gneiss, and how much he owed him; he thought about Bock, mostly in sentimental terms. While she'd been alive, even though they'd been apart, he'd never missed her this much. Knowing that she could never come back, that her memory would fade, that he would never see her again, not even an image of her, made her absence much more palpable. In some ways, he envied the Gobblers for their ability to lose memories so quickly, but in another way he had never felt more keenly what they must be missing. Even this memory of loss and sadness would one day be precious to him.

In the midst of this, Biz had a row with Globe.

She cornered him on the second day after his return. 'What's the deal with that barbecue explosion story?'

'Run it, but don't identify the victim,' he told her.

'Why?' She was petulant. 'If some Gobbler was plotting against the government, surely we should name that person, in the public interest.'

'You've never shown any concern for public interest before.' Biz regretted his own irritation, and tried to calm himself. 'What do you care if the Gobblers know or don't know who's behind the plot? Besides, we almost never name anyone but Joe. And in this case, anonymity is more effective as a weapon of fear. If the terrorist could be your next-door neighbour or the person that serves you at the Synthetron, that brings it closer to home.'

'But if we name the person, this Bock or whatever her name was' – she had obviously read the full report – 'it may alert her co-conspirators and maybe encourage them to give themselves up.'

'For fuck's sake!' Biz blew up. 'This poor woman was trying to fill a barbecue gas bottle and it took the top of her fucking head off. Now, you want to spin that into a homegrown terrorism story, that's fine; that's what we do. But don't come to me with any crap about imaginary co-conspirators. Run the fucking story, don't use names.'

Globe was taken aback. She couldn't understand Biz's reaction, but she didn't want to take the argument any further in case the battle became personal. 'Okay, okay,' she said. 'Jesus.'

After she left, Biz sat down, with his head in his hands and stared at his desk. His hands were shaking. But he still had so much to do. He tried to push his emotions and fears aside. He hoped he'd been successful in convincing Globe that her "homegrown terrorism" story really was just spinning mileage out of an unfortunate accident. If he hadn't convinced her, he had exposed himself again. Either way, it would all be out in the open very soon.

23.

Biz left the Bastion early on the morning of the funeral. He was bitter, despondent, guilty. Adrenaline coursed through his veins, and he felt sickly and weak, as though his courage was deserting him. He thought of Knead and Gneiss, the mentors who had shaped his life with such heavy hands. They couldn't help him today. Today, he would have to be his own master.

The funeral was a suitably sombre affair. Bock's parents were surprised and delighted at the number of mourners – over thirty people. Trinket and Caper were very proud at such unusual attendance, even though they didn't know most of the people there, not even the Sharp from the Bastion, who must have been connected to their daughter somehow, though they couldn't remember how. Instead of asking him, they stared at the only decoration in the room, the small bunch of flowers by the unmarked urn containing Bock's ashes.

The ceremony was short. The citiburb official delivered the standard departure obsequies. 'Bock's Freedom has been taken from her; she will now be bound by the earth forever. Let us honour her memory by setting it free, and in forgetting Bock, free ourselves from the sadness we feel at her passing.' The urn was lowered into an anonymous hole the ground, and all present bowed their heads.

The Gardeners at the graveside had all known Bock as a principled, intelligent young woman, the intellectual equal of them all, except perhaps for Gneiss. They remembered, and would remember far more about her than her parents did, so they had no need to fake or exaggerate their sadness. They knew, too, that she'd never been as confident in herself as she should have been, despite the adoration she inspired on YouStar and the esteem in which the Gardeners held her. She just couldn't translate any of that into the kind of self-assurance that Gneiss, for example, showed. She preferred to carry the load rather than drive the train. She had been a worker. And that was the reason for her death – if she had not been working on their project behind the scenes, she would still be alive.

The urn went into the ground and the mourners made their way to Caper and Trinket's house for a wake. Trinket was apologetic as she welcomed the guests to her standard citiburbian home – Gneiss had sprung the idea of a wake on her only the day before, and she hadn't thought to cater for so many. Gneiss pleaded with her not to worry, saying that they really did not expect anything much, and besides they would all be gone soon. He even suggested that Caper and Trinket retire to their Cocoons so Bock's friends could have a quiet Flurient in the garden to mark her passing. The parents agreed with relief.

The crowd, consisting of half a dozen co-workers, the Gardeners and Biz, gathered in the back yard. Until this moment none of the Gardeners had looked openly and frankly at Biz. They'd stayed circumspect at the funeral, acknowledging each other with curt nods and downcast eyes but acting as if Biz was not even there. They were nervous, anxious to get the meeting over and done with and go back, safely, to their own homes.

But they also understood that this was the beginning of the real revolution, and that from now on the stakes would be much higher. To say it was a critical moment was to understate the gravity of the situation – everything hinged upon the actions and words of this man, Biz, whom they did not know, and had never known or encountered. All they had to go on was Gneiss's assurance, and even though he'd never misled them before, it was a tense situation.

Standing around in awkward expectation on the deck of this strange home, the bolder Gardeners – they were all quite bold, or else they would not be there at all – regarded Biz. His close-cropped hair and angular features made him look every inch the Sharp he was, which made many of them suspicious. They wanted to trust Gneiss's claim that Biz was true to their cause and that his allegiance was the product of many years of indoctrination in what is right and just, but they were trained in caution and paranoia. They darted furtive glances around the yard's perimeter, looking for the telltale gleam of secreted listening devices or cameras. But they looked in vain and saw nothing but the normal sights and sounds of an average dwelling in an unimportant street in an unremarkable piece of citiburbia.

After a short, awkward period of small talk and Flurient sipping, Bock's co-workers left one by one. When only Gardeners remained, Gneiss spoke, low and softly.

'As you all know, this is my former student and current Bastionado, Biz. Biz, this is Lens, Cluster – '

'No names,' Biz barked. Gneiss stopped, mouth open, and cast an approving glance at the young man.

'Frens, this man has come here at considerable personal risk to join us,' Gneiss continued. 'Everything we have achieved up until now has been trivial compared to what will happen next. Each of you controls between five and twenty Gardeners, and you must pass on what you learn here today to the members of your cells. Our organisation has grown, but until now we haven't really achieved anything. This is different. Biz has come here to tell us how we're going to achieve true freedom. Biz – '

'I couldn't have said it better,' Biz said with a terse smile. There was no going back now.

At that moment, the front door crashed and splintered under the weight of a battering ram. Black clad figures spindled like spiders over the garden walls. In a split second, the Gardeners were surrounded by a heavily armed team of Liberty Guards. The biggest and probably bravest of the Gardeners, a delivery driver named Distaff, lunged at the Liberty Guard in front of him, plunging the air embolism gun he'd been fingering in his pocket into the man's neck, unerringly targeting the carotid artery. The Guard fell and Distaff quickly stomped on his head, crushing it. Terrene grabbed the fallen Guard's weapon and fired it indiscriminately, wounding one of his own men but cutting down two Liberty Guards. In the confusion, several Gardeners scrambled over the fence into the waiting arms of yet more troops, who beat them where they landed; the revolutionaries' screams echoed around the neighbourhood. The Liberty Guards had been told to hold their fire, and they did, but they were free to use clubs and the butts of their weapons, smashing Gardeners in the face and buckling knees. Gneiss stood stock still, rooted to the spot with horror until he was brought down by solid crack to the side of his head and blood poured from the gash. The melee was short but brutal, and within less than a minute the Gardeners were all subdued, most of them bleeding, lying face down and struggling to get their hands behind their heads as per the screamed instructions of the Guards' commander.

Biz remained standing. He smiled grimly at the cowering group. 'You fools,' he said. 'Now you're all going to experience first-hand the efficacy of our Enhanced Interrogation Techniques, and when you've given up the names of the people in your cells – and you will – you'll take the Freedom Ride. And when you do, remember, it's because you trusted this man.' He pointed at Gneiss.

He watched the Liberty Guards manhandle the revolutionaries into handcuffs, while around the yard others kept their weapons trained menacingly on the prisoners' heads.

Gneiss arched his back to lift his head off the deck. 'What the fuck, Biz? I thought you believed in us? I taught you better than this.'

Biz sneered. 'You taught me, did you? You taught me that lies and manipulation and dissembling are the tools of men who get what they want. You taught me that sincerity is for fools and honesty is a cheap façade. You taught me that the end justifies the means, any means, and that the end is always justified if you claim nobility of motive, whether that accords with truth or common good or not. You taught me that we are all just after power, and that no sacrifice for the sake of power is too great, if that sacrifice is someone else. Even a supposed loved one, like me. Or like Bock. I learned more from your actions than your empty words.'

'But you swore. You promised,' Gneiss pleaded. His face was twisted and his voice rattled with anguish and physical effort.

'I promised not to betray you and Bock. When you let her die in a shed, you betrayed me again. My word became as worthless as yours.' Biz thrust his contorted face close to his tormentor's, and whispered tautly, so the Liberty Guards couldn't hear, 'You know, the funny thing is, if I am ever in a position to do so, I may well give the Gobblers back their minds, grant them real freedom – freedom of choice. If I do, it will be my gift to them, not yours. Not the leavings of some grubby manipulative Gobbler who claims to speak for them all, but the legacy of the greatest Psyman the free world has ever known. I'll be remembered forever. You? You're already forgotten.'

He turned on his heel and walked into the house, where Trinket and Caper were being held by a brace of Liberty Guards amid the ruins of their home. 'Take them too. Erase them. Erase them all. Show them what Freedom really looks like.'

24.

The Bastion was abuzz when Biz got back. Reports of the raid and arrests had filtered back very quickly, and all of his colleagues wanted to know more. That a conspiracy of the kind that Gneiss had headed could exist had flabbergasted everyone, all the way to the very top. As Biz strode down the hallways, people called out to him, slapped his back and gave him the thumbs up. It was by far his finest hour, and he tried, with limited success, to keep the grin off his face.

At last he attained his office and sat down, exhausted. He may have swelled with pride at the reaction of his peers, but guilt and depression nagged at him. Did it have to be so brutal? So very final? He guessed it did. He wondered what would have happened if Bock hadn't died. The Gardeners would still be plotting, and he may even have taken a hand in it. Still, conjecture was pointless. The thing was done. Very soon, Gneiss and his gang would be dead, the other Gardeners would be rounded up and dispatched, and the Gobbler public would be none the wiser. There was no need for a trial or anything of that nature. Long ago it had been established that one only had to be designated as a terrorist or enemy of the state for one's life to be forfeit. It was a handy expedient that provided an economical solution to all kinds of sticky problems, and avoided any compromising revelations.

Biz tried not to think about what he owed Gneiss as his teacher and friend, preferring to think of Gneiss the manipulator who had rearranged a young man's life for his own ends.

He'd had a right to settle the score, and they were even now, he thought bitterly.

And yet none of it would bring Bock back.

He was shaken out his reverie. Radiant, beaming Globe had come to congratulate him and share his glory. She was effusive; like many others she found it hard to fathom that Biz had smashed such a diabolical plot from within the Bastion without ever saying a single word. It didn't make sense, yet it had happened. And she was keen to spin it into a massive victory over terrorism, a great and lasting triumph for Freedom.

Biz put the brakes on her enthusiasm. 'Nothing of this gets reported,' he said, mildly.

'What?' Globe was incredulous. 'You must be joking! This is the story of the year. The decade. The century.'

'Think about it. Whenever we report on what we call a terrorist plot, it's always some clueless Gobbler doing something stupid. The common thread is that it's always just one dolt working alone, and it's never, ever a real threat. Now look at this case: dozens, perhaps hundreds working together to present a genuine danger to our rule. Do we really want the Gobblers to get hold of that information? To learn that a revolutionary group could operate in secret for years?'

'But it's a big story and it needs to be told. We can have the entire population cowering over the threat that group posed, and quavering at the thought of the instant justice meted out!'

'The population was never under threat – *we* were! Not only that, we are talking about concerted group action. If we implant the idea in the public mind – however feeble – that such a thing is possible, where will it end? They may come out of their Cocoons and start talking to each other about it. If even one person should ponder what motivated that little group of thugs, or how they got away with it, our whole system could unravel. There might even be other Gardeners out there. We don't want to encourage them.'

Globe was going to say more but thought better of it. They had both noticed Knead standing quietly in the doorway, observing. They stopped and looked at him.

'Well said,' he nodded to Biz. His mouth was smiling but his eyes were serious. He looked at Globe. 'You can go.'

Knead waited until she had closed the door behind her. 'Ah, the conquering hero.'

Was there a hint, maybe more than a hint, of facetiousness in his tone?

'Care to accompany me to the Cabinet room? Your fellow members would like a debriefing.'

Biz had anticipated this, indeed he had counted on it, but he hadn't expected Knead to be so dour about it. After all, he'd foiled a substantial plot. But he'd done it alone. He hadn't involved his mentor, the Cabinet leader who had entrusted him with so much – even at the end when it was a done deal. He'd dealt directly with the local Liberty Guards without bringing any other Bastionado into his confidence. Perhaps this would go badly for him? They might find his actions incompatible with those of a true Sharp, and sack him from the Cabinet. Or worse, send him off with Gneiss and the others.

He followed Knead to the Cabinet room. They walked in silence, two pairs of heels clicking curtly on the diamond floor.

As he entered, the Cabinet members all acknowledged him solemnly. Biz nodded back, and took a seat next to Knead, who began the proceedings.

'The success of your venture notwithstanding, we have questions surrounding its development and circumstances,' he said.

Of all the Cabinet members, he looked the most peeved, but he had the most right to be so. He was the one to whom Biz should have confided, and that lack of confidence may have reflected particularly badly on Knead as Cabinet leader.

Lucent nodded. 'You are to be congratulated, young man,' he said. 'But we need to know these things: where and when the plot began, at what point you were initiated, and why you chose not to share its existence or your daring plans with your colleagues or superiors.'

For the next hour and a half Biz answered their questions in plain speech, with almost naïve honesty. He explained to them his accidental reunion with Bock and Gneiss after his Face-cast, and their description of the plot in broad outline at that time. The only details he omitted were those relating to his own CO_2 metamorphosis and the way Gneiss had manipulated him, which he thought were irrelevant and would only have prejudiced his standing as a Sharp.

He told them that he had, in an oblique manner, discussed the issue with Particle after his return, and gained sufficient understanding of the process to determine that the Gardeners would never be able to achieve their goals; they were simply not capable of producing genuine change. So he decided to let the matter rest, and wait until he had a chance to insinuate himself into the group as an undercover operative.

'Once I knew they could never succeed, I felt safe enough waiting for an opportunity to do something about it. If I'd acted in the first instance, we would have secured the leader, Gneiss, and his assistant, Bock, but the other members of the cabal would have gone free. If I'd divulged the information I had to my colleagues or superiors, I believe that would have been the outcome. I realise now that I have deeply misjudged the capabilities and discretion of my colleagues, most notably Knead, and for that I apologise.' He hung his head in an approximation of shame, which appeared to soothe his mentor; Knead nodded gently to Biz, in forgiveness.

'The death of Bock, my former friend, gave me the opportunity I'd been waiting for.'

The Cabinet members all nodded. They were at least

half-convinced. Knead pressed Biz for more details: exactly how had the existence of the group been revealed?

Biz explained that he had long been suspicious about his teacher, and had manipulated him into blurting out the truth through a combination of shrewd questioning and the liberal consumption of Flurient. 'He believed he was a Sharp, but of course his crude application of carbon dioxide in poorly metered doses made him much less astute than he believed. Once a kernel of truth was out I was able to elicit the whole story by assuming a pretence of empathy.'

The Cabinet members appeared to buy this, except for Knead, who knew Biz well enough to wonder if the empathy had actually been genuine.

'This Bock, the dead girl,' Psyllium asked, 'she was your girlfriend, correct?'

'Just a friend, Doctor, with "was" being the operative term,' Biz replied, with a straight face and a deadpan voice. 'When I first went to visit Gneiss after my Face-cast, I had no idea they were together. When I found out, it changed nothing; my intent was to find out what Gneiss was up to, and that remained my focus. You may not be aware that I have formed a liaison with Globe in Conflict Spin, so my relationship with Bock was as dead as she is now.'

'I see. And what made you… What gave rise to your suspicions about Gneiss?' Lucent asked.

'It was his teachings,' said Biz, his confidence growing. 'They were deviant, if not outright subversive, throughout my entire schooling. He frequently had us turn away from our Educoon screens, and delivered lectures that I now know to be seditious. Among other things he taught an erroneous definition of Freedom. He laid heavy emphasis on what he called the qualities of personal integrity and responsibility, the role of the individual in the face of injustice, and the responsibility of citizens to question their government – in fact, a whole doctrine of individualism.' He could hear Cabinet members suck in their breath; he saw exchanges of meaningful glances around the panel. He continued, 'Of course as a young boy, particularly before your visit, Doctor,' he nodded to Psyllium, 'I had no idea that what he was saying was so controversial. He was the only teacher I'd ever known, and I had no knowledge or interest in what other students were being taught. It wasn't until I came here to the Bastion that I really began to understand how he had subverted my education and that of my classmates.

'Once here, my suspicions grew, and the more I pondered them the more I knew I had to act. But I was a junior, making unsubstantiated accusations against a teacher of many years standing, even if he was a Gobbler. I had to first prove to myself that what I recalled from my childhood was accurate. It was only then that I stumbled on the Gardener conspiracy.'

The questioning continued, but where in the beginning it had been pointed interrogation, it slowly became a more interested probing for details. Zeal, the Minister of Education, was made uncomfortable several times, and she had the good grace to blush. There would have to be a major investigation into the teaching hierarchy, and more than likely a purge. New restrictions on the purchase, use and contents of gas bottles would undoubtedly be introduced. Educoon usage would be even more strictly monitored.

Through all the questioning and discussion, Biz was convincing, his answers apparently unrehearsed, and eventually even Knead seemed satisfied that the young man's motives had been pure. After what seemed like an extraordinarily long time, Knead put both hands on the table and stood up.

'I think we have heard enough,' he said, looking around at his colleagues and noting their barely perceptible gestures of affirmation. 'I think I speak for all of us when I say that you are to be applauded for your perceptiveness and initiative, but castigated for your inability, or rather your refusal, to trust your Cabinet colleagues and share this information with them. In particular, I am personally affronted.' He looked at Biz, but his expression didn't conform precisely to his words; he looked almost paternal. 'Do you understand that?' he asked.

Biz, who felt very much like a son being chastised by a doting father, nodded. 'Yes, sir.'

'Good. Leave us, but wait in the anteroom.'

Biz excused himself. He sat in the outer room for thirty minutes while an occasionally strident debate raged in the Cabinet room. He couldn't make out what was being said, but the raised voices led him to believe that they were discussing his punishment. He grew cold. When the room went quiet, meaning that the decision had been made and the details were being quietly finalised, he became afraid.

At last, Knead opened the door, his face hard-set, and invited Biz back in. The Cabinet members were all looking at him, but he couldn't tell if it was with curiosity, anger or something approaching regret.

Knead spoke. 'If you are to reach your true potential in this organisation, you must learn to collaborate with your fellow Cabinet members. You will never again undertake such a reckless adventure. Never work on a suspicion or idea without first consulting your colleagues. You will take advice and, where necessary, direction from other Cabinet members, including myself. Is that clear?'

My god, thought Biz. I'm going to be exonerated. 'Yes, sir.'

Knead again looked around the table, observing the subtle inclination of Cabinet members' heads. He drew a breath.

'While you were mourning your ex-girlfriend and mounting your spectacular raid, we have been suffering through a tragedy. As the leader of this chamber, it has fallen to me to resolve it. That is why I need to impress upon you the need, the absolute obligation, to do as we say. Can I trust you to do that? Will you let me down?'

'No, sir, I will not.' Biz's voice was stronger now, but he was confused. He could read nothing on the faces around him; even Zeal had regained her composure.

'After a short illness, one that arose quickly and accomplished its ends with terrible efficiency,' Knead said slowly, 'our dear leader has left us. It began the day you left to visit your friends, and the end came yesterday. We need someone of ambition, clarity of vision and initiative to take his place.'

Biz understood in a flash. His expression grew calm, his demeanour cooled, and he tried to hide his elation. He nodded.

Knead returned his nod. 'Excellent. Thank you, Joe.'

The Reprint
by
Nick Bruechle

Who is Jakob Petersson? He wants to be the man his ex fell in love with, rather than the easygoing stoner his friends prefer. But right now he is neither.

And wait – did he commit a brutal crime last night?

Jakob's search for identity, meaning and the truth will reveal the dark secret of the deceptively idyllic city of New Elysium, and for that he will pay the ultimate price.

The Reprint is a thought provoking exploration of personality, a desolate portrayal of depression and drug addiction, and a mysterious adventure in a dystopian future.

The Reprint is now available at nickbruechle.com

9 780648 569985